# SIX MONTHS

Deborah Fullwood

*To my family*

# PROLOGUE

The waiting

Zoe read the last paragraph of 'normal people ', closed the book, clutched it to her chest and sighed. This was the fourth time she'd read the book, and every time she fell more in love. Not with Connell himself but with the love that grew between Connell and Marianne. It was the intensity and simmering passion that Zoe had fallen for. Not that it bore any resemblance to real life. If anyone knew that there was no such thing as soul mates, it was her. She sat up on the bed with a deeper more troubled sigh, and reached for her phone. Finding her favourite moping song, she pressed play, slumped back onto the bed and let her mind wander

As Ellie Goulding sang soulfully in the background about true love and heartbreak, Zoe's thoughts drifted to the teenagers she taught, particularly the girls. How could they ever be expected to have realistic ideas about relationships with Connell and Marianne still commanding pole position on the best selling paper back chart and now streaming on Netflix. Zoe remembered feeling the same when she'd read the twilight saga as a teenager. Romance, beauty, love and eternity- so delicious but so unobtainable. No wonder the divorce rate was so high!

As a secondary school teacher in a large mixed comprehensive,

Zoe had always felt some sense of responsibility to try to prepare her students for the outside world. As much as she wanted them to have dreams and aims, she also felt it was important for them to realise that the odds were against them ending up as glamorous Instagram influencers or footballers girlfriends, it was much more likely they'd be working full time and paying a mortgage, dealing with their fair share of heartache, as the society they lived in demanded they wanted more of everything. She had to admit though working with young people who happily chatted about what their mansions would be like when they were 'loaded', regularly lifted Zoe's spirits, and occasionally put a dent in her hardened cynicism. Even in the most difficult times of her life.

And this was one of them she thought. Just as she felt the burn of tears behind her eyes, her mobile buzzed beside her, snapping her back into the room, and pulling her from the danger of sinking into another marathon of heart wrenching sobbing.

'Hi' she exhaled into the phone, trying to sound normal.
'Zo, you having a bad day? Shall I come over?' as always there was no keeping her grief from Sam, her long suffering best friend.
'No, really Sam, I'm fine' Zoe whispered, her voice breaking on the last word, 'I just can't believe I'm alone again. I'm 27 and the thought of starting again...' she trailed off. Sam knew exactly how much pain her friend was in. She also knew there was nothing she could do to erase her friends heartache and suffering. She knew whatever she said would be inadequate, but knew it was her job to try anyway.

As Sam took a moment to consider what new angle to take in order to console her distraught friend, her mind flashed her a recap of the cause of this upset, and reminded her just how unexpected it was. Zoe and Ryan had met when they were 18 and 19 respectively, and had been inseparable immediately. Ryan had just fit with such ease, that none of them had doubted Ryan was Zoe's soul-mate, just like none of them had ever doubted that the couple would stay together forever. Ryan had become part of Zoe's family, and had fit in with their group of friends. They all loved him. They were all missing him. The shock announcement had come only a few weeks earlier. Zoe and Ryan had been attending the wedding of one of her school colleagues (although Zoe had recently left the school to take on a promotion in a different school the following September, this it turned out, was some small relief).

On a girls night out the week before the event, there had been some serious analysis and discussion (helped along by their favourites, Prosecco and a couple of cocktails) about whether Ryan would propose at the wedding, or wait until their trip to Madrid at the end of August. They had all agreed Madrid, and so Zoe felt no cause for concern when Ryan spent the afternoon of the wedding flitting around the beautifully decorated marquee. If anything, she'd told Sam in one of their less emotional exchanges since the event, she'd felt proud that her partner made so much effort to fit in with her colleagues. She hadn't worried when she'd lost track of him for a couple of hours, she'd been having a blast on the dance floor with Tamasyn, one of her best friends who by some happy coincidence knew the groom and so had also been able to attend the wedding. Nor had she even worried when Ryan had been late home from work several times in the two weeks following the wedding. Such was her confidence that he was her life partner and nothing, or no-one would ever come between them.

This certainty was the reason Zoe's world had crumpled so totally when Ryan had left her two weeks after the wedding to move in with Kate, Zoe's fellow teacher and colleague, someone that she had mentored and supported through her own personal difficulties. And although Zoe had no particular attachment to Kate it was this sense of double betrayal that had left Zoe winded, feeling isolated and vulnerable, making the job of her real friends so much more difficult. 'What a bitch' thought Sam, and then spoke aloud, having decided to apply the 'time is a healer' slant to today's counselling.

'I know how raw you feel, but six months down the line you'll feel so much better. Honestly, in six months it'll be like your heart was never broken at all' soothed Sam.
'Six months?' gasped Zoe 'six minutes is an eternity'
'I know, and if I could fast forward six months for you I would in a heartbeat, but some things you have to live through. You can get through this Zoe. Six months. By February things will be different, I promise.' The concern was clear in Sam's voice, and Zoe knew she meant it.

Six months, Zoe considered this silently. Is that all Sam seriously thought it would take for her to feel better. Maybe she was right. Zoe did a quick inventory of how she felt, while Sam hung on the other end of the phone waiting for her to say something. Her arms and legs felt like dead weights, her stomach light and fluttery, filled with anxiety. In her chest, where she knew there should be a light rhythmic pounding, it felt like there was a dead weight, maybe her heart had been replaced with a cold stone. If that was the case someone had also lodged a tennis ball in her throat making it difficult to swallow, let alone speak in her normal upbeat tone. Above each eye there was a pounding pressure that just made her want to close her eyes and sleep off eternity.

No. Sam was wrong. It would take far longer than six months to recover from this heartache. At that moment she truly doubted she would ever recover at all. 'Ok' she humoured Sam 'let's see how I feel in six months'.

And so the waiting began.

# CHAPTER 1: THE HEARTACHE

The nights were the worst, Zoe sobbing into her pillow, wondering what she could have done to avoid this outcome, how could she have avoided losing him? Sleep would come in the early hours, when Zoe's body, exhausted from hunger and emotion, would give way to a restless slumber. Zoe resented losing consciousness as it only meant she had to wake and rediscover her loss over and over, each time as raw as the first. 'This pain' she thought night after night, how can I bear it? Let alone recover from it.

The days were equally as excruciating and long. Each morning Zoe found herself crippled with grief, wanting to get out of bed, but unable to. The summer holidays were a blessing, she wasn't sure she could cope with a class full of hormone fuelled teenagers in the this state, but then again, with no work, she had no focus, no reason to get out of bed, eat or socialise. The days dragged in a blur of Daytime TV and Kleenex. Zoe had never considered heartbreak before. She'd read about it in the twilight saga when Edward left Bella, but only now could she really appreciate the numbness and utter desolation it brought. The thought of The twilight saga heroin lifted her spirits some- she recovered didn't she?- only she had got her love back, and Ryan wasn't coming back. He had made it very clear. Sam had told her, that even if he said he'd come back it would never be the same now he'd betrayed her. Zoe could see her point, but the thought of life without Ryan was still too raw to concede that she could ever refuse him re-entry to her life. He was after all her whole world.

It was four weeks into the holiday when the hammering on the door awoke Zoe from her daytime tv daze. How long had the door been knocking? The last thing she'd been watching on tv was loose women, but now it was bargain hunt. 'Oh man' she mumbled to herself 'three and a half hours passed and I didn't notice, is this it? Am I a zombie?'

'I can hear you talking to yourself' Sam was shouting through the letterbox 'it's pissing down out here, open the friggin' door!'

'Oh shit' Zoe thought as she scrambled to the front door. I really am losing it. She opened the door to see her sodden best friend in what appeared to be a gym kit. Yes, really losing it - Sam didn't own any sports wear and if she did it would be by mistake, she wouldn't actually wear it!! Zoe shook her head to try to eject herself from this surreal dream-like state she seemed to have entered. Sam shoved past her into the house.

'Right' Sam's voice was scarily forceful Zoe noted with apprehension. This tone could only mean one thing- Sam felt she had a purpose now in her friends recovery. This filled Zoe with dread. While Sam had felt useless, she'd let Zoe's self indulgent behaviour persist, cooed down the phone to her, and mainly let her get on with moping. Zoe could sense this period of grace was over as far as Sam was concerned, and that her best friend would shortly be putting her on some sort of recovery regime that Zoe was nowhere near ready for. She found herself bracing herself in anticipation of Sam's next words. They weren't really what she was expecting.

'What sort of workout shall we do?' Sam asked flicking through YouTube video thumbnails on the TV screen.
'What?' Zoe's frown revealed her confusion
'Well you're down a dress size with all your moping, and I've only got four days to lose four pounds' Sam explained, as though

Zoe would immediately know what she was talking about. Zoe's continued look of confusion prompted her to embellish her somewhat brief explanation.

'Before Madrid. I picked up the details off your desk the other day and then i phoned up and pretended to be you to change the booking. So now we're going together! It'll be ace.' Sam was in full speed talking flow now 'actually there was meant to be a £70 charge, but I explained the whole story to the woman, and her boyfriend had done the same to her last year, anyway she put something down about bereavement and did it for free' Sam's smile was triumphant. Zoe had to smile back. In their group of friends, Sam was known as the 'warbler' she could talk anyone into anything just by befriending them and telling them her life story. If you sat by Sam on the train, you were friends for life. She would frequently start a story and go off at so many tangents that by the end of the monologue you were five stories removed from the original tale. It was one of many endearing qualities of her friend that Zoe loved.

Zoe and Sam had met fifteen years earlier, when Zoe was just eleven. Two years younger than Sam they seemed an unlikely pair to become best friends. They had met back in the day that neither of them were afraid to wear gym gear and they both attended the same freestyle class. It was of course the time of Adele's power ballad reign, not the best music for freestyle, but there had been plenty of pop music too. They'd loved flinging themselves around to the Katy Perry and Lady Gaga.

From these beginnings, their friendship had grown. They had started going on girls nights out together in their teens, their dancing not much more reserved than it had been in class when they heard any of their favourite songs. Despite both being 90's born, they shared a love of 80's music and their night out venues were often chosen to reflect their old school music taste! They eventually chose their university together, Sam heading off two years before Zoe, but staying on for a fourth so that there was a two year overlap. Zoe often considered those two years as the best of her life- even though she was in a fledgling relationship with Ryan, they were so carefree. So much fun, so little commitment.....

'Zo, you're still in your pyjamas' Sam's words interrupted Zoe's reminiscence. Zoe looked down. It was true enough. She was wearing her favourite marks and Spencer's pyjamas that she'd had at least five years. The grey cuffed trousers with pink spots were stretched and comfortable as was the pink top with an image of cows jumping over the moon. Looking at her crumpled nightwear, Zoe tried to work out when she had last got dressed. She couldn't remember. Although she'd been taking a long soak in the bath each day, the most she'd achieved was alternating these pyjamas with her cream and red reindeer set that Sam had bought her the previous Christmas. But what was the point in getting dressed? Zoe felt the sickness rise up to the lump in her throat and the tears behind her eyes begin to form again. Sam noticed it too.

'Zoe! Stop that before you start. We've got stuff to do. Now go and get your kit on. Have you eaten today'? Despite Zoe's broken heart, she had been forced to eat reasonably regularly by her concerned mother, who had brought over Zoe's favourites cottage pie, tea cakes and spaghetti bolognese on a regular basis. The emotional trauma and self-neglect in her mothers absence had still resulted in some weight loss though. Every cloud mused Zoe.

She nodded in response to Sam's question as she walked back out of the lounge towards the front door, and headed up the stairs to find her gym kit. Zoe loved her house. She'd bought it on her own after university, while Ryan was finishing his studies and couldn't afford the mortgage contributions. He had lived with her of course, but they had never got around to changing the mortgage deed, and when he'd left, Ryan had been clear that he had no intention of trying to claim any stake in her house.

Zoe had been relieved, but Sam had been outraged he'd even raised the point when it was him leaving her.

Her bedroom was her favourite room. Although it wasn't huge, it was plenty big enough to fit the large antique bronze coloured bedstead that her nan had bought her for her housewarming. It was intricately decorated with brass flowers and swirls, and was made up in beautiful Next bedding with cappuccino coloured satin stripes at the top. The bedding had cost more than she'd intended to spend, but Zoe thought it was worth it for the comforting feel of the cool satin on her cheek as she drifted into sleep.

Behind the bed, Zoe had painstakingly painted vertical stripes that alternated between the cappuccino colour of the bedding and gold leaf varnish that she'd found online. The specs of gold, reminded her of those in goldschlager, which was a liquor concept she didn't 'get' if she was entirely honest. But on her wall the flakes of gold set off her brass bedstead perfectly and made her bedroom twinkle in the sunlight, which was fitting for Zoe, whose love of all things pink and sparkly surpassed that of your average woman.

Zoe paused for a moment in the door way of her bedroom, trying to work out where she would find something to wear that wasn't a track suit that had really been purchased for the purposes of lounging. She decided her safest bet would be the black running leggings and matching Nike Women top that she had purchased when her friend Leyla had tried to get her to complete a couch to 5k plan. 'bloody hell' she chuckled to herself 'it'll be almost realising it's sport set destiny'. The smirk on her face pulled her up short. What, after all, had she got to be giggling about. In that brief second she'd forgotten herself and her misery, but now it came crashing back down around her. What was Sam thinking? Barging in here disturbing her melancholy. Trying to get her to exercise. As she pulled off her pyjamas, and located her most sturdy bra, Zoe considered her options for getting Sam to leave her alone so that she could return to her tormented sofa state. But even as she tried out the sentences in her head she could see Sam's concerned, hurt expression and Zoe knew that within fifteen minutes, she'd be lurching around the lounge in a bid to help her friend burn some calories.

'I can't find the clubbercise workout that we always used to love' Sam reported on Zoe's return to the lounge 'we'll have to do our own one just with music... Bloody hell, no wonder you're depressed' Sam had made her way to the stereo and turned it on. She flicked off the Lana Del Ray album that Zoe had been listening to and raised her eyebrows in her friends direction. 'They're not all sad songs' Zoe's tone was defensive, but there was no need, Sam already had her phone synced with the speaker and an Amazon workout playlist playing. As Sam skipped and span around the dining room table, Zoe felt her spirits lift, ever so slightly, for the first time in a month.

The next forty minutes passed in a blur of jogging on the spot, jumping jacks, squats and sit ups. Zoe and Sam were unashamedly sweating and panting as they began to perform some cool down stretches. Despite neither of them exercising very actively, they had both qualified as dancing teachers in their late teens, and so had a competent understanding of anatomy and physiology. It wasn't that they didn't want to be fit, it was just the usual time constraints of adulthood that had meant they eventually stopped dancing altogether, although on a girls night out everyone knew that the dance floor was where you'd find them between trips to the bar.

As Zoe collapsed onto the floor, Sam headed to the kitchen and came back with two glasses of water. They sat beside each other on the floor sipping the cool liquid slowly. Eventually, Sam, her breathing rate now returned to normal, broke the silence. 'Am I thin yet?' she asked innocently, Zoe giggled her reply 'size zero already!'. The girls burst in to laughter. Although Sam and Zoe weren't overweight, neither were they ever likely to be a size zero!

Zoe was 5'6", two inches taller than Sam. She had long dark hair that much to her frustration wouldn't grow past the line where her bra fastened. Her hair dresser, Lucy, frequently told her that people's hair often had a natural length that it wouldn't really grow past, but Zoe still hoped that one day she'd have hair down to her backside. Zoe's skin was pale, she got this from her dad, quite annoying considering her mom only had to look at the sun to turn a shade of golden brown. Instead, from her mom's genes she'd inherited her battle with her waistline. She was a size 12, but made no secret of the constant struggle to maintain it. Her and Sam had tried every main stream diet at one point or another, slimming world, weight watchers, fasting, boot camp, fat burning soup diet, you name it. The problem really was their love of food and alcohol. Zoe really didn't get people that went out for a meal and didn't have a dessert, or went on a girls night out and had diet coke. Life was too short.

This shared philosophy was another bond Zoe shared with Sam, who also battled to keep her size 12 figure. Being the same dress size as your best friend was great for clothes sharing, but Sam's slightly shorter frame meant that their feet varied a size and so shoe swapping was out. Sam's hair was light brown with a natural curl that Sam usually left unaltered. Only on special occasions would she let Zoe straighten her hair, as it was considered too much effort. Sam's laid back nature complimented Zoe's 'control freak' tendencies perfectly. Sam's skin was darker than Zoe's, but then everyones was, and her eyes pale blue in contrast to Zoe's dark green. Despite all the obvious differences, on nights out they often got asked if they were sisters. It amused them that men clearly thought that being a similar height and sharing a hip measurement must make you related despite looking nothing alike!

Sneaking on the scales earlier, Zoe had realised her recent heart-ache had caused her to shed a few pounds. She'd suspected as much during her daily 'naked in front of the mirror' fat inspection. Still, she wasn't light, even with all the grief she weighed 10st 4lb. Sam and her often wondered if other women completely lied about their weight all the time, or if the pair of them had bones made of some metal alloy, as their size 12 colleagues claimed to be 9st, confusing Zoe about where her extra stone and a half was stored. Perhaps they had heavy organs they'd mused a couple of months earlier. Sam had announced mid- workout that she was up to 10st 7lb, and wanted to be 4lb lighter in 4 days time. Although they both knew it was extremely unlikely, neither of the said anything, because this was the greatest cement of their friendship. Supporting each other blindly through fad diets, exercise plans and unwanted weight gain. This is what gelled the girls together.

'oooo, all that jumping about has made me really hungry' Zoe burst out laughing at her friends predictability, she should have known Sam would think she deserved junk food after exercising so vigorously. Despite having set out the 'four day, four pounds' regime only an hour earlier, Sam was already thinking of her next food-fix. 'Should we go out for something to eat?' She questioned, then hurriedly, remembering her friends fragile mental state added 'or we could get take out?'. Zoe thought about it for a moment, she hadn't felt this good in a while, the exercise had done its job and flooded her brain with endorphins. She actually felt almost human again. 'You know what?' she began, Sam looked at her expectantly waiting for the instruction to find the take away menus. 'I'm actually feeling the best I have in a while, let's take advantage. What day is it?' Zoe asked, realising she had no clue. 'It's Friday, Friday' Sam began singing and both girls winced at Sam's lack of musicality. Something else they had in common- their lack of ability to hold a note or carry a tune. Sam left Zoe's at 5.30pm, promising to call and book a table at their favourite bistro in town, and to meet Zoe on their 'shoe changing bench', at 7.30pm.

# CHAPTER 2:
# LINTFIELD CITY

The place Zoe and Sam knew as town, was actually the cathedral city of Lintfield, but as the medieval place of worship was the only thing making it a city, Zoe and Sam had only ever thought of it as a small town, in the heart of England. Lintfield had very little deprivation, and seemed to be home to many of the countries middle aged eccentrics! Zoe and Sam loved it. There weren't many shops in the town, but there was a Next and a Dorothy Perkins, that usually offered an option in those nightmare 'need something for tonight' situations.

The reason a place with such bad shopping was loved so much by committed shoppers Zoe and Sam, was the restaurants, bistros, cafes and bars. They were never short of an option for somewhere to meet for lunch, coffee, afternoon tea or cocktails. Tonight they'd be eating in The Lemon Grove, their favourite Mediterranean restaurant. Zoe was surprised at how her mouth watered at the thought of food, it had been a while. As she lathered her hair in the shower, she considered what she would choose from the menu. Her heart lurched as she recalled the last time she'd eaten at the restaurant with Ryan, when she'd been happily oblivious to the heartache that would follow only days later. She'd thought he had taken her out to make up for working late, on reflection he'd probably been trying to break up with her that night but had lost his nerve. Zoe wondered how she'd feel going back there so soon when so much had changed. 'Only one way to find out' she muttered to herself as she ducked her head under the stream of water to wash out the shampoo.

Once out of the shower, Zoe dried and straightened her long dark hair, whilst humming along to the songs playing on shuffle through her I pad. She looked in the mirror at her pale skin, her eyes were circled with dark rings, she looked weary, the sort of weary that only a broken heart can inflict. With a heavy sigh, she opened the top drawer of her dressing table and peered in at her make up selection. Wow, those circles were going to need some attention- she rummaged around in the cosmetics and retrieved her Yves San Laurent Touché Éclat. In the fifteen minutes that followed, as she applied her makeup, Zoe began to feel more like her old self. Finally she applied her false eyelashes and considered her reflection. She was impressed with the results, and amazed at how much better she felt about herself, maybe she'd recover after all, well in another six months.

Despite it being a while since Zoe had got dressed up for a night out, she automatically headed to the drawer that contained her best underwear, and selected a pink bra with a lace overlay. As she slid the matching french knickers over her hips, her phone beeped, with a picture message off Sam. The picture was of a grey dress, no text at all, but Zoe knew the code well. It basically meant 'don't wear your grey dress that's like this one'. Zoe, who had, in fact been considering the grey dress, stood biting her bottom lip whilst she considered her other options. It seemed so long since she'd gone out that she couldn't remember with any accuracy what her 10st 4lb options were. That was the thing with being a yo-yo dieter, Zoe thought, you had to have options available for the upper and lower limits of your weight range, plus all the intermediary stages. Zoe slid open her mirrored wardrobe and began sifting through the section containing her Friday night wear. She settled on a cappuccino coloured straight fit midi dress with small sleeves. The dress was figure hugging and as Zoe slid it on, she realised that for the first time in her life, she was probably on the lower end of a size

12. Although Zoe knew heartache was not a diet she would recommend, she was pleased with the reflection she saw in the mirror. Her silhouette was still rounded and curves at the hips and bottom, but the weight she always carried around her ribs and in her lower back seemed to have melted away. Zoe slid into her high nude coloured stilettos and admired herself again. She hadn't looked this good in a while. Picking out a matching bag, she slipped her heels back off and headed to her dressing table to accessorise.

*****

She was the first to arrive at the 'shoe-changing bench', just before 7.30pm. The bench was on the corner of the main street, and was traditionally where the girls met on a night out, to slip out of their folding shoes and slip into their stilettos that they always carried into town. Zoe glanced up the street as she slid her folding ballet pumps into their tiny drawstring bag and then into her handbag. She could see Sam striding towards her purposefully in the grey bodycon dress she'd warned Zoe off wearing, as Sam approached, she grinned and waved at Zoe. Zoe reciprocated her friends warm greeting, as she clipped her bag shut and got to her feet.

Within moments Sam was standing at her side, her flat shoes replaced by grey suede sandals that fastened at the ankle. Sam's bag was a jade green colour, that matched her earrings and bracelet. Zoe loved green and resolved to treat herself to a dress in the colour of Sam's bag the next time she was online. 'You look great' Zoe told her friend, 'I *love* that bag'. Sam stood back and looked Zoe up and down. 'You're not so bad yourself' she giggled, as she clasped her friends hand and they started to totter along the cobbled main street.

The girls made their way through town at a leisurely pace. Unlike many evenings when they had shuffled their way through town huddled beneath an umbrella, this evening was warm, with the sun still shining over the top of the guildhall building. Zoe had always loved going out in the summer when there was no need for tights, coats or umbrellas. It gave her a sense of freedom, that with a pang of regret she realised she now truly had. She shook her head to clear the miserable thought, she needed to take advantage of her new found positivity and enjoy the impromptu evening with her loyal best friend.

As Sam squeezed her hand and interrupted her thoughts, Zoe realised she had unintentionally gripped Sam, while her mind had been pre-occupied with Ryan. Loyal Sam had of course given her an encouraging squeeze back, no doubt reading Zoe's mind accurately, as only a true best friend can. Whatever happened in Zoe's life, she knew she was truly blessed to have Sam as her best friend. She glanced across at her girly soul mate and grinned. Her grin deepened when Sam reciprocated with what could only be described as a ten gigawatt smile.

The girls knew their routine well, and both stopped outside a little cafe bar called glimmer. They headed inside for a pre-dinner glass of medium white wine. Traditionally, this was the catch up drink, but Sam had been with Zoe so much lately, supporting and comforting her through her break up, that there was really no need to catch up at all. It was nice all the same to stick to the routine Zoe thought as the first heavenly sip of chilled Pinot Grigio slid down her throat. Sam occasionally drank wine with Zoe, but she much preferred cocktails and spirits and prosecco if she was drinking wine. Tonight, rather than joining her friend with a Pinot, she ordered a gin and tonic in a large gin ballon with plenty of ice and strawberries floating on top.

They treated themselves to the full works at The Lemon Grove restaurant, three courses and a bottle of Prosecco to share. 'That cheesecake was to die for' Sam sighed as they left the restaurant arm in arm. 'Not the best start to the diet mind' she continued. Zoe didn't respond. It had been a while since she'd been out, and the wine had gone to her head, she was too busy navigating the cobbles in her four inch stilettos to reassure Sam about their binge. As it was, Sam was in high spirits and didn't notice her friends lack of conversation.

Without speaking the girls both automatically headed into The Sun. Another part of the routine they knew so well. The sun had recently been refurbished, the battered tables and fabric covered benches had been replaced with high tables surrounded by brown and cream faux leather bar stools. Where the sticky patterned carpet had once been their stilettos now clicked across pale wooden flooring, and at the bar the real ales had been superseded by cocktails and flavoured shots of noxious liquors. The girls both ordered another glass of Prosecco and settled onto some of the faux leather stools.

Although Zoe and Sam came out often, Zoe felt different tonight. She realised that the men ogling them from the bar weren't just a joke anymore. She'd have to start interacting with some of them if she was going to meet someone to replace Ryan and avoid a life of loneliness. The thought made her heart sink and her stomach turn. 'Come on Sam, lets get some shots to cheer me up' Zoe shrilled at her friend in the hope of distracting herself from the thoughts rushing through her mind. Sam's face flashed concern for a split-second, and then her easy smile returned 'sure thing sister!!' She laughed as she slid off her stool, flicked her hair over her shoulder and shimmied her dress back down to an appropriate length all in one fluid movement.

Zoe watched Sam approach the bar, flashing her smile and flickering her eyelashes at the groups of men she passed by. Their gazes followed her as she weaved her way through the busy bar area. 'There's an art to this' Zoe thought, 'and Im sure I used to know the ins and outs of it all'. Although Zoe had met Ryan fairly young, she had been out and about with her girlfriends from the age of fifteen. She recognised all the attention seeking tricks as she watched Sam, but noted that Sam's techniques had evolved exponentially since those tentative beginnings back in the 00's. How hadn't she noticed her friend turning into an irresistible siren exuding sex appeal from every pore? Zoe's eyes widened as she realised that she had some serious catching up to do.

'S'up?' Sam eyed Zoe questioningly as she returned and slammed the shots on the table in a grand gesture. Without waiting for a response from her friend, she half turned back to the bar and held her glass up in a salute, Zoe noticed some guy wink at Sam, and maybe even blush a little, 'courtesy of Kirk' Sam stated still smiling towards the bar. As she raised her glass towards her mouth, Zoe grabbed her arm . *That* is what's up!' She half laughed half wailed at Sam. 'How will I ever catch up with you and your temptress skills?' Now it was Sam's turn to laugh 'you already are a temptress Zo! We just need to fine tune your skills- release your inner goddess! Kirk's friend said you were *mighty fine*'. Zoe felt encouraged, and glanced back towards Kirk... And his Danny DeVito like friend. He stared right back into her eyes' then made the crudest blow job gesture Zoe had seen in a long time. Zoe thought she might cry.

Having necked their shots, they exited the Sun by stumbling through the door onto the street, giggling as they collided with a snooty looking couple headed towards the theatre. 'Mojito time' Sam chirped as she led Zoe by the hand down the stone steps into The Cellar cocktail bar. Zoe was really feeling the effects of the alcohol now, but as long as she didn't let her thoughts drift to Ryan, she was feeling pretty good.

As they nestled their way into the bar, the girls both ordered a mojito, and stood in the crowded little room, bouncing their hips to the music, and glancing around at the groups of people near them.

As Zoe glanced over Sam's left shoulder, a pair of blue eyes met hers. She looked at the owner of the deep blue eyes, and found they belonged to a tall, maybe 6 foot, blonde haired man, with a kind face and a smile that showed off his perfect teeth. His smile seemed to be aimed in her direction. Zoe frowned a little and glanced over her shoulder to locate the Emilia Clarke look alike behind her, that she was sure the guy must have been smiling at. The only thing behind her was a wall. Zoe turned back towards him and now he seemed to be chuckling at her, and wow, his blue eyes were sparkling.

Zoe's breath caught in her throat, and her stomach fluttered. As he was drawn back into the conversation in his group, Zoe stole glances at mr blue eyes. Once or twice she met his eyes again, each time he smiled and she was rendered senseless. Each time he looked away, she mentally kicked herself for having gawped back at him rather than returning his easy, sexy smile. Although Sam didn't comment on her friends obvious interest in one of the guys standing in the group behind them, she did steal a quick glance at the group and note what a fine specimen Zoe had her eyes on.

Sam felt relieved at Zoe's obvious attraction to a member of the opposite sex, she'd been really worried about coming out tonight and drinking with Zoe. Alcohol could make everything seem so much better or so very much worse. She felt pleased that it looked like Zoe was going for a happy drunk night, she even fantasised that her friend could hook up with the blue eyed guy permanently and be over her Ryan heartache for good. Just last week she'd read in Cosmo that rebound love was the best thing for a broken heart. Yep, Sam had a pretty good feeling about mr blue over there, and from her friends wide mouthed gawp, so did Zoe!

As the group of men left the bar, they walked right past Zoe and Sam who were half way through their second mojitos. The cocky dark haired member of the group, who seemed to be in charge and was leading the way for the group, winked at Sam as he passed and Sam smiled back. Zoe didn't notice. She was too busy holding the gaze of mr blue. This time she managed a smile, which was instantly returned as he passed, and then he was gone. Up the stone steps and out into the night. Zoe looked at Sam wide eyed. 'Go after him and get his number!' Sam responded without being asked a question. The look from her friend told Sam this would be too much too soon, and so Sam continued. 'There'll be plenty more blue eyed boys after a lovely lady like you Zoe. Now, drink that mojito! The Feathers is calling me for a pornstar martini!'

\*\*\*\*\*

The cocktail was deep orange with a shot of Prosecco sitting alongside it. Zoe's head was beginning to spin, so she watched as Sam took large gulps of her own sweet cocktail. They always chose PS martinis here, they were the best in town. Zoe glanced at her watch, realising she had no idea what the time was. It was already ten to midnight, which explained why the dance floor was beginning to fill up with groups of girls gyrating as they flicked their hair and waved flutes full of fizz in the air. Groups of horny teenage boys surrounded the dance floor, watching the women move to the tunes. No question thought Zoe, the Feathers was pretty rough!! Sam must have been having exactly the same thoughts as she glanced over at Zoe and raised her eyebrows. The girls burst into laughter. Although they loved the cocktails here, they weren't really fans of either the music or the clientele.

Glancing around, Zoe noted there were no mr blues, just scrawny men with rodent like features and moustaches grown from fine down rather than serious facial hair. Also, she discovered on her way to the ladies, many of these men had serious roving hand issues. Zoe was always amazed that men still thought, on a night out, it was acceptable to feel women up. They went all week without grabbing a woman's bum, but it was as though on a Friday night, they got a free pass. On the short walk to and from the bathroom, Zoe had her bottom squeezed twice, pinched once and even rubbed. This was another reason her and Sam weren't massive fans of the venue. Still, lintfield didn't have late music bars in abundance and so they tolerated it for a quick cocktail now and then!

*****

It was a quarter after midnight when the girls stepped off the cobbled street into 'Afters'; one of the two late night bars in addition to the Feathers, that hosted a DJ and had a dance floor. The other venue, Club Chameleon, was frequented by those ten years Zoe's junior, and so Afters was the older persons choice in Lintfield. And in all fairness, it was pretty good. It's two floors were all red leather and wood, with lots of booths, sofas and stools to sit at. The music was usually 80's and 90's on a Friday night which suited Zoe and Sam perfectly. They loved all those cheesy 80's hits from fame and flash dance, but also enjoyed bouncing around to Mr Brightside and other party songs. There was no doubting it, Afters suited them perfectly!

They headed straight for the busy bar, where Sam used her elbows, breasts and smile to get to the front. As she was waiting to be served, Zoe glanced around and spotted him. There he was, gorgeous mr blue eyes, standing by the flashing quiz machine, laughing with his friends. 'Woah' Zoe subconsciously breathed causing Sam to follow her gaze and smirk a little. Then he looked over at them, and caught them staring. 'Shit' Zoe exclaimed, 'why does that always happen? Whenever I look at him he catches me in the act. He must think I'm a real bunny boiler'.

'Nonsense' scolded Sam 'he must be looking at you lots to catch you looking at him! Why don't we head over there and talk to him? I wouldn't mind spending a little time with the dark haired Adonis' Sam winked at Zoe. Zoe blushed, and rather than face the humiliation of being caught staring again, snatched their recently purchased drinks from the bar and headed toward the dance floor in the opposite direction to mr blue and

Sam's Adonis.

As they got to the dance floor Sam began to protest, but the DJs perfectly timed mix blended into one of Sam's favourites, maniac, and Zoe's telling off was forgotten as her fickle friend began strutting her stuff on the dance floor. Zoe smiled at her affectionately then threw her head back and joined in Sam's tuneless singing with the chorus.

As they danced, the DJ, Cal, winked and waved at the girls. They knew him pretty well, as their friend Tamasyn had recently had a passionate fling with him. It hadn't lasted, but there were no hard feelings. Cal was a nice guy, and his love affair with Tam meant he always played their favourite songs when they were on a girls night out. Tonight was no exception, and he followed up Sam's favourite 'maniac' with 'take on me', Zoe's favourite song to sing and dance to. She just loved Morton Harket's voice, the lyrics and especially the video. Zoe closed her eyes and let herself go. She'd slowed up on the drinking, and had recovered very slightly , her head wasn't spinning as much now, she just felt deliciously tipsy, sexy and confident. She wiggled and sang to her hearts content gazing only at Sam who smiled and danced with her, singing to her best friend as only the closest of girl friends do.

As the song came to an end and Tiffany's 'I think we're alone now' kicked in, Zoe felt someone's eyes on her back at the same time as she saw Sam glance over her shoulder. Sam's eyes widened a little causing Zoe to turn around. He was standing less than a metre away from her, his blue eyes gazing into hers, his perfect teeth smiling at her. He took a step closer and leaned in to her ear so that she could hear him. Oh wow she thought, he smelled delectable.

As he spoke his lips brushed her right ear, causing her breath to catch in her throat 'that was some nice dancing' he murmured. Zoe was struggling to get a grip of herself. She felt certain he could hear her heart pounding, and blushed at the thought of him knowing the effect he was having on her. Thank goodness it was dark! 'Aren't you going to speak to me?' He was leaning in again. This time, as his lips brushed her ear, his right hand skimmed her left hip. It was like an electric current passed through her body wherever he touched her. She needed to get a grip and say something, but she seemed to be rendered speechless.

Thankfully Sam had spotted her friends discomfort and cut in to buy Zoe a little breathing space 'Zo, I'm just off to the ladies. Do you have any powder with you?' Zoe opened her bag on autopilot, but could thankfully feel her breathing rate slow. Sam leaned forward as she took the Clinique powder from Zoe's hand and instructed in a low voice 'be calm, be cool, you can do this!' And then she was gone, headed up the stairs to the ladies, but not without drawing the attention of at least eight men on the way Zoe noted with a smile. And just like that Zoe was calm, Sam really did know her she mused before turning to blue eyes and saying 'sorry, I'm Zoe, so you liked my cheesy dancing huh?!'

As they chatted the sparks continued to fly. His name was Pete, he was a manager at a local wine merchants, he was gorgeous, he was sexy and he seemed to be interested in her. Zoe was amazed. She was also amazed that she had recovered her ability to flirt, must be like riding a bike she thought. Pete bought Zoe a Prosecco, and then another, Zoe started to worry where Sam had got to. As she glanced around the bar anxiously, Pete said 'she's standing outside talking to Alex, do you want to head out to them?'

Zoe nodded and headed off towards the door. As she stepped outside and the cool night air hit her, so did the extra Prosecco. Her head felt woozy, and her stomach was starting to churn a little, she needed her bed. She looked around hopelessly for Sam, frowning as she tried to focus her very drunk eyes. Pete tugged her hand and pointed to where Sam was leaning up the wall kissing Alex the Adonis passionately. He smiled and said 'Alex is the charmer of the group, it seems he charmed your friend'.

Zoe looked over to where her friend was leant up the wall, one knee up next to Alex's hip, hands firmly planted on the back pockets of his jeans pulling his body towards her in a passionate embrace. Zoe turned back to Pete and tried to smile, but suddenly felt lost and abandoned by her friend. Her concern must have shown on her face because Pete pulled her into his arms and rested his chin on her head as she sank into his chest, and then in one fluid movement he was tilting her chin up to his face and leaning down towards her. Zoe parted her lips as Pete's warm mouth met hers, she felt his arms embrace her more tightly as his mouth pushed against hers softly and then more urgently. Zoe tilted her head further letting him explore her mouth, she tried to let herself go, to lose herself in the moment, but there it was, Ryan's face, as clear in her mind as though he was standing right in front of her.

She pulled back from Pete, and gave her head the slightest of shakes to clear the image of Ryan from her mind. Pete tilted his head slightly as though considering what to do next and then planted a chaste kiss on her lips, whilst looking into Zoe's eyes. He was gorgeous, what was wrong with her? She parted her lips once more as he pulled her back against his body. She could feel the urgency of his kiss, as he kissed her harder again, she tried to kiss him back with the same intensity, but all she saw was Ryan.

Suddenly Zoe was backing away from him, shaking her head at his confused expression. 'No' she said, 'No, this is wrong...this feels so wrong' She looked at his confused frown, and could feel the hot tears behind her eyes begin to form. Suddenly she was running, away from Afters, away from Pete and away from the image of Ryan in her mind. Once she was safely back in her house, Zoe let the tears fall, hot and salty and intense from the alcohol. She cried and cried, only stopping to respond to Sam's persistent text messages demanding to know she was ok. Zoe's tears fell heavily, shaking her body, never ceasing until she fell into a restless sleep. Her alcohol induced slumber bought her no real peace, just distorted visions of Pete and Ryan and painful reminders of how broken her heart truly was.

# CHAPTER 3: THE MORNING AFTER

Zoe tried to open her eyes but the throbbing in her head and threat of light flooding her pupils stopped her. She took a moment to take stock of why she felt so bad, as she recounted her night with Sam in her head, she tried to recall exactly how much she had had to drink. Clearly way too much. As her weary brain walked her through the previous evening, his blue eyes flashed in her minds-eye and her memory of the previous night suddenly became crystal clear. Zoe groaned and rolled onto her stomach, tucking her arms beneath her pillow and burying her face in the top of it. 'What an idiot' she muttered to herself, her voice full of disdain for herself.

Without moving her face or opening her eyes, Zoe slid open her bed side drawer, plucked out some paracetamol, dropped them in her mouth and negotiated a glass of water to her now raised head- eyes still tightly shut. She let her head drop back on her pillow and with deep breathes once again considered the previous night. The thought of Pete's blue eyes and friendly smile made her feel warm inside, but then she recalled herself running, or rather staggering quickly, down the street, having behaved like a complete lunatic, this made her feel less warm inside and more like she wanted to curl up and die of embarrassment.

Zoe rolled back over onto her side and tried to breathe deeply. She thought about his electric touch, his perfect teeth, his hands on her hips and in her hair and his lips on hers, warm and soft and intense.

With her mind more happily engaged Zoe drifted back to sleep, this time she dreamt about Pete in her bed, kissing her passionately, touching her, the dream was just getting interesting when she was awoken by the buzzing of her mobile. Drowsily, Zoe clawed around on the floor by the bed and retrieved her bag, abandoned there the night before, she pulled out her mobile and saw it was Sam. 'Hey' Zoe spoke quietly 'you ok?' Sam asked? 'Yes, but my head has a group of work men hammering inside it' 'mine too' groaned Sam. 'Coffee and catch up at 2? Costa?' Sam's concise conversation was the usual following a heavy night. The girls always spoke first thing, just to check the other was fine, arrange a meet up and then they'd leave well alone until an hour when they were reasonably well recovered.

Having agreed a meeting with Sam, Zoe clicked on the radio to her favourite local station and put the volume low so she could just hear it when lying quietly. She dozed on and off until 11 am, then got out of bed and headed for the shower. Her mind continued to drift to Pete, his blue eyes and his sexy kiss. It was a welcome relief from thinking about her loss, and Ryan-less future, but with this welcome relief came frustration at herself. Why had she been so stupid, she didn't have his number or have anyway to contact him, not that she would anyway now; he probably thought she was a right head case. Zoe stopped mid-lather at this thought. Was she a right head case? Probably, she conceded. 'Grrr' she growled at herself to express her anger and frustration at the turn of events last night. She'd never seen him out in Lintfield before, so was unlikely to see him out there again. As she turned off the shower, she resigned herself to the fact she wouldn't see Pete again, and anyhow, even if she hadn't gone off on one, there was nothing to say he would have taken her number anyway, let alone called. In fact, she told herself forcefully as she towelled herself dry, he was probably only after one thing anyway. Her friend Louise was always meeting men that were only after one thing, why would Pete be any different?

Her friend Lou was desperate to settle down and have children, she'd been on the look out for the man to make this happen for over five years. Sam and Zoe hadn't known Louise very long compared to their own friendship, but knew she had been married reasonably young, at 23 and was all for having babies straight away.

Sadly, within months of her wedding to her childhood sweetheart, she'd come home to find her husband in bed with her (former) best friend. According to Lou she had come home from work early and heard noises upstairs, thinking it may be an intruder she had crept up to her bedroom, mobile phone in one hand and knife in the other. She had walked in to her bedroom to find her best friend, fucking her husband senseless in her marital bed. According to Lou, who had the humour to laugh about it now, they hadn't even had the courtesy to stop when she walked in. They had apparently paused to look at her with pained expressions, but when she'd stormed out expecting her husband to follow her begging for forgiveness, she'd had to wait a full ten minutes, and listen to their noisy mutual climax, before either of them showed their face downstairs.

Ever since, Lou had dated relentlessly, but with no success in finding mr Right. Sam said it was because she was scared of getting hurt again, Zoe wasn't sure; the probability was that she ought to have met someone by now, after all she'd been on hundreds of dates. Maybe Sam was right and Lou liked the company and the idea of settling down, but was actually commitment phobic, or maybe there just weren't any decent men out there. Zoe considered Lou's situation as she applied her eyeshadow and added her false eyelashes, and decided that whatever the reason, she would rather be alone than spend years going on dates with men that had no redeeming qualities at all.

By the time Zoe walked into Costa at the top of Lintfield town, she was feeling much better. Her head had stopped pounding and she didn't feel like she might throw up any second. Those extreme symptoms had been replaced with feeling chronically tired and anxious. Oh the joys of a hang over.

She spotted Sam in their favourite place in the window in one of the high backed leather chairs that coffee shops always put at the front to make the place look comfortable and inviting. Unfortunately, if you weren't timely enough to grab those chairs, the alternatives were hard dark wood dining room chairs that weren't conducive to a long gossip session over creamy hot chocolate.

Sam had already purchased their costa staple hot chocolate with cream, marshmallows and caramel syrup. Not the healthiest of drink options, weighing in at over 300 calories, but it had the much needed sugar for a hangover pick me up, and the heat was just what Zoe needed, as her hangovers always brought a shivery chill that she could never understand.

Two hot chocolates and two slices of fruit toast each later the girls had analysed the previous evening and were moving on to their plans for heading to Madrid the day after next. They discussed the clothes they were travelling in, the clothes they would take and split up bulky items like hair dryer and straighteners between them. As they were flying hand luggage only, they headed to super drug to stock up on mini-toiletries that would comply with the airport security checks.

As they headed through WhSmiths to the bureau de change at the post office, Sam let out a high pitched squeal. Zoe spun round to see that somebody had grabbed Sam's waist from behind and was now laughing with Sam at how she had jumped. That somebody was Pete's friend, Alex. Zoe felt herself turn crimson, had Alex noticed her run away like an idiot? Had Pete told him how unhinged Sam's mate was? Was Pete here with him? As the thoughts rushed through her head and she looked around the shop warily, Zoe noticed that at the moment she could actually be dancing naked and Alex wouldn't notice. His head was bent down towards Sam's face and he was talking in hushed tones, loosely holding her friends right hand. Sam was all smiles too.

Zoe felt a little confused, how had this happened? How hadn't she noticed these two weren't just snogging, but were actually really into one another? They must have spent ages chatting when she was talking to Pete, Zoe realised, after all, they'd headed to Afters around midnight, and she hadn't got home 'til 2.15am. That was a long time unaccounted for. Wow. He looked smitten and Sam was all a show of girly gigglyness. Zoe felt terrible, the last few weeks had been all about her, and even today, over hot chocolate, the focus of their conversation had been how Zoe had felt when Pete had kissed her and why she'd runaway. She hadn't even asked if Sam and Alex had exchanged numbers.

Zoe realised she was staring at Sam and Alex with a start and began to back away discreetly, promptly tripping over a push-chair wheel, and disturbing their quiet dialogue. She knew she'd broken the spell as they both looked over and Sam said clearly 'Zo, this is Alex, remember him from last night?' Zoe smiled and took a step back towards them. 'Yes of course, hi Alex' Zoe said, her crimson blush returning as his eyes met hers.'You ok?' Alex asked 'Pete said he scared you off, he doesn't normally get girls running down the street in their stilettos to get away from him' Alex's laugh was sincere, but Zoe felt embarrassed and ashamed of her foolish behaviour. Her face betrayed her and Alex added 'don't sweat it. Pete can look after himself. He was kinda disappointed though, he said he really liked you'

Zoe's breathe caught in her throat and she tried to think of what to say next, could she pass her number on? Should she? Maybe she could send Pete a message to say she was sorry. As

Zoe opened her mouth to speak, she realised that she'd missed the moment. Alex's head was bent once again to her friends, and they were back in their own whispered world. Zoe turned dejectedly and headed to purchase some euros.

Pete had liked her. He'd been disappointed. This lifted Zoe's spirits. But that was before she'd rejected him wasn't it. And what did Alex mean when he said 'he doesn't normal get girls running down the street in their stilettos to get away from him'? Did that mean Pete had a lot of girls swooning over him? Only too happy to kiss him back? Probably, Zoe thought. After all, he was clearly out of her league. Maybe that was how he secured a steady flow of women through his bedroom, chose vulnerable women, slightly below his standard so that they'd feel grateful. She had after all hasn't she? Had she been used? How humiliating!

At that moment Zoe felt relieved that Sam had taken control and changed the Madrid booking. She needed some space between her and this place. She completed her purchase and turned away from the counter to find Sam standing next to her with a dreamy expression on her face.

Zoe couldn't help but smile. 'Sooo, tell me all the details!' Zoe was impressed with the enthusiasm she had mustered for her friend, and listened intently as they walked towards Next and Sam gushed about Alex. They had arranged to meet for a drink that evening before Zoe and Sam departed for Madrid.

Sam was now all anxiety and agitation about what she could wear, when everything that was a possibility was clean for their trip to Madrid. 'That's easily fixed' Zoe laughed as she dragged her friend in to Dorothy Perkins and headed to the concession rail. Sam selected some dark blue skinny jeans and a black tunic that fit tightly over her hips and hung off one shoulder. She told Zoe she would wear her nude shoes and use her matching bag. Zoe's nod of approval reassured Sam and the girls began on their walk home, hugging goodbye by their bench and arranging for Sam to be at Zoe's by 9am the day after next to drive to Birmingham airport for a midday flight.

Once home, Zoe put on her favourite leopard print loungewear, and settled down on the sofa to watch re-runs of Friends on Comedy Central. She'd seen them all plenty, but still enjoyed them. She was laughing at the episode with Ross's spray tan when her mobile beeped. Glancing over at her iPhone Zoe saw Sam's name and frowned, Sam hadn't said she'd text from her date, Zoe hoped nothing was wrong as she unlocked her phone screen and opened the message.

OMG Pete here!
Askin bout u....
Any msg 4 him?

Zoe began typing her response and deleted it several times. What should she say? As she tried a fourth attempt, her phone began to ring 'Sam!' Zoe gasped as she answered the phone 'what have you said?' The voice that responded was not the one Zoe was expecting. Instead of her friends high pitched tone, the voice was deep, she vaguely recognised it but it was out of context. 'Not Sam no' the voice said 'and what should she have said?' There was an edge of humour in the voice, and as he spoke Zoe could see his blue eyes twinkling. The voice belonged to Pete. The familiar embarrassment, that Zoe had come to associate with remembering the night before, took over and she felt herself turn red. 'So,' Pete continued talking, he seemed to be coming to her rescue, as she couldn't find a single word to squeeze out. 'I just wanted to check you're ok, and say sorry if I offended you last night.' His words caused Zoe's heart to flutter. 'You really didn't offend me Pete, and I'm fine'

Zoe felt a surge of relief as she found the words to respond. 'I'm glad you're ok' Pete continued, 'anyway, I enjoyed meeting you, but I can take a hint and you needn't worry about me having the wrong idea again if we see each other out. I just wanted to clear the air, what with my mate and yours seemingly infatuated with each other'. Pete's tone was business like. It brought a lump to Zoe's throat, but she managed to keep it together. 'That's very considerate of you Pete, thanks for calling' Zoe's voice was even but whispered. 'See you round then. Enjoy Madrid.' He said, and with that he hung up. Zoe sat on the sofa, hugged her knees and cried, but for the first time, her tears weren't about Ryan, the blue eyes causing the hurt belonged to someone new, but some-one lost all the same.

# CHAPTER 4:
# WELCOME TO MADRID

When Sam appeared at her doorway the morning, of their flight, Zoe was ready to give her friend a piece of her mind about letting Pete use her phone to call her. Zoe had thought about it intermittently since the call. It wasn't that she minded Pete's call, it was just that she was so ill-prepared for it that she'd had no chance to say any of the things she should have said, no chance to defend herself or her bizarre behaviour the night they had met and shared a kiss.

As it was, Sam looked really sheepish and practically fell onto Zoe hugging her. 'Is it true? Did Pete call you off MY phone? Alex just told me now. I'm so cross. Apparently he just took it when I was in the loo, strode off outside with it, and came back with it a couple of minutes later' the words were gushing out of Sam's mouth. 'Alex thought he'd just got your number off it, but now he's saying Pete may have text and phoned you! But its not in my texts! You look really cross- I'm so sorry Zo. I shouldn't have left my phone, I'm so stupid. How fucking presumptuous of him' Sam stopped to take a breath and Zoe took the opportunity to cut in. 'Don't worry Sam, it's not your fault. You're right about presumptuous though, how rude! He was obviously in a rude mood, as he basically told me to forget what happened as there's no chance of a re-run!' Sam's eyes were wide and questioning and so Zoe relayed their brief conversation with more accuracy. Sam huffed and groaned in all the right places before changing the subject to a more favourable topic, their trip to Madrid!

By 9.30am, the girls were on the train from Lintfield to Birmingham international airport. Zoe had checked she had everything at least thirty times by the time the train pulled into the station at 10.20am. The girls wheeled their air hostess size cases out of the station, and towards check in. Zoe felt excited at the prospect of a few days away with her best girl, and realised that she was in a very small way, pleased to be going with Sam rather than Ryan. She was young (ish) and free, she thought, and she was determined to have a good time!

As soon as they were checked in, they headed straight for the executive lounge, stopping only to purchase some fashion magazines from WhSmiths. Sam had access to the lounge through her bank account, and they were excited to have a couple of glasses of wine and a look through the latest trends in Cosmo and Red. They found a quiet corner beneath the departures screen and settled their bucket chairs beside one another. Sam headed off to get drinks and came back with two glasses of fizz, a stack of mini-pretzels and a selection of tiny, cellophane wrapped cakes that didn't look all that appetising if Zoe was honest about them. Still they sat drinking wine, flicking through the magazines and eating every unappealing snack in sight!

With half an hour to go before boarding, whilst Sam was collecting their third glass of bubbly, Zoe picked up her I-phone for a last glance at face book. As she thumbed down her newsfeed, she noted Sam had recently become 'friends' with Alex. It was too much temptation for Zoe. She clicked on Alex's profile, and was stalking his friends in moments. She'd almost given up filing down the list when she caught site of those eyes. Vivid blue, even on the tiny thumbnail on Alex's friend list, there he was-Pete Saunders. Zoe's heart lurched as she clicked on his name to view his profile.

'You stalker!' Sam's interruption caused Zoe's phone to bounce out of her hand and skim across the floor. Zoe cringed and turned bright red as she scrabbled on the floor to retrieve her phone, and Pete's profile. Sam was giggling uncontrollably, thoroughly enjoying her best friends clumsy embarrassment. 'I'm not stalking him' Zoe muttered through clenched teeth, as she heaved herself back into her bucket seat, 'I was just curious.... And a little bit stalky' Zoe laughed, joining in Sam's delight.

Sam grabbed the phone out of Zoe's hand and said 'well I'm only too happy to be a stalker, lets see what we can view. Oooo Saunders, Zoe Saunders, yep, I like it! Relationship status: single, interested in: women, good bloody job!! That's about all we can see, but we can...'. Zoe couldn't see what Sam was doing, but as she passed the phone back, Sam smirked and Zoe huffed as she spotted that Sam had saved the profile image of Pete and his twinkling eyes as her lock screen wallpaper. 'Now that....' Zoe emphasised each word as she changed her wallpaper back to her and Sam on a girls night out '... Is stalky!!!'

The girls found their seats on the plane at 11.40am. Zoe was feeling a little bit tipsy, but as she wasn't a massive fan of flying, this suited her just fine. Zoe had paid extra when booking for her and Ryan, so that they could have the seats right at the front with the extra leg room. As Sam tried to wrestle her wheeley case into an overhead locker, a very attractive male flight attendant lifted it out of her hand and slid it into the space effortlessly. Sam smiled graciously and thanked him 'no worries, here to be of assistance' he winked. Sam's face said it all as she turned to Zoe eyes wide and mouth open. 'Only one of him Zo, we'll have to share' the girls giggled in unison as the attendant headed down the aisle to assist an elderly couple with their bags. Neither Sam or Zoe could resist peering over the top of their chair backs to check out the rear view as he walked away! It was one of those film type moments, when they almost certainly would have turned back in time both breathing out the word wow as they sank back into their seats.

But as they turned back their eyes widened further as the young, dark haired, tanned pilot stepped through the aircraft door. The girls glanced sideways at each other and sniggered simultaneously.  The flight attendant strode back up the aisle and shook hands with the pilot. The banter that followed, about a recent night out in the city, suggested the men were good friends. They chatted for another minute before the flight attendant picked up the phone for the in cabin intercom. 'Hello, my name is Mark and I'll be leading your cabin crew for the flight down to Madrid today. Working with me I have Marie and Charlotte. Our pilot is William Southall and he's assisted by co-pilot Dan Thomson' as he said this he smiled at his friend and raised his eyebrows.

The girls glanced at each other again, wordless code for 'their names are Mark and Dan', Mark continued 'we'll be heading off ten minutes later than planned, but should be landing as scheduled, please sit back and take your ease and my team and I will be back in ten minutes or so for your flight safety demonstration'. Mark replaced the phone handset, muttered something quietly to co-pilot Dan and then turned directly to Sam and Zoe. 'So ladies, you know our names are Mark and Dan, how about you tell us yours?!'. Usually Zoe would leave this sort of thing to bubbly Sam, but the wine was providing plenty of Dutch courage. 'Im Zoe, this is Sam. So, lead flight attendant and co-pilot, hope you boys are going to keep us safe' Zoe and Sam were both stunned at the ease with which she purred the sentence. Their audience were both smiling and nodding their heads in response and in approval. 'I'll make sure you're very safe' Dan grinned, 'and Mark will make sure you're well looked after'. The girls grinned as Dan winked 'laters' and retreated to the cock pit.

Mark completed his safety demonstration with frequent sideways glances at the front row, and then took his place in the cabin crew seat opposite the girls, ready for take off. 'So, are you girls hooking up with your guys in Madrid?' Mark's question was a classic 'find out if they're single' ruse. 'No, no men in our lives at the moment' Sam chimed, all smiles. Zoe glanced sideways at her friend, wondering if she was the same person that had been infatuated with Alex just hours before. 'So,' Mark was continuing 'Dan and I are on a stop over tonight if you fancied meeting up for something to eat? Maybe some drinks?' His smile was relaxed and easy, and Zoe noted what straight, white teeth he had. 'That sounds great' Zoe's own voice shocked her. She wouldn't usually be so confident, maybe she should begin everyday with a glass or two of wine she thought. She returned Mark's warm smile and then looked out of the window to watch the ground fall away beneath them. Mark was busy working for the remainder of the flight, only getting around to collecting Sam's number as they were landing. As the girls disembarked the aeroplane, Mark winked and held his thumb and little finger up to his face signalling that he'd call later that day, once he'd flown back to Birmingham, and back to Madrid again!

*****

The girls were through customs and heading out the arrivals door in minutes, Zoe loved travelling hand luggage only, it saved so much hassle at the crowded luggage carousels. As they headed out the sliding doors, Sam dropped back a little to let Zoe take the lead. The one thing the girls had never had in common was their organisation, or lack of it, in Sam's case. Zoe was meticulous in everything and had pre-planned the trip in micro-detail as soon as it was booked. She led the way straight onto the airport shuttle bus, paid the €5 fee, and within moments, they were on route to the terminal at Plaza de Colón, in the centre of Madrid.

The weather was glorious, but the air conditioned bus meant that the girls could enjoy the journey without suffering from the 32 degree heat. 45 minutes later the girls dragged their air hostess cases, off the bus, and simultaneously fished inside them to retrieve their sunglasses. Zoe slid her Dior sunglasses over her eyes, and tipped her face up to the sun, the heat felt blissful on her cheeks. Sam reached over and squeezed Zoe's hand- they grinned at each other, grabbed their cases, and Zoe began leading the way South along Paseo de Recoletos.

The girls took their time and took in the sights as they strolled along the Gran Via towards Calle Valverde and their 4* hotel. Their room was basic, but clean and modern, with a balcony looking onto the narrow street below. Zoe headed to the bathroom to freshen up whilst Sam began unpacking the few items she had brought in her tiny case. Zoe splashed cool water on her face, and then patted it dry with one of the clean, but slightly off white, towels that she noted had an embossed crab on it, matching the picture from the hotels logo. She sat on the edge of the bath, closed her eyes and took a deep breath. Here she was, on her romantic city break to Madrid, single, with a girlfriend for company. Not the way she planned it, but even a week ago she'd never have imagined being here- 'it's all progress' she muttered under her breath before heading out of the bathroom and joining Sam on the balcony.

Within an hour, they were sitting in a small square across the other side of the Gran Via, sipping their first cool beer. With Zoe and Sam loving food as they did, Spain was perfect, as every drink arrived with a small snack or tapas plate. With their cool Estrella, they were munching on juicy green olives, almost the size of golf balls! They sat with their legs outstretched in the sunshine, watching the world go by and enjoying the warmth of the sun on their skin. Zoe had changed into a bold print strapless dress in red and blue, and Sam had on a strappy coral sundress with white lace trim at the top and bottom.

Zoe had no idea what they would do with their time here, she had planned a day by day itinerary of sightseeing for her and Ryan, but didn't really want to drag Sam around on it. Although

Sam enjoyed seeing the sights, she rarely enjoyed the military operation Zoe made of it! They were on their second drink, looking through their tour guides and planning their days, when Sam's phone rang. It was Mark the flight attendant. They'd just landed and were still keen to meet up! As Sam chatted and giggled, she signalled to Zoe to get a pen and hand her a tour guide. Zoe obligingly routed in her bag, then handed both to Sam. Sam circled a small street, Calle de Tetuán, on the map in the front of the guide, and then scrawled 'Casa Labra 6pm' in the margin. Zoe looked at her watch and frowned- it was already 5pm!

Once Sam had hung up the phone, they hurriedly made their way back to the hotel room, giggling in a haze of girly excitement. They quickly showered in turn and huddled by the mirror to apply their make up. Zoe dressed carefully in a cream floaty mid-thigh dress, that was covered with butterflies. As she bent down to put her highest heeled nude coloured sandals on, Sam laughed. It didn't matter how hot it was, or how far they had to walk. They always wore their heels. Sam had dressed in a navy blue halter neck play suit, exposing her falsely tanned smooth thighs, and accessorised with nude sling backs and clutch bag. 'Oh my god- I have butterflies' Sam shrieked as they left the hotel 'who's having who then?' She continued. 'What?' Zoe laughed, 'I thought it was an innocent drink! And that you lurved Alex!!' Sam held her right index finger to her lips in an exaggerated gesture and said 'hmmmmm, what happens on tour and all that! And innocent my arse! Bagsy Mark the foxy flight attendant!'

By ten past six they were headed down Calle de Tetuán, to casa labra, an old bar serving cold beers and hot tapas. Mark and Dan were sitting on high stools at a table outside. Without saying a word to one another, Sam and Zoe both slowed to check their reflections in the shop windows and check out their dates for the evening. Mark was wearing a short sleeved white polo shirt with blue jeans and white trainers. His sandy brown hair glinted in the sun as he chatted to his friend Dan. In contrast Dan's hair was black and shiny, his teeth were gleaming Hollywood white as he laughed at Mark's conversation. He was wearing a pale pink polo shirt that was snug over his biceps, slim fit jeans and white converse. Zoe's tummy knotted- he was looking really good, just her type, more so than blonde haired Pete she mused to herself. And in that second Zoe realised she wasn't out for an innocent drink, she was there for Dan, and to make up for the mess she'd made of Friday night. She was out to prove that Sam was right, that she could get over Ryan. She could move on, and for the first time since Ryan had left her, she was determined to prove it!

From the moment they greeted the boys, it was clear that their pairing preferences matched the girls. Mark pulled Sam a stool up next to him, and Dan was all smiles at Zoe. They ordered beers, croquetas, Bacalao and tortillas española. The Bacalao, battered cod pieces, were delicious and Dan laughed at how hungry Zoe was.

Dan's laugh was easy and relaxed, his smile sparkled and when he laughed his whole face radiated happiness. Zoe found herself relaxed in no time, Dan's happiness was infectious. He chatted about his job and all the interesting places he'd been. 'You don't always get leisure time built into your stopovers though, and to have a stop over with two lovely ladies for company is a real bonus' he smiled warmly as he spoke to Zoe. As she held his gaze she noticed his hand lift slowly and thought how romantic it was that he was going to brush hair hair off her face, or stroke her cheek, her stomach clenched in anticipation. Surely he'd follow it with a kiss, in the milliseconds that followed, Zoe had imagined how soft his lips would be, how he'd pull her stool towards him whilst still kissing her, how his hands would tangle in the back of her hair as the kiss grew more passionate. And then, he picked a sizeable piece of batter off the corner of her lip and said 'I've needed to do that for the last five minutes'.

The spell was broken and Zoe was the colour of a beetroot! 'Oh my god' she thought to herself 'I'm the least sexy woman in the world, no one will ever want me, why do i keep making such a fool of myself?' Thoughts like these ran through Zoe's head until the waiter brought out tortilla española. The small Spanish omelettes with potatoes were golden and looked delicious, but Zoe had completely lost her appetite. For the hour that followed, Dan and Mark continued to entertain them with stories of their trips and travel, occasionally interacting as a group, but mainly chatting as two discreet couples. Zoe tried to smile and laugh but that small incident had left her feeling an idiot, and running through her head as though on playback, were all the times Ryan had been late and she'd believed his excuses, the wedding where he'd been missing, the night outside Afters with Pete where she'd made a complete idiot of herself. Zoe could feel her sorrow engulfing her, and really wanted to be back at home in her favourite PJs, on the sofa by herself, no one to try to impress, no one to remind her how hopeless she was at getting or keeping a man.

'What do you think Zo?' Sam's voice cut into her thoughts 'Another drink here, then move on?'. Zoe felt like heading back to the room alone, but looking at Sam's face, she knew her friend was enjoying herself, and Zoe knew she owed Sam for all the care and attention she'd given her in recent weeks. 'Sure' Zoe managed a smile, and Sam's hand was promptly in the air ordering a bottle of white wine for them to share. The white wine helped. Zoe began to relax and enjoy the late evening sun on her skin, she smiled more freely again and told Dan a little about the ups and downs of teaching teenagers.

It was only when they all stood up to move on that Zoe realised just how much the wine was helping, and just how tipsy she was. Dan held her elbow to steady her. His hand was warm on her skin, but even with her senses diluted by the white Rioja, she noted that it didn't tingle like when Pete had touched her. There was no electric shock. It was still nice though, and still made her feel warm inside, or was that the mixture of wine, beer and tapas? Zoe giggled aloud at her internal dialogue. Dan looked down curiously at her 'I'm a little tipsy' Zoe smiled up at him in way of explanation. Dan smiled back and the warm feeling returned, definitely not the wine, beer tapas mix. Definitely the handsome pilot Zoe thought triumphantly, as she took Dan's hand in hers and gave it a squeeze.

As they strolled slowly along the Madrid side streets, the sun began to sink below the roof tops causing odd shaped shadows to fall on the ground ahead of them. Zoe sighed contentedly, the combination of warmth, sunshine and alcohol was definitely good for her mental health she mused, as was the pilot on her arm. Having heard her sigh, Dan was now smiling at her 'it is a beautiful city' he said as though Zoe's sigh had told him what she was thinking 'with some excellent company' Zoe added and grinned back at Dan. It was true- she was enjoying his company, he was so easy to be with, she felt truly relaxed, so much so that she had no idea where they were or where they were headed, but she felt safe. But, she thought as Dan squeezed her hand tightly, where were the sparks, the electricity, the tension? Maybe you only get that if you're drunk on first laying eyes on each other, she'd have to ask Sam!

Mark and Sam were five shop fronts ahead of Zoe and Dan, she noticed as they slowed down and glanced back along the street to their slower companions. As Dan and Zoe increased their pace to catch up, Sam and Mark headed down some steps that reminded Zoe of the entrance to the Cellar bar in Lintfield.

The bar below the street had some similarities to the cellar bar- it was small with low ceilings, but that was really where the resemblance ended. The lighting in this bar was fluorescent blue, making everybody look slightly alien. They had entered in the centre of the wall opposite the bar, which took the whole length of the cellar and had colour changing down lights over the optics, making it really difficult to tell which spirit was which.

Either side of where they had entered, the floor was raised and people were dancing to some euro pop, some rather drunkenly.

Zoe tried to shake away an uneasy feeling that crept over her, as she reflected that Dan and Mark wouldn't take them anywhere too seedy. Would they? Sensing her concern, Dan held her elbow and guided her to the bar behind Mark and Sam. 'This place has the best measures of Anis in town! Worth suffering the clientele for!' He laughed in Zoe's ear. 'Anis?' Zoe questioned, then wondered if it was something she should really know about. Would Dan laugh at her ignorance? Goodness- this dating was a minefield! 'It's a Spanish spirit made from distilling aniseed' Dan informed her just as Mark lifted 4 shot glasses of Anis, over his head as he turned away from the busy bar. 'Down the hatch' Mark exclaimed, as him, Sam and Dan tipped the liquid down their throats. Zoe tried to ignore the anxiety butterflies forming in her stomach, and followed suit.

Although she wasn't a massive fan of the burning liquid, by her second shot, Zoe was sensing it had the properties she looked for in an alcoholic beverage! She and Sam were on the raised dance floor, shaking their hips to Clean Bandit's Solo. The boys were standing just off the dance floor, chatting with each other, and casting admiring glances in Sam and Zoe's direction. Just as she started singing the chorus, Zoe noticed Sam's eyes widen. Zoe was too drunk to read her friends expression accurately, was her singing worse than usual? Had one of her false eyelashes come off? Before Zoe had chance to run through any more scenarios, she felt a pair of hands slide across her bottom, around her hips and onto her stomach. She was all drunken confusion, Dan wasn't on the dance floor a moment ago, how had he moved so quickly. As she reached down to put her hands over Dan's, the horror of reality hit her hard. The hands were big and hairy, they weren't Dan's hands at all. As she tried to pull away, they grabbed hold of her tightly and spun her around so that she was chest to chest with a large, thick set man with a snarly face and a thick lips set into a sneer. He had coarse black facial hair that was turning grey, his face was wrinkled and his teeth yellow. As Zoe struggled to slide out of his grasp the man jeered, released her waist and grabbed her wrists.

Oh god, he was going to force himself on her. As she bobbed her head from side to side, trying to wriggle free, she was aware of cheering and laughter coming from the men surrounding them. Where was Sam? Zoe turned back to look at her captor, just as he leant in to kiss her. The stench of his breath turned her stomach and she yelped, just as a fist came from out of nowhere and hit the side of the twisted face with such force it made a crunch. Zoe hadn't got a clue what was going on, but was aware she was being dragged by her right wrist up the stairs out of the bar.

At the top of the stairs, Dan stopped dragging her, and held her by her shoulders, squarely in front of him. He looked her up and down as he spoke 'are you ok, god I'm so sorry I couldn't get to you. They'd surrounded you! Did he hurt you? The bastards! Thank god you're ok'. Zoe glanced away from Dan's concerned face, back down the stairs just in time to see the men pouring through the door, Snarly face in the lead. The side of his face was bleeding and already beginning to swell. Man, he looked pissed. 'Come on!' Zoe was suddenly aware that she was being dragged along by Dan again. They were running, her heels clinking on the paving, her head was spinning and she wanted to throw up but she kept going, blindly following Dan as he held her hand tightly, never letting go once. As they turned another corner he pulled her into a dark, narrow alley way and pressed his finger to her lips to signify their need to be quiet. She tiptoed behind him down the alley way as it became darker and narrower. Her chest was heaving and her heart racing, she had to stop and breathe. She leant against the cool brick wall and tried to steady herself. Her head wasn't spinning anymore, the adrenaline coursing through her veins had sobered her up almost instantly. She wanted to cry, where was Sam? Dan's face was suddenly lit by the screen of his mobile phone. He was reading a text. He held it up so Zoe could read it.

'We're both fine. Back on Gran Via. Meet at Con a Che in 15 mins?' Dan typed with speed 'Yep - we're both ok too. Cu in 15'.

Dan slipped the I-phone back into his pocket and leant against the wall opposite Zoe. 'I am so sorry Zoe.' Dan's face was barely visible in the dark of the alley, but she could tell from his voice that it was pained. 'Dan, you saved me! I'm sorry for get- ting us into that mess in the first place!' Dan took a step closer to Zoe and gently put his hands on her waist. 'Hope you're still pleased we met up'. Zoe smiled, even though Dan couldn't see. 'Of course I am' she whispered, as she covered his hands with hers. He winced, and she realised his right hand must be bruised from hitting Snarly's head. She gently picked it up and took it to her mouth, softly kissing each knuckle in turn. Dan sighed and gently pulled his hand away from her mouth, and then, his warm soft lips were on hers. Kissing her so softly and gently that it seemed inconceivable a few minutes ago he had bruised his knuckles by punching another man in the side of his head! As Zoe reached her arms up around Dan's neck. His back stiffened and he lifted his head. Zoe heard them too. The drunk men from the bar were at the end of the alley way.

Dan gently pulled her further into the alley way and around a corner. It was entirely concealed from the alley way entrance, and was pitch black. As they stood in silence, listening to see if the men entered the alley, Dan pulled her against his chest. He smelt so good. Zoe could hear his heart beating in his chest. It wasn't pounding like hers, but a steady, strong rhythm that made her feel safe and protected. They heard the men move away, but neither of them broke their embrace.

Dan's hands started to rub the small of her back and she lifted her hand to the side of his face. The pitch black heightened her senses as she felt the shape of his square jaw, and moved her hand to stroke the back of his head and his smooth black shiny hair. His mouth was suddenly on hers again, but this time his kisses were more intense. Their softness had been replaced by an urgency. She felt wanted. He pushed her so her back was against the wall, his hands moving from her hips, up onto her rib cage. Oh my, Zoe thought, there's the electricity! She kissed him back with a need that matched his urgency. His hand was on her thigh now, slowly and softly working its way up to her hip, but this time it was beneath her dress. Just as Zoe let out a small gasp, she felt Dan's pocket vibrate. His phone! Sam and Mark! They broke away from each other instantly. 'Oh shit!' Dan laughed 'we'd better hurry up!'. The text was telling them they had a seat at the restaurant, and were ordering food. What did Zoe and Dan want? Hmmm Zoe thought, she knew what she wanted at that moment, and it wasn't food!

*****

They arrived at Con a Che exactly 15 minutes after Mark had sent the first text, but Zoe knew they'd never have made it if he hadn't sent the second one! After a quick run down of what had happened, four portions of chocolate con churros arrived and the conversation dropped as they all munched on the sweet fritters. Every now and then, much to Zoe's pleasure and excitement, Dan's thigh would brush hers, or his hand would find her knee beneath the table, and squeeze it enticingly. Zoe's heart was still beating faster than normal, but she knew it wasn't because of snarly face now! She glanced sideways cautiously and found Dan doing the same. They smiled at each other and once again there was a squeeze on her knee below the table. Zoe saw Sam catch them smiling at each other, and readied herself for some ribbing, but Sam's phone gave a timely shriek and Sam jumped up to move away from the table and speak to the late night caller. Zoe pondered who could be calling at such an odd hour, when Mark's words cut into her thoughts. 'Your friend is great. Smart, pretty, funny. Shame she's so hung up on this Alex guy!'.

'What?' Zoe sounded more shocked than she'd intended, but really? Sam had told Mark about Alex? Oh my goodness- she must be infatuated with him to overlook the gorgeous flight attendant! As Sam headed back to the table, a few minutes later, she was beaming. 'Sorry about that, where were we?' she asked as she took her seat next to Mark. Luckily, Zoe noted, Sam had no recollection that she'd caught Dan and Zoe's electric eye contact just prior to receiving the call. 'Who was that?' Zoe took action to avoid Sam remembering, by asking her friend about her call. 'It was Alex' Sam grinned, then, seeing Zoe's puzzled expression, continued to explain 'I know it's Sunday, but its bank holiday tomorrow, so they're in The Sun having a few quiet beers'. As soon as Sam said 'they', his face was in her head; blonde hair and blue eyes. Zoe blinked the image away and smiled back at Sam. 'Of course, I forgot it was bank holiday'.

As they finished off their second round of chocolate con churros, Zoe let out a yawn, she suddenly felt exhausted! 'That'll be all that adrenaline leaving your system from earlier' Dan said to her, as though reading her mind. 'Come on Mark, let's walk the ladies back to their hotel'. Zoe felt a sense of desperation. She didn't want the night with Dan to end just yet. She hadn't had opportunity to revisit what had happened in the alley way; and she really wanted to! Once they were back at their hotel, in their shared room, there'd be no opportunity, and then the boys were flying again in the morning.

Zoe felt panicked at her missed opportunity, she desperately wanted to stay and have another drink, but the others were already standing and heading away from the table. As Zoe struggled to resign herself to a companionable walk home, her own phone began to buzz with a withheld number. 'Hello?', Zoe's greeting was more of a question, as she really didn't know who would be calling her at this time of night. 'Zoe?' His voice was familiar, short and sharp, but she couldn't quite place it. 'Are you ok? Alex said you were attacked!'. Holy shit! Zoe had dropped the phone on the floor, and Pete with it, Pete! What was Pete doing calling her? Zoe was aware she was now on her knees scrabbling under the table for her phone, and as she grabbed it and thrust it back at her ear, she could hear his voice 'Zoe? Zoe? Are you ok?'

Zoe took a moment to catch her breath and compose herself, as it seemed, once again she was making an absolute idiot of herself in front of this man. As she stood with the phone to her ear, her eyes met three confused expressions on her companions faces. 'Sorry' she eventually spoke into the phone, 'my phone slipped out of my hand. I'm fine. I erm wasn't really attacked,' as Zoe bumbled her way through her sentences, she tried to collect her thoughts and get a hold on herself. Sam and mark had turned and started walking again, but Dan was just standing watching her curiously. He sensed he wasn't welcome to hear the conversation and turned to join the others. Zoe saw a look of hurt on his face before he turned, but was just so relieved that he wasn't watching her humiliate herself on the phone to Pete, she dismissed it from her mind instantly.

'Some pervy old letch just grabbed me is all' Zoe felt her heartbeat slowing a little. 'Alex exaggerated! I'm fine'. There was a pause 'grabbed you how? Did he hurt you?' Pete's voice was calm and measured. Zoe could see his face in her minds eye. Her thoughts wandered to their kisses that night, how much she'd loved being with him, right until she'd gone mental and run out on him.

'He just felt me up a bit and tried to kiss me, honestly Pete, I'm fine' The softness in Zoe's voice mirrored Pete's calmness. 'You need to be careful Zoe. Two girls on your own like that, it could have been so much worse' Zoe could feel the concern in his voice, but just didn't get it. Last night he'd basically told her that he had no interest in a re-run of Friday night, but now he was acting all concerned? Zoe didn't understand him. As she

53

drew breath to respond, she started walking in the direction of her companions. Dan sensed her movement and turned back to look at her questioningly.

'We're fine Pete. Dan punched the guy in the face and we ran away and we're all fine.' There was an icy silence on the end of the phone. Eventually a cool voice asked 'who is Dan?' Oh shit Zoe thought, she'd clearly been wrong to assume Sam had told Alex the whole story, and even if she had Alex clearly hadn't told Pete an accurate version of the truth. Zoe swallowed hard. 'He's the pilot that flew us here. We were having a drink with him and his friend..' Pete cut across Zoe's words 'is he still with you?' Zoe could sense the direction this conversation was taking, and although she didn't want to be back on bad terms with Pete, she knew there was nothing she could do to avoid it. 'Yes he is' Zoe's voice was almost a whisper, but Pete's cut back in immediately 'enjoy the rest of your break with your pilot Zoe.' And then he was gone. Holy shit he was changeable- such hard work! 'I don't need it', Zoe thought to herself as she speeded up to join Dan. 'Not when I have a pilot waiting for me!' And although that's what she told herself, it wasn't Dan's kisses that were on her mind as she looped his arm for the walk back to the hotel.

They were back at the hotel in minutes, Sam and Mark, leading the way again, were already collecting the key from reception when Zoe and Dan entered the lobby. As Sam and Mark said their farewells, Zoe stood awkwardly, not knowing what to say to Dan. She was still shook by Pete's call but knew she needed to focus on the man infront of her, who seemed much kinder than Pete. She glanced at Dan. She knew wanted to see him again, but was so out of practice, she didn't know what to do.

Sam was now hugging Dan too, and thanking him for taking them out, and saving her friend. Zoe felt panicked; he'd be gone in a moment. 'I'm heading up then Zo' Sam squeezed Zoe's arm as she spoke, kissed both boys on their cheeks and then headed to the lift. Mark immediately leaned in to kiss Zoe on the cheek, winked at her and headed to the bar with a 'see ya' called back over his shoulder. Now it was just the two of them, standing in the centre of the lobby. 'Thanks for a great night' Dan smiled as he spoke, and put his hands on Zoe's shoulders.

As Zoe looked up into his smiling face, she knew he wasn't going to revisit what had happened in the alley. She knew if she wanted another kiss, she was going to have to get it, and so she reached her arms around his waist and pulled him closer, until his lips were really close.  Dan's first reaction was a smirk as though he thought he was being teased, but Zoe's face told him all he needed to know. The creases of laughter at the corners of his eyes vanished and were quickly replaced by a look of desire. Without taking his eyes off hers, Dan began to manoeuvre Zoe back through the lobby and out of the hotel, back into the street. 'I don't want an audience' he whispered in way of explanation. Zoe couldn't speak, she couldn't take her eyes off his. All thoughts of Pete dissolved as she nervously thought of what might happen next.  God she felt excited!

The heat of the evening air hit them as they left the hotel, and Dan pulled her by her hand a little way along the street, he pushed her back against the wall, where the cool bricks rubbed roughly against her shoulders. Dan grabbed her wrists and held them against the wall above her head, and pushed all of his body against hers. They still hadn't broken eye contact and Zoe was desperate for him to kiss her, as he had in the alley way earlier. As his lips finally came down on hers, it was better than before, the tension and anticipation made the hardness of his mouth electric on hers.  His kiss was passionate and sexy, and made Zoe want more and more. He loosed her wrists and let his hands work their way down her arms, past her elbows, onto her shoulders, and then he was rubbing her breasts. Oh wow, she was seriously turned on. His hands moved down her sides to her waist, and Zoe brought her arms onto the back of Dan's head. They continued to kiss, neither one able to get enough of the other.

Just as Dan's hand reached for the hemline of Zoe's dress for the second time that evening, the glass door to the entrance of the hotel burst open, and a tear streaked Sam tumbled into the street. Zoe was at her friends side in an instant. 'what's happened?' Zoe asked, fearing news from home of an accident or some other devastating event. 'It's Alex' Sam gasped, as she sank to the curb. Zoe joined her friend on the roadside, and hugged her knees, waiting for Sam to complete her sentence. 'He's dumped me. Pete told him we were on a double date tonight, and Alex said it's just too early in our relationship for me to be breaking his trust'. Sam was sobbing heavily, her mascara streaked face contorted with hurt and disbelief.

Dan was standing at the curb uncomfortably. 'It's just a misunderstanding' Zoe tried to reassure Sam 'Pete has made a mistake and was just trying to look out for his friend'. Zoe was aware she was defending him, but didn't know why. Why had he done this to her friend? Dan cleared his throat and broke Zoe's train of thought. Zoe stood up and led Dan out of her weepy friends earshot. 'Dan, I'm sorry - I need to help Sam sort this out', Zoe could hear the disappointment in her own voice, and felt as good as treacherous. Sam had looked after her so many days and nights lately, Zoe owed her friend a shoulder to cry on. Dan smiled at Zoe as he gently stroked her cheek. 'No worries Zo, I'll add you on facebook, then maybe when I'm back in the midlands...' he left his sentence incomplete and Zoe hanging as he leaned down and gently kissed her lips, then turned and walked down the street.

Zoe watched for a few seconds as he walked away, before turning back to her friend, helping her to her feet and leading her back in to the hotel, and the comfort of their little room. By the time Zoe had got them both undressed, and taken both her and Sam's make up off her friend was a little calmer. 'I can't believe that Pete said that, how did he know?' Sam eyed her friend questioningly. 'It's my fault' Zoe confessed, and proceeded to fill Sam in on the weird phone call she'd had with Pete and hour or so earlier.

By the time the girls had talked through the details of the conversation, and had speculated on why Pete would behave in such a way, it was 3am and they were exhausted. They both drifted off to sleep with the light on, but Zoe's sleep was restless with muddled dreams of Pete, Dan and snarly face. She awoke at 8am, feeling as tired as she had at 3am, and more confused than ever about her love life, where it was at and where it was going.

# CHAPTER 5: ALL GOOD THINGS.

Sam was still fast asleep, so Zoe put her headphones in and put her iPhone onto shuffle. The first song her phone selected was Fun, we are young. Zoe loved the song, it gave her some hope that Nate the lead singer was much older than her and still singing like a teenager. As she listened and tapped her foot under the white cotton hotel sheet, she decided to have a peek at Facebook and twitter. She hadn't got the hotel WiFi code and knew it would use all her data allowance, but couldn't resist, and as soon as she saw the little red notification sign next to the friend icon, she didn't care how much it cost. She clicked excitedly, expecting to see Dan's brilliant white teeth smiling at her from a profile picture, but it was Mark's face she saw.

Zoe's heart sank as she clicked accept. Why hadn't he added her straight away? As if it could sense her change in mood, her iPhone shuffled on to Lana Del Ray's summertime sadness. As Zoe listened and read her newsfeed, she realised what Sam had been talking about- this album was kind of depressing! The Speech bubble icon on her homepage turned red, and Zoe clicked to see who was messaging her. It was Mark, on the way to Barajas airport, asking if Sam was ok as Dan had explained what had happened. They exchanged a few messages, and Zoe thought what a nice guy he was- shame Sam was hung up on Alex.

When she awoke, Sam was less hysterical, but still miserable. Zoe was incensed at Pete's obvious ill-informed interference, in fact, she thought, someone should tell him how wrong he was and how much misery he'd caused.  She was decided in an instant, and while Sam was getting a cappuccino at breakfast, Zoe pulled out her phone and typed a Facebook message to the blue eyed profile picture quickly.

'I can only assume you're responsible for my friend being miserable. Just FYI there was no need for your interference, Sam did nothing with Mark, except talk about how great Alex is.... I guess she was misinformed'

Zoe spotted Sam returning, and quickly pressed send and tucked her phone away.  She discreetly checked her phone a few times as they got ready to go out, but found no response, not that she's really expected one.  Pete didn't seem the type to admit when he was wrong, let alone apologise.

The girls spent the rest of their time in Madrid sight seeing, sunning themselves and drinking Sangria.  Although their time was enjoyable and relaxing it was overshadowed by Zoe's desperate heartache and now Sam's disappointment at what might have been with Alex.  They didn't hear off either Pete or Alex until they were in the airport, ready for home.  Zoe had gone to look at some sun glasses, leaving Sam to guard the luggage, when she returned, Sam was all but jumping up and down. 'He's text me Zo!', Zoe grabbed her friends outstretched mobile phone and read the message from Alex:

'Sam, I'm so so sorry, seems my source is crap and I've made a shitty mistake. I really hope U can forgive me. I'll be at the airport to meet your flight and drive you home. Missed U xxx'

Zoe breathed a sigh of relief for Sam.  Pete must have got her message and relayed the information after all.  Sam's beaming face told Zoe all she needed to know about whether Alex was forgiven or not. Gosh, maybe Sam had met her man, just as Zoe had lost her Ryan, what a cruel twist of fate that would be.

The flight home was uneventful, with the girls sitting in companionable silence sipping a glass of white wine and reflecting on events. Sam was reading her novel, but as the most motion sick person she'd ever known, Zoe avoided anything with text. She was listening to her favourite favourite 80's playlist, and thinking about all that had happened in the last week.

As they began their descent, Sam grasped Zoe's hand. 'Sorry that I didn't help you recover after all, I meant to, it's just that I think I'm falling for Alex and I was gutted that he didn't want to see where it could go.' Zoe smiled at her friend. 'No thanks to Pete' she murmured. 'Don't be too hard on Pete' Sam whispered back conspiratorially 'he was only looking after his bestie, just like you when you clearly messaged him telling him what's actually what!". Zoe smiled back at her friend. Not much got past Sam!

They were soon off the flight and through passport control, as they had only hand luggage. Although it was only 7pm, Zoe felt tired - flying always had that effect on her. As they walked through customs, she felt relieved that Alex was picking them up - it meant she could relax in the back seat, and would be soaking in the bath at her house in no time at all. Just as Zoe's mouth turned up into a smile at the thought of solace in her own house, Sam shrilled 'Alex! There he is!' Zoe glanced over in the direction Sam was grinning and sure enough spotted a beaming Alex, standing next to a rather sheepish looking Pete.

As Sam raced to wrap her arms around Alex's neck, Zoe hung back awkwardly wondering what time the next available train would get her home. As she looked helplessly from side to side she was sure she could feel him glowering at her.

Zoe felt so awkward she could feel her cheeks turning red and the welling of tears in the back of her eyes. Why had he come with Alex? Just to make her feel even more ridiculous for her behaviour the other night? After all, he'd made it very clear he wasn't interested in a re-run of any sort. No doubt she'd also be getting a lecture about the risk of bars in Madrid in his cool tones soon enough. As she stood feeling helplessly abandoned by Sam, who was still nuzzling into Alex's neck, Zoe risked a glance up and looked straight into Pete's azure blue eyes. That was all the invitation he needed, he was in front of her in four long strides.

'Zoe, I'm sorry I told Alex what you'd told me. We both jumped to the wrong conclusion about Sam..... And you. Sorry'. Awkward thought Zoe. He obviously thought that she'd only chatted to Dan too. She needn't have worried what to say though, within a moment of speaking, Pete had picked up Zoe's case, turned his back on her and was striding towards the exit, Sam and Alex in tow. Zoe followed them to a black Audi TT with gleaming silver alloys. The car was waxed within an inch of its life. Sam will love this Zoe thought, she always liked her men to have nice cars. Just as Zoe turned to check her friends expression, Pete pulled keys out of his pocket and popped the small boot. Lifting both girls cases into the boot space, and moving around to open the passenger door, it became clear to Zoe it wasn't Alex's car at all. As Sam and Alex scrabbled into the tiny 2+2 rear seats it also became painfully clear that Zoe would be riding up front with moody but gloriously handsome Pete. Marvellous.

The cool black leather felt delicious on Zoe's bared shoulders. She was wearing her favourite black strappy jump suit and pink wedges, and didn't feel too shoddy considering she was just off the flight. Amazing how seeing Pete had caused an adrenaline rush to dispel all her earlier tiredness!

Sam and Alex were already kissing passionately on the back seat, so as Pete headed around the front of the car to get in the driver's seat, Zoe flicked down the sun visor to check herself out in the mirror. Yep. She looked ok. At least Pete wouldn't be too repulsed by the fact he'd been with her on Friday. Even though, just now walking around the car in his jeans and polo shirt, he looked way out of her league. He slid into the seat beside her with effortless grace and confidence, and glancing over his shoulder at Sam and Alex chuckled, 'guess they missed each other' as he smiled at Zoe with those brilliant white teeth she noticed how his eyes crinkled in the corners. Her stomach fluttered and she found it impossible not to smile back at him. He held her gaze for just a second longer before his smiled dropped, as if he'd remembered he wasn't interested, then he started the engine and reversed the car out of the spot quickly, with expertise.

As Pete glided the sleek black car onto the motorway, he flicked on the stereo. Zoe was surprised to hear The Long and Winding Road by The Beatles burst out of the speakers and looked over at Pete curiously. 'Best band of all time, obviously' was all the response he gave her, eyes glancing to her only momentarily before he fixed his gaze back on the road ahead, 'definitely fantastic' Zoe said 'I really love their early music, and the other music of that time. My favourite film is Dirty Dancing'. He glanced sideways and she felt she had to continue 'We can work it out is my favourite Beatles song' she said. Pete gave an interested nod, eyebrows slightly raised approvingly, but he didn't speak. Why was he so hard to communicate with? He wasn't distant on the night they had met, maybe they were both just drunk. But come to think of it, she hadn't really noticed him drinking much at all.

As they continued along the motorway, the silence settled and grew in the car. Zoe enjoyed listening to The Beatles, but was struggling to think of things to say. Sam and Alex had yet to come up for air and were clearly unaware of the awkward atmosphere in the front of the car, that was thickening by the moment. 'So,…. How's your week going?' Zoe finally managed, she knew it sounded forced and false but to her surprise, Pete seemed a little relieved and seemed to loosen up as he responded by telling her all about the wine tasting he had hosted at his company's cellars the night before.

As he told her about the range of red wines he'd had on offer, Zoe felt confident enough to take her turn in the conversation 'sounds wonderful' she smiled at the side of his face 'although I'm a white wine kinda girl. Pinot Gris if available, or if not a very predictable New Zealand Sauvignon Blanc'. Pete took his eyes from the road to glance at her, and although he smiled, his gaze was intense. 'I'll do my best to remember that'. Zoe's tummy did a familiar somersault and she looked away quickly, breaking the spell and losing the moment.

They chatted about their jobs and families the rest of the way home, but Zoe noticed he didn't mention her love life. Sam must have warned him to avoid the topic. Pete was relaxed again and seemed to be easy company. Zoe remembered why she had taken to him last Friday. Her heart fluttered at the thought of the previous week and she felt herself flush a little. 'So', Pete began his sentence quietly 'when are you going to be in town dancing to A-Ha again?'. There was a mischievous glint in his eye and Zoe couldn't help but giggle. 'If I'm in town and A-Ha is playing, I'll be dancing' she laughed 'my music taste is somewhat old school!'. Pete reached out and squeezed her hand, sending a jolt of electricity through her, 'Well it would be a crime to waste those moves' he laughed, just as Zoe's phone began to shrill.

Sam, disturbed by the noise, leant forward over Zoe's chair. 'Who's that Zo?' She asked. 'Not sure, it's an unknown number' Zoe responded as she slid her finger across her screen to answer the call with a curious 'hello?'. The voice on the other phone responded loudly enough for the whole car to hear 'Hey sexy! Surprise! It's Dan, so, when are we going to meet up to finish what we started?!'.

By the time Zoe had explained that now wasn't a good time, and Dan had agreed to call later, they were at Sam's house, where no surprise, Alex clambered out of the car too. Sam and Zoe hugged and promised to speak first thing, then Zoe climbed back into the car and into an atmosphere as thick as treacle. Pete's face was like stone. He drove straight to her front door in silence, making Zoe wonder how he knew where she lived. He practically jumped out of the car and had Zoe's case on the pavement in moments. Zoe took a deep breath. 'Thanks so much for bringing me home Pete' she smiled at him but he didn't reciprocate it. 'And....erm.... Just in case we don't bump into each other again, I wanted to apologise for my behaviour last Friday night.' She hesitated, as she checked for a reaction. He stood in front of her unresponsive. 'It wasn't you Pete, it's me' Zoe could feel herself panicking as she realised she was saying things she'd had no intention of ever speaking aloud, let alone to Pete.

When he finally responded, the disdain in his voice knocked the breath right out of her lungs. 'Don't take the piss Zoe. It doesn't suit you. It wasn't me? You run off down the fucking street, but it wasn't me? I notice you didn't have that problem with your fucking pilot friend! Have a nice life Zoe!'. He was in his car and speeding away down the street before Zoe could recover enough to say a word. What the fuck! She thought. What on earth had she done to deserve that? Ok, her behaviour Friday night had been a bit crazy, but she was just trying to apologise wasn't she? And why bring Dan up? It's not like it was any of Pete's business. Was he jealous? Zoe's heart fluttered at the thought, Pete, jealous? The idea excited her, but she kept herself in check. As if Pete Saunders would be jealous over her, and it was him that had made it clear he had no interest in a rerun.

Zoe shook her head and picked up her case. As she headed into the house, she expected the tears to begin rolling, but they didn't. Instead, she poured herself a large glass of Sauvignon Blanc from the fridge and headed to the bathroom. A soak in the bath with some Ed Sheeran was all she needed to recover.

# CHAPTER 6:
# SUMMERTIME'S END

Zoe was awake by 7am, having had an early night and having slept peacefully for the first time in weeks, she felt rested and as positive as she had for what seemed like an age. It was Thursday, she had four days before starting the new term as Assistant Headteacher at her new school. It was time to get a grip and get organised. Zoe got showered slowly, making a mental list of everything she needed to get done, and then straightened her hair and tied it into a messy side bun. A trick she'd learned an hour earlier off a YouTube video, whilst she was eating her blueberry wheats! She did love modern technology!

She dressed in a high neck black playsuit play suit that showed off her slightly tanned legs, it's design had blue flowers and a brown belt and so she chose her brown flat sandals and brown leather long strapped bag. Another aspect of her somewhat controlling personality was her need to coordinate and match! Unlike her close friend Leyla, who had attended Zoe's leaving do in a red skater dress, leopard print wedges and a turquoise clutch bag! Another of her exact opposite friends that complimented Zoe perfectly! Leyla was also a teacher, Zoe had in fact trained her and that's how they had met and hit it off. Leyla was still at Zoe's previous school; Zoe would miss their chats but knew it was time for a new challenge. A bit of her was relieved at the thought of being able to reinvent herself; no need to tell anybody about Ryan. She was sure she wouldn't miss the whispering and sympathetic glances she'd have got at her old school.

Zoe's leisurely start meant that it was 9.50am before she began her leisurely walk into Lintfield. She headed straight to Costa when she arrived and called Sam while she waited for her medium skinny chai latte to arrive. Having relayed the telling off from Pete, Zoe realised Sam was being very cagey about what she said, 'erm Sam... Am I right in thinking you have company?' Zoe asked. 'Maybe' giggled Sam. 'Alex stayed over' Sam gushed. Zoe realised how happy this man was making her best friend and smiled back into the phone. 'You enjoy your last day off work and we'll speak later' Zoe signed off and Sam hung up with her usual kiss down the phone.

Zoe took her latte to the window and sat down to write her shopping list. She was just gazing out of the window thinking about what to do with her new year 11 group for their first lesson when she saw him. Pete was strolling easily down the street in a light grey three piece suit looking relaxed, successful and well, just plain gorgeous. He was laughing at what the person next to him was saying, but Zoe couldn't quite see his companion. Until he stopped and a petite, tanned blonde in midi dress and stilettos stepped out from behind him. Zoe felt embarrassed, as though she was spying on him. She had to get out of here and skulk away before he noticed her. She was feeling the best she had in ages and certainly didn't need another telling off from blue eyes. As she gathered her things and quickly finished her latte, she kept a check on him with furtive glances. They were laughing and his eyes were as sparkly as they had been the previous Friday. Zoe felt hurt, but knew this woman was far more glamorous and beautiful than she could ever be; she was perfectly matched to Pete.

They were standing a couple of shops up from Costa now, and so she decided to make her move. As Zoe was sneaking out of Costa and back onto the Main Street, the blonde stood on her tiptoes and planted a kiss on each of Pete's cheeks. He was all smiles and Zoe felt deflated, although she knew she had no reason. As the blonde tottered off up the hill, Pete glanced up and spotted her. 'Shit' Zoe muttered under her breathe as she turned on her heel and headed down the hill as quickly as she could.

*****

Zoe spent the remainder of Thursday and most of Friday getting prepared for the new term. She was just considering what to order for her Friday take-out tea when her mobile buzzed, it was Leyla. Leyla's family were all keen sailors and she had spent the last month yachting around the Greek Islands. Zoe had forgotten she was arriving back the previous night. Leyla updated Zoe about her holiday adventures and enquired tentatively about Zoe's emotional state. Zoe began telling Leyla about her adventures when her friend cut in 'tell you what Zo, I can tell you're past the pyjama and ice cream phase, let's meet up for a glass of Chablis and catch up properly.' Zoe knew Sam and Alex were out on their first official dinner date, and that the alternative was take-away for one, and so agreed readily. '8pm by the Library' Leyla declared before hanging up.

Leyla also lived in Lintfield, in a set of very stylish new apartments on the main road into town. Zoe loved Leyla's company. She was confident, charismatic and above all good fun. She was also a fabulous conversationalist and as a result had fit easily into Zoe's more established friendship group when she'd first met Leyla, three years earlier.

Amongst Zoe's work purchases, was a bag from Dorothy Perkins, that was less work related and more confidence building! Inside was a black cami-style top, a faux leather skirt with a long zip down the back and a pair of black stiletto sandals the fastened around the ankle. With the end of summer sales, the whole outfit had cost just £39, which made Zoe feel completely justified in buying it. She'd hardly been spending anything wasting all her time on the sofa anyway. Besides, she needed to make the most of this weight loss! Zoe got showered and ready excitedly, without thinking about her heartache. She only had a slight wobble as she pulled open the jewellery drawer in her dressing table and spotted her favourite Coeur de Leon jewellery that Ryan had purchased for one of their anniversaries. She closed the drawer quickly and put her Tiffany jewellery, that she'd just removed, back on to avoid any tears in her newly applied mascara.

Zoe picked up her Michael Kors handbag and shoved her powder and lipgloss into it along with her cash card and £30 in cash. She picked up her iPhone to put in and noticed a Facebook notification on her home screen, showing she had activity on her profile. She opened the app quickly whilst slipping her feet into her folding flats. The notifications had been indicating two new friend requests. Unusual. Zoe didn't get many friend requests as she didn't generally meet many new people. She clicked and stared as she saw Dan's brilliant white smile on one thumbnail and Pete's saturated blue stare on the other.

Zoe's stomach lurched and she laughed at herself 'hmmmm' she mused to herself 'which one of you boys is making my stomach turn?!' As she set her house alarm, balanced her heels under her right arm and closed the front door she clicked accept on both requests. Dan was clearly a 'treat them mean' guy she thought as she strode her way into town, and goodness knows what Pete Saunders was all about. Maybe he felt bad for shouting at her... although why would that make him send her a friend request? Who knew. What she did know though, was that Pete Saunders was rapidly becoming the most complicated, difficult, interesting and attractive man she had ever laid eyes on.

*****

She arrived at the library before Leyla and couldn't resist revisiting Facebook. She clicked straight onto Pete's profile and scrolled down his page. He rarely updated his status and the photos he was tagged in were all other people's uploads. He was a mystery. He was also out of her league Zoe reminded herself as she glanced up and saw Leyla turn the corner. Leyla was wearing a grey mini dress with tigers printed all over it. She had her trusty leopard print wedges on, and was carrying a clutch bag that looks like a hardback book in a shade of mustard yellow! Such kooky taste, Zoe loved her individuality and envied her confidence. Leyla was taller than Sam and Zoe, but a similar build, although she was better endowed in the boob department. Leyla's hair was naturally curly and she wore it big and bold. Another tribute to her confidence. The girls hugged and headed straight for The Vineyard, a restaurant with a bar area and great wine list.

Zoe loved to drink wine with Leyla as Sam wasn't all that fussed and preferred gin. Leyla ordered a bottle of Sancerre and they settled into a window seat. Leyla was of the opinion that if you were going to drink wine, you should drink the good stuff, Zoe always knew that a bottle Leyla ordered would be another level of delicious.

They sat and caught up for two hours over the bottle of Sancerre, with Zoe filling Leyla in on all the details of her summer. 'Sounds like you have been busy!' Leyla shrieked at one stage of the conversation, and then more considered when Zoe had completed her tale 'To me it sounds like Pete actually likes you Zo'. Zoe explained that it wasn't the case and the girls moved on to other topics of conversation, including how much they would miss being at the same school when Monday arrived. Leyla had done her teacher training at Zoe's school. They'd hit it off straight away and had been friends ever since. Leyla securing a position at Zoe's school the previous year had cemented their friendship, but now Zoe was leaving.

At 10.30pm Leyla announced that it was Queens Head time and off they went. The Queens Head was an old coaching inn, that still had the original cobbled courtyard, now covered by a conservatory. The pub had a much older clientele than afters, but Zoe and Leyla liked the live music. Their other girls friends dismissed the pub as grotty and so it was only when Zoe and Leyla headed out as a twosome that they got to go and see the bands.

Currently the duo that were performing at the back of the courtyard were playing a version of 'your sex is on fire'. The girls grabbed a glass of Sauvignon Blanc from the bar and headed straight to the area in front of the makeshift stage. All of Zoe's friends loved to dance and Leyla was no exception. They danced and swayed until the band and music changed to heavy metal. Laughing, they both headed to the door at the same time. 'I'll dance to most stuff' Zoe laughed, 'but heavy metal is a bridge too far!'. Leyla linked Zoe's arm 'I concur' she exclaimed, dragging Zoe towards the entrance to Afters.

As soon as they walked in, Zoe saw Tam and Louisa at the DJ booth talking to Cal. Zoe and Leyla waved and headed to the bar. The next hour passed without incident, Leyla and Zoe danced with Louisa and Tam, they chatted and drank Prosecco. Zoe was leaning over the bar ordering another round when she heard Leyla mutter 'oh shit' next to her. Zoe spun round to see what the problem was and found herself looking at Ryan. Her Ryan who had viciously broken her heart and left her devastated was standing by the entrance with his best friend James and some of his other friends.

Zoe closed her eyes and took a deep breath to assess her feelings. She felt drunk and sick and also like she might burst into tears to thoroughly humiliate herself. Leyla put a protective arm around Zoe's shoulder as she paid the bar man with her other hand. As Leyla retrieved their drinks, she tried to shepherd Zoe in the opposite direction, but Zoe was frozen to the spot, her eyes flickering about the bar as she tried to locate Kate, the harpy who in her eyes had stolen her man. As Leyla continued to try and scoop Zoe away from the scene, Ryan spotted her and headed straight over to them. James followed and he and Leyla stepped a respectable distance away from the couple in order to give them some privacy for what Leyla suspected may turn into a slanging match with her carrying a hysterical Zoe home.

'Zoe' Ryan began speaking softly and cautiously. 'You look amazing; I haven't seen you look like this for ages'. Zoe knew she wasn't thinking particularly rationally at the moment, but was sure she could sense some disappointment in Ryan's voice, as though he'd hoped she'd be a blithering wreck. Well, there was no need for him to know she had been until a week ago was there? Zoe smiled 'thanks, that's nice of you'. Her voice was serene but she could hear the control in it and wondered if he could. They spent the next few moments swapping pleasantries about Zoe's new job and where they had both been so far that evening. When Ryan excused himself to go to the gents, Zoe was relieved, but as soon as he'd gone, James replaced him. 'Zoe, how are you?'

His question seemed to be one of genuine concern. Zoe and James had always got on famously and she missed his company. 'Getting there' she replied honestly with a slight smile that gave James a hint of how vulnerable she actually was. 'Oh Zo' James began 'he's an idiot.' He paused but Zoe didn't respond and so he continued. 'We all miss you Zoe. His new girl is psychotic, deranged, jealous and controlling. This is the first time he's been out with the lads, and he's only allowed because she's on a hen do'. James's words were pouring out, as if he knew exactly what he wanted to say before Ryan arrived back. 'I know I shouldn't be saying this, but I think he knows he has made a massive mistake Zoe. I think he misses you and regrets it. You must have seen his eyes light up when he saw you. Can you just...'

James's words trailed off as Ryan reappeared with a tall glass of Stella Artois in one hand and a glass of white wine in the other. He handed the wine to Zoe and James seemed to dissolve into the background. As a lairy group of men tried to get to the bar behind Zoe, Ryan gently took her by the elbow and pulled her out of the way. Zoe's heart lurched; the familiarity was agony. Zoe was overwhelmed with the sense of belonging they had together and as she looked up into Ryan's eyes, she knew he was thinking the same thing. As he leant down to speak to her his hand went to her jaw line and it felt natural, as though it was meant to be. Ryan's eyes were glistening now with emotion and as he leant towards her ear she heard his voice catch as he whispered

'Zoe, I miss you. I'm so sorry'. The lairy men behind jostled Zoe forwards and the spell was broken. Zoe felt herself falling into the gloom again. She needed to protect herself. She reached up and pecked Ryan on the cheek and then turned and practically ran away to find Leyla. They were in a taxi in minutes, Zoe drunk and slumped against the window, Leyla rifling through her clutch to find her mobile that was ringing. Zoe wasn't paying attention particularly, but heard fragments of Leyla's conversation; 'oh hi Sam.... Better than expected.... How?... OMG the bitch!.... Ok, will do'.

The next thing Zoe knew was when she opened her eyes in her own bed, to glaring sunlight. It was 9am and she'd slept just fine. Zoe lay still for a moment as she recalled the events of the previous evening. She was just trying to recall the details of Leyla's taxi phone call when her bedroom door opened and Leyla was standing there a cup of tea in each hand.

'Good morning!' Leyla' smiled at Zoe, 'I invited myself for a sleepover when you zonked out, I thought you might wake up traumatised, but I can see you're surprisingly fine!', Zoe pulled back the duvet on the other side of her double bed and Leyla climbed in, carefully handing Zoe one of the steaming mugs of Zoe's favourite Clipper Fairtrade Tea. 'I was trying to remember who you were talking to in the taxi' Zoe said as she blew into the mug of tea.

'Yeah.... I need to tell you about that, but I'm not sure how your gonna take it' Leyla paused to check Zoe was giving her full attention and then continued to answer Zoe's query. 'It was Sam checking you were ok after seeing Ryan, which is obviously what you'd expect from Sam, it's just how she found out you'd seen Ryan that I'm not sure you're gonna like.' Leyla pulled her phone out of the top pockets of her dressing gown (that was actually one of Zoe's she'd obviously removed from the clothes drier in the spare room). 'It would seem that Tam thought it would be appropriate to post a status about you and Ryan being reunited' As she spoke, Leyla turned her phone around to show Zoe a screenshot of Tam's status from the night before. Zoe nearly choked on her tea as she read 'great to see these two back in negotiations!' Beneath the status were two pictures, one of Ryan leaning into Zoe's ear looking all intense, and the other of Zoe kissing Ryan on the cheek! Beneath the photos a number 72 next to the thumbs up signed showed how many of Zoe and Ryan's friends had liked the status. Lots it would seem.

'Oh my god! How could she publicise that we bumped into each other like that, and all those people have seen it!'. Leyla reached out and gently removed her phone from Zoe's grasp and put it facedown on the bedside drawer. 'That's probably the most liked status she's ever had' Leyla mused, and then went on 'the thing is Zoe, Tamasyn doesn't always get it right. None of like her as much as we like each other, well, except for Louisa. We all just put up with her because she's a long time friend. But after last night I'm not sure I would trust her as far as I could drop kick her.'

After Leyla had left, and Zoe had de-tagged herself from the photos, Zoe tried to get on with her day, but she kept coming back to what Leyla had said about Tam not being trustworthy. She couldn't get away from the fact that Tam had taken advantage of her like that and that Leyla's opinion probably wasn't entirely inaccurate.

# CHAPTER 7: NEW TERM, FRESH START?

Zoe was already wide awake with nerves flooding her stomach when her phone alarm rang at 6am on Monday morning. She readied herself for her new job, feeling sick, but was pleased with her appearance as she stood in front of her hallway mirror at 7am. The idea that teachers worked 9am-3pm was a complete myth; Zoe was used to being at school for 7.30am and leaving anytime between 5pm and 9pm, depending on her workload, parents evenings and meetings.

As she swung open her front door she was surprised to see a tall cream cylindrical package on her doorstep. She picked it up and slid off the end of the tube. Inside was a bottle of Pinot Gris, her favourite, with a note written in fountain pen with scrawled writing that read. 'Sorry for the outburst the other night. Hope your new job is everything you want and need x P x'. Zoe hadn't given much thought to Pete since the whole Ryan incident, but felt positively joyous at his note and the fact that he had thought of her and gone to the effort of remembering and delivering her favourite wine. Although, what did he mean by 'want and need?'. He was so very mysterious.

Zoe's first few weeks in her new job absolutely flew by. Her colleagues seemed nice, and so did her classes, with the exception possibly of her year nine Physics group. Zoe wasn't sure what to make of them yet and would reserve her judgement she thought! Her 'buddy' tasked with looking after her as a new member of staff, Harriet was lovely. Really caring, and just the sort of friend Zoe thought she might need after deciding Tamasyn probably shouldn't stay on her Christmas card list for too much longer!

The weeks comprised teaching her new groups, carrying out many lunch duties, meeting the teams she would line manage, attending and running various training, and getting to know the rest of the senior leadership team. This week had been particularly busy and by the time she arrived home at 5.30pm on Friday Zoe was absolutely exhausted and completely committed to having a soak in the bath and an early night.

Zoe opened the fridge and spotted the bottle of unopened Pinot Gris, she poured herself a glass as the bathtub filled and in no time was soaking with bubbles up to her earlobes! Zoe soon felt the effect of a large glass of white wine on an empty stomach, and felt the overconfidence that only alcohol can induce. She picked up her iPhone and tapped her Facebook app icon. Before she knew it her status had been updated to show a picture of her hand emerging from the bubbles, holding her glass, with a statement that read 'enjoying a glass of chilled white! Thanks P x' she felt smug that nobody would be able to crack her code! She hadn't tagged him after all. She didn't know, but felt pretty sure he wouldn't like being tagged and his new girlfriend almost certainly wouldn't appreciate it. Zoe took a gulp from her wine and slipped deeper into her bath. Within moments her phone buzzed on the bathroom floor, as she unlocked her screen she immediately saw that profile picture with those blue eyes! He'd commented on her status! Zoe gulped and clicked to open the notification. 'You're very welcome :-)', as she clicked to like his comment, an instant private message popped up. Pete!

'How's the bath?' Zoe gulped again. How should she respond? Should she text Sam to ask? As she tried to consider what Sam would do, another message popped up 'you're leaving far too much to my imagination....'. Zoe nearly dropped her phone! He was flirting with her! Gorgeous Pete, who she was sure thought she was way beneath him! OMG, now she really didn't know what to respond. Another buzz, and a third sentence 'need any help scrubbing your back?' Zoe squealed involuntarily! Wow! Zoe actually felt herself squirming with pleasure and embarrassment, oh well, her mom always said honesty is the best policy. She began typing 'I'm blushing...'. His response was instant 'I bet you are Zo, kinda cute x'. What now? More honesty... 'I'm not sure cute is what I should be aiming for :-0'.

This time his response took longer, Zoe was out of the bath and drying off, convinced that the interaction was over, when her phone finally buzzed again 'maybe not Zoe, but it's what you are. I like it xx'. Zoe dried and straightened her hair in a haze. Sipping her wine she recalled the night outside afters, his eyes, his lips, just him. When her phone buzzed again she practically fell off her dressing table stool trying to reach it immediately! This time her heart skipped a beat for a completely different reason. The text message was from Ryan. 'So, who's Pete and why is he buying you wine?'.

Although Zoe ignored all of Ryan's messages, by the time she climbed into bed she'd received sixteen messages from him, all questioning who Pete was, how she knew him, and at the most offensive whether she was fucking him! Although she missed Ryan so much, this man texting her now, she didn't know. Why was he being so confrontational when he'd left her? It was him who'd replaced her so very easily, how dare he question her for beginning to try to move on with her life?

Zoe cried herself to sleep with her longing to have back the Ryan she loved, but also with a new sense of loss. Had her Ryan gone forever? Zoe's dreams were confused that night, with dreams of Ryan and Pete that made no sense at all. When she woke on Saturday morning, for the first time in nearly a month, Zoe couldn't face getting out of bed. She decided to spend the weekend in a haze. Back in her loungewear on the sofa, she began to browse Netflix for a box set to watch when a loud hammering at the door set her adrenaline rushing and heart pounding.

'I know you're in there you bitch' a voice shouted through the door. Zoe peered through the corner of her bay window and saw Kate, the vile Kate that had stolen her Ryan, standing on her doorstep, red with rage. Another bang bang bang on the door was followed by a further tirade of abuse. Zoe felt her heart thumping. What should she do? Tam or Leyla would have opened the door and given her a mouthful, but that really wasn't Zoe's style. Zoe slid down the wall and sat hunched under the window. She quickly typed a WhatsApp message to Sam 'Kate hammering on my door and seems crazy'. Sam was online in moment's 'on my way', Zoe breathed a sigh of relief. She really did have the best friend. Zoe considered her position, Sam lived about a six minute drive away. They were going to be a long six minutes.

Zoe heard the letter box lift as Kate tried to peer into her house. She heard her kick the door before another tirade came 'don't you dare try to come onto him again! He told me you followed him to Afters. Then kissed him and got your friend to post pictures. You're so pathetic Zoe. No wonder Ryan can't stand you'. As Zoe sat huddled beneath the window, listening to insult after insult, silent tears began to stream down her face. Why would Ryan have told so many lies about her, why had he lied about their chance meeting and why was he messaging her about Pete?

Zoe suddenly realised that the abuse had stopped and that there was silence outside. She heard a car pull away. Kate had finally left and Zoe released her sobs loudly and without reserve. The door tapped gently and she heard Sam's comforting voice 'it's me Zo, open up'. Zoe opened the door and sagged onto the shoulder of her friend, her body wracked with tears. Sam gently asked Zoe what had happened. Zoe continued to sob and as she lifted her head to tell Sam, she realised that Alex was standing half way down the drive, hands in pockets staring awkwardly at his feet. Sam realised Zoe had noticed and shrugged at her friend

'I thought we might need back up?' Zoe was so upset, she really didn't care that Alex was seeing her at her worst and turned to head into the house.

Sam and Alex followed. Zoe was conscious with Alex there and Sam, sensing this, dispatched him to the kitchen to make tea. With Alex safely out of earshot, Zoe relayed all of the events from the night before up to her arrival, including the messages she had received from Ryan the night before. Sam was wide eyed in disbelief by the end of it. 'What an absolute nightmare. I wonder if Ryan has told her he has made a mistake. Do you think he will come back Zoe? Would you have him back? How did Kate leave it? What has Tam got to say for herself? Why would James say all that?'. Zoe reached out and put her hand across Sam's mouth. 'All questions I have already thought Sam, none of which I can answer' Zoe was feeling suddenly matter of fact about the situation. Alex walked into the room tentatively, carrying two cups of steaming hot tea. 'Thank you for coming to save me Sam, thank you Alex, but I am honestly fine and don't want to ruin anymore of your day'.

Sam and Alex finally left about thirty minutes later, but only after convincing Zoe to join them for drinks later that evening at their local The Swan. It was a gastro pub that had a warm and homely feel and somewhere that the girls would usually use for lunches rather than Saturday night drinks, but Zoe didn't object to the thought of a quiet evening out rather than staying home waiting to see if Kate showed up again.

Zoe spent the afternoon watching her favourite romance films, she loved the Tom Hanks oldies like sleepless in Seattle and You've got mail, and today was no exception. She had always been 'old-headed', and it transferred into her film taste as well as her music preferences. As she wept at the ending of 'The Holiday', she realised she hadn't moved since Sam and Alex had left and that it was dark outside. She headed for the shower to prepare for a night with the lovebirds Sam and Alex. As she pulled her skinny jeans over her tight black bodysuit, she thought about her friend and Alex. He seemed like a genuinely nice guy, but Sam had gone all in so quickly, Zoe hoped that Sam wouldn't get hurt again. Sam had a tendency to jump straight into new romances, often paying the price later by discovering a wife, girlfriend or general lack of interest on the blokes part. Alex didn't seem like the others, but Zoe would reserve her judgement until she knew her friends heart was protected.

As she pulled her ankle boots over her jeans, she reflected again on her time with Ryan the previous evening, had he said he had regretted his decision, she had been tipsy and couldn't entirely recall. She knew one thing though, if she had bumped into him six weeks ago, she would have got down on her knees to beg him back, but now, something inside her had changed, and whilst the ache and loss was still there, she wasn't 100% certain that she would jump at the chance to have him home. That was progress, definite progress, she thought as she grabbed her mulberry handbag and headed out the front door towards The Swan.

\*\*\*\*\*

Zoe entered the pub 15 minutes later and easily spotted Sam sitting in the corner with Alex and some other men she didn't know. She was relieved to see that Pete wasn't there, as much as she loved his blue eyes, she couldn't bear another run in with him after the day she had had. She waved and headed to the bar.

Zoe ordered a lime and soda just as Sam joined her at the bar, Zoe ordered Sam a G&T as her friend checked she was ok and hadn't had any more unexpected visitors. "Do you fancy a girls night next Saturday' Sam enquired. "Alex is off out with the boys for Jakes birthday'. 'Who is Jake?' Zoe asked and Sam laughed. 'Zoe, you've been so busy staring into Pete's baby blues that you haven't noticed he and Alex are a group of five guys that hangout together. Jake is the one with a cheeky smile and auburn hair, he is a mechanic'. Zoe was about to defend herself, but realised she hadn't noticed the other guys around Pete at all. She had indeed been too busy gazing a the gorgeous Pete. 'Girls night sounds great Zoe said and squeezed Sam's hand as they collected their drinks from the bar and headed to the table at the rear of the pub.

Sam returned to her seat next to Alex, and Zoe noticed the way he stopped his conversation and turned to smile at her. Sam beamed in return before placing her drink on the table and turning her attention back to Zoe. The girls chatted about Sam's brother as he had recently got a new job, before Alex turned his attention to Sam, whispering in her ear. Zoe suddenly felt like an outsider and was relieved when someone sat in the seat next to her. The rugged looking man was stocky and muscular. He had auburn hair and Zoe immediately knew it was Jake, Saturday's birthday boy.

Jake had a masculine but kind, round face that was welcoming and friendly. He was shorter and stockier than Pete and Alex but clearly looked after himself and was in good shape. His hands gave away his physical job and Zoe noticed the shortness of his nails. She had always (weirdly) loved men's thumbs, and Jake's tanned hands and short nails were appealing. Jake was so friendly that Zoe was at ease speaking to him for the next fifteen minutes or so, at which point they were joined by another man, dark skinned with shiny black hair and a straight nose. Jake introduced him as Jaiden, group member number four. Jaiden was also friendly, he was an ICT consultant and as he and Zoe chatted, they realised they had both studied at Birmingham university and were able to reminisce about Friday nights in 'Old Joe's' at the 'Guild' or student union. They laughed about events that they had probably been at together without knowing. Zoe felt really at ease and was enjoying herself despite the incidents of the previous night and that morning.

As Zoe laughed with Jaiden, her phone beeped, signalling a text message from an unknown number. Zoe read the text with interest. "Hi Zoe, sorry I haven't been in touch for a few weeks. I had my phone stolen in Marrakesh and have only just got hold of your number again. Mark and I are flying into Birmingham for a stopover on Saturday. Are you and Sam free to meet up. It would be great to see you. Dan x'.

Zoe, having text Dan a couple of times and received no response had assumed he'd blown her off and so was thrilled to read the message. Feeling happy that he hadn't rejected her After all, she nudged Sam. Sam read the message over her shoulder and shrieked with excitement before holding her hand over her mouth to contain her excitement as she glanced sideways at Alex. Zoe began to text back immediately 'Great to hear from you. We are in!!'. The texts that followed arranged for the girls to meet their Madrid acquaintances In The Mailbox at 8pm. Zoe looked questioningly from Sam to Alex and Sam shrugged. Zoe decided to discuss it later.

As she placed her phone back on the table, excited at the prospect of seeing Dan, movement out of the corner of her eye caught Zoe's attention and she looked up to see the gorgeous Pete enter the pub with the blonde she had seen him with in Lintfield town after she had returned from Madrid. Their eyes met and she was sure Pete's eyes widened before her regained his composure and headed to the bar with his date. Zoe's heart was pounding as she watched him with the beautiful blonde.

The evening went on and Pete remained at the bar laughing and talking with his date and speaking to his friends when they headed to the bar for drinks. Only occasionally glancing in Zoe's direction. As Zoe continued to chat with Jake and Jaiden, she swapped the occasional flirty text with Dan and looked forward to meeting up with the pilot on Saturday, although she knew her attention was really at the bar with Pete and the petite blonde he was sharing his laughs and smiles with. She knew it was ridiculous, but she just couldn't get him off her mind. Suddenly the guys around the table cheered at someone in a jovial fashion and a man that Zoe guessed was Matt, the fifth member of the quintet strolled over to the table, pint in hand.

Jake was in the gents and Matt took the opportunity to take his seat right next to Zoe. Jaiden introduced them, but Matt's response was far from the one Zoe expected. "Zoe, the famous run away' Matt laughed. Zoe pretended to laugh along but she felt humiliated. Matt had not been there on that night out, and Zoe knew Pete had shared the story. The fact that he had laughed at her with his friends made her heart pound with embarrassment and anger.

She waited until an appropriate time had lapsed before excusing herself to the ladies. As she turned the corner on the home run to the sanctuary of the ladies, she came face to face with Pete and found herself looking straight into his beautiful eyes. 'Zoe, Alex said you had a tough day' his face and tone were gentle. Zoe knew he hadn't heard what Matt had said, but her face burned with embarrassment and she was desperate to get to the ladies for some privacy and solitude.

She looked toward the bar where Pete's date stood waiting for him. 'Huh? Yeah, I guess so.....You'd better get back' Zoe said, trying to get him to leave her. She couldn't bear the humiliation she was feeling and somehow Pete made her feel he was looking into her very soul. He glanced toward the bar. 'Katya, the girl I'm with, it isn't what it looks like'. Zoe's heart was pumping. Why was he saying this now? When he had clearly mocked her to his friends. Zoe felt irrationally hurt.

'What?' She responded snappily , 'it doesn't matter to me, it's nothing to me' she replied curtly, only thinking of how she could get to the ladies before the tears burning the back of her eyes were released. For a millisecond she thought she saw hurt and dismay in his face before he reset his stony poker face. He whispered so quietly that she could hardly hear him, 'that's a

Shame' he paused and looked straight into her eyes 'I had been thinking that you could really mean something to me'. And then he was gone. Returning to his wide eyed, smiling Katya. Zoe was rooted to the spot and had to force all her efforts to continue to the ladies where she promptly locked herself into a cubicle and let the silent tears roll down her face.

By the time Zoe emerged from the ladies Pete and his date, Katya, were nowhere to be seen. Zoe was simultaneously relieved and downhearted. She hadn't had time to process what he had said, and was questioning what she had heard altogether. She returned to the table with a smile pasted across her face. She wouldn't be telling Sam of the latest incident, her friend had already spent too much of her last months invested in Zoe's dramas, it was time to give her some space to build what was clearly a blossoming relationship with Alex. Zoe was so happy her friend seemed so content and she would be making a real effort to get to know Alex too, even if it meant unpleasant confrontations with Pete. Her friends happiness was so important and it seemed Sam may have found her perfect match with Alex.

Zoe stayed for another fifteen minutes or so and then made her excuses to Sam about needing to get up early to mark a set of exam papers. It was true and Zoe hated having work hanging over her. Leyla was the sort of person that started her work at 8pm on a Sunday night, but it wasn't Zoe's style and it wasn't unusual for her get home on a Friday and get it done straight away.

The workload in teaching had been unbearable at the beginning of her career. Planning a single lesson used to take her an hour as she learned her trade. Then as she progressed up the responsibility ladder quickly, her weekend planning was quickly replaced with managerial tasks and organising her teaching team. She was given the responsibility as Director of Science Faculty at just 24, and found it a real challenge, but that had enabled her to progress quickly and all those weekends of working hard had paid off now she was on a senior leadership team. She still got to teach, but the load was far less as her other duties took most of her time. Her new role involved spending time with colleagues in school and working to improve their classroom practice. It meant that there was limited work she could bring home, which was a complete change from her previous roles, but a very welcome change. She was enjoying having her Friday evenings to herself.

Zoe had arrived home as sober as she had left. She felt given the events of the day and previous evening that she needed a clear head. She also felt that her liver deserved a bit of a break after the last few weeks. They had been a rollercoaster, but she felt that things were settling down a little now. Ryan hadn't text again and Pete was clearly involved with someone else. Zoe would look forward to a fun night out with Dan the next weekend, but focus on herself for now and try not to think about relationships, after all, they had caused her more than enough trouble in the last couple of months and she was ready for some peace now that she was recovering from her heartache.

*****

The next morning, as planned, Zoe was up and exam papers marked by 9.30am. With the whole day ahead of her she considered what she would do. She had struggled all summer with the prospect of having days to herself, but today for the first time she was looking forward to the solitude and the hours of freedom. Although she had never really thought about it before, Ryan had been quite controlling in their relationship. Always having strong views on anything that she suggested doing. He wasn't like it in the early days of their partnership, but over the last few years, he had become increasingly controlling over where they did and didn't go.

Zoe had always loved to do slightly random things, like a Segway rally, cooking classes, open air theatre, just a broad mix. At the start of their relationship, Ryan had always said her sense of adventure was what had drawn him to her, but over the last 18 months in particular, she had found herself frequently wasting money as she bought tickets to events with Ryan's agreement that he would refuse to attend on the actual day. Zoe frowned as she put pieces together in her head, that she had never acknowledged, let alone processed. It dawned on her that Ryan had begun to leave her way before the affair. He had slowly been withdrawing for the last two years and she hadn't even noticed. Zoe felt unease rise in her chest and knew she needed to quickly snap out of it to avoid it taking over her again. She quickly headed to the shower to get ready for a day of solitude, shopping in Birmingham. She loved that she had taken a momentary decision and now she could go ahead and do it. Maybe single life wouldn't be so bad after all.

By 11.15am, Zoe was disembarking at grand central. She couldn't remember the last time she had spree shopped alone and felt exhilaration at the prospect. Zoe had decided to focus on choosing an outfit to wear on Saturday night when her and Sam met up with Dan and Mark. She had put Dan firmly out of her mind since he hadn't responded to her texts, but now that she knew his phone had been stolen, she allowed her mind to drift back to the night in Madrid and how fantastic it had felt to be leaning up the wall of that dark alleyway in Dan's embrace, both their hearts pounding from adrenaline and lust, and both of them desperate to see where the night would lead. Zoe didn't consider Dan boyfriend material, after all, he was forever flying to and fro and staying in different countries. But she did know that the distraction would be good whilst she fully recovered from the loss of Ryan and it was clear that Pete was not the option that she had hoped he would be.

Though her thoughts kept drifting to those sparkling blue eyes, she made herself a promise to invest her energy into enjoying some commitment free fun with Dan. She would focus on not getting attached and the six months recovery that Sam had mentioned back in August would pass by in no time. Zoe's heart lurched at the thought of recovering from the loss of Ryan. She had thought she'd be wedding dress shopping by now. How could she have been so wrong? She had truly believed they would be together forever. She had believed he was her soul-mate and now he was gone. Zoe panicked as she felt the hurt hit her full force in her chest. What was she doing pretending to be over Ryan and trying to shop to impress another man. Her emotions were beginning to spiral and so head down, she plunged into the first shop she saw to distract herself from the gloom and emotion that threatened to engulf her once more.

Zoe found herself browsing shop after shop before settling on a dress and sandal combination. The dress was emerald green and perfectly matched Zoe's colouring. The hem brushed the middle of her thigh and the long sleeves tapered at the wrists. The moment she tried it on, she knew it was perfect. She paired it with a new pair of black sandals, her favourite wrap around the ankle style, but this time with a chunky block heel. Zoe was pleased with her reflection and headed to the till before she could change her mind. She had intended to eat lunch alone, to demonstrate that she was a strong independent woman, but the earlier wobble over Ryan had highlighted that perhaps that wasn't the case. Too much too soon could leave her sobbing into her sushi all alone, so she opted for the earlier train and a costa in Lintfield.

Zoe sat in hers and Sam's usual spot in the window of costa, drinking her hot chocolate and idly scrolling through Social media. She had friend requests from Jake and Jaiden which she immediately accepted. She smiled as she saw selfies of her and Sam taken the night before, along with shots of Sam and Alex that Sam had eagerly uploaded to her timeline the previous evening. Then she spotted that Pete had been tagged into two pictures by Katya Giraldo. The first picture was a selfie with Katya holding the phone whilst their heads touched ear to ear.

In the second, Pete smiled at the camera whilst Katya kissed his cheek. Zoe's heart fluttered again at what might have been, but she couldn't deny Katya's beauty. It was no wonder Pete liked her.

Zoe clicked Katya's profile page. It was private but she could see Katya's profile pictures. Mostly pictures of Katya surrounded by other glamorous looking women and beautiful men. It seemed she had a very different life to Zoe's. No doubt a better partner for the manager of a wine merchants. Zoe clicked off the profile of the beautiful Katya and onto Dan's profile. Just like Pete, he didn't share much on social media either, but she could look at his face via the photos other had tagged of him. Looking at his face set her heart racing as she remember his hands all over her. She peered into her shopping bag and imagined his hands over her new green dress. She would forget Ryan and she would forget Pete. It was time for Zoe to enjoy herself with her sexy pilot Dan.

The rest of Zoe's Sunday passed quickly. She strolled home from town, but noticed how quickly the evening were drawing in as it headed towards mid October. When she got home it was gone 4pm. She headed upstairs to hang up her new purchase and then got into her loungewear, a long conversation with her mother was followed by a rewatch of 'A star is born', along with copious amounts of sobbing. Zoe headed to bed early and slept as soundly as she had in a very long time.

# CHAPTER 8:
# THE PILOT

Zoe's week was uneventful, but seemed to drag. She had a late meeting and an open evening which meant that it seemed she had little time at home, being busy usually suited her, but for some reason, this week seemed flat and uninspiring. She found time to chat to Sam most days. Things were going well with Alex but she still hadn't told him about their planned outing with Mark and Dan. Sam suggested that they book a hotel room for the weekend and so Zoe checked a comparison website and booked a room at Jury's inn. When the girls met up on Saturday afternoon, they were both excited to spend an evening away as they used to do frequently. Zoe had showered and straightened her hair already, but would do her make up and get dressed at the hotel.

The girls checked into the hotel at 4pm and spent time lying on their beds reminiscing about previous nights out in Birmingham. They played songs that they loved to dance to and evaluated all the things that had happened over the previous few months. Zoe found she could talk about Ryan a little easier now, without getting upset, but the sense of hurt and humiliation she felt at him having left her for a work colleague still made a lump rise in her throat and her skin redden with a mix of anger and distress. Sam knew to mostly avoid the topic of his infidelity, but as Ryan had been such a large part of Zoe's life for so long, he came up frequently in conversation.

The girls began getting ready in earnest at 6pm, and whilst they each applied their make up in the long dressing table mirror, the conversation turned to Sam's 30th birthday in the coming month. Sam and her parents had arranged a traditional party with a DJ and bar, in a function room at a local golf club. She had invited Alex and wanted to know if she could invite his four friends. Zoe's heart fluttered a little at the thought of being near Pete again, but she knew that with Sam and Alex so close she would have to get used to being an acquaintance at least.

Sam was excited at her friends measured response and text Alex straight away. The boys were in Liverpool for Jake's birthday night out. Pete's love of The Beatles wasn't exclusive to him, it seemed that all of the group shared the love of the band. They had headed to Liverpool to do a 'Beatles tour' and then see the Cavern Club's resident Beatle tribute band. Sam had told Alex last night about her plans to stop over in Birmingham with Zoe, but she had been less than honest about their plans to see Mark and Dan. She had agreed with Mark that they would meet up 'by chance'. Zoe didn't feel easy about it, but it was Sam's relationship, and her decision.

They had agreed to meet Dan and Mark for food at a pizza restaurant in Brindley Place before heading into the bars. They stepped into the restaurant exactly at 7.30pm. Scanning the restaurant, Zoe was quickly met by two smiling faces. Dan and Mark were clearly pleased to see them and Zoe instantly relaxed. Dan's face was so familiar, even though she hadn't seen him since August. He felt like coming home, relaxed and easy. Unlike every time she saw Pete, which always felt awkward, despite his sparkling eyes and warm smile. Zoe reflected that, given the first night they met, she had run down the street to get away from him, it was unlikely to ever feel anything other than awkward.

The group chatted and laughed whilst they ate pizza and dough balls. The white wine they drank was cool and refreshing and Zoe felt relaxed and happy. As they left the restaurant around

9pm, Dan put his hand on the small of her back and she felt a spark of excitement run through her body like a surge of electricity. The chemistry from Madrid was still there and Zoe was looking forward to exploring it further!

Brindley Place was an area around Birmingham's central canal system. With conference and performance venues, the city library and so many restaurants, bars and clubs near by, it was always a hive of activity, but Saturday nights were when it really bustled with groups of people spilling out of the bars and pubs, catching up over cocktails, overlooking the scenic canals and cobbled bridges. White fairy lights in trees gave the area an added touch of elegance. Zoe loved it here and so did Sam.

They headed into a crowded cocktail bar as a group and began to weave their way to the get drinks in a snake like line. Mark leading the way followed by Sam and Zoe. Dan was behind Zoe, and placed his hands lightly on her hips to avoid getting separated. His touch made Zoe tingle and transported her back to that night in Madrid outside the hotel. She wondered what would have happened if Sam hadn't burst out the hotel upset about Alex. She hoped Sam's half-truth with Alex didn't cause a similar chain of events tonight.

Cocktails and beers in hand, the group made their way back onto the terrace. The evening was mild for early November, but the wine and chemistry between her and Dan was no doubt contributing to the warm fuzzy glow that Zoe had inside. Mark and Sam were immediately engaged in conversation about a new release film they had both seen in the last week. Dan turned to face Zoe directly. 'We have some unfinished business' he said, staring straight into her eyes, 'you look amazing and I'm not sure how long I can keep my hands off you'. Zoe was sure she was blushing, but her confidence was bolstered by wine and the raspberry martini she was sipping. She returned the intensity of Dan's gaze and said 'why do you need to keep them off me' and then she reach up and kissed him on the lips. Dan returned her kiss and then looked into her eyes and sighed. 'I fly out again on Wednesday' he said, 'then I'm busy pretty much to the New Year'. Zoe felt a twinge of annoyance at Dan's disingenuous way of telling her he wasn't interested in a relationship. She had never been a game player and always preferred to be honest and frank. She found Dan's approach underhand, but, it was her that had decided herself that Dan would be some light hearted fun. Maybe him saying this now, however deviously, was for the best and now they were both clear. Zoe shrugged and gave Dan a sly smile 'who's to say I won't have my wicked way with you tonight and want nothing more to do with you?'. Dan's eyes widened and they both burst out laughing.

The four friends bar hopped for the next couple of hours, enjoying each other's company and laughing both as a group and as two discreet pairs. Zoe saw Sam checking her phone and decided it was probably time for a ladies based catch up. The girls headed off to find a quiet spot where they could catch up on each others' headspace, and the boys headed to the bar for another round of beers and martinis.

Once in the sanctuary of the ladies room, Zoe and Sam began to evaluate the evening. 'So Dan still has the hots for you Zo!'. Zoe laughed and then shared with Sam Dan's indiscreet way of telling her that it was on fun only terms. Sam was wide eyed, but said 'well, if it suits you Zoe, that's fine, but don't do anything to cause more hurt, ok.'. Zoe nodded but internally she knew Sam had hit the nail on the head. Zoe couldn't honestly say she wouldn't get hurt, but knew she had to try to have some fun and move on, and Dan was super sexy after all. She decided it would be best to change the subject.

'So, have you told Alex who we are with?'. Sam nodded slowly whilst pulling a face showing she was nervous. 'Just about 45 minutes ago. I sent him a message saying guess who we bumped into', he messaged back a few minutes ago with a smiley face, so maybe all is ok?'. Zoe nodded and tried to smile at her friend. 'I know it isn't what you would have done Zoe, but nothing will happen between me and Mark, and I don't want anything to go wrong between Alex and I'. Zoe's expression softened. 'You really like him don't you Sam'. 'Yes, I think I'm probably in love Zo'.

As Zoe and Sam embraced at Sam's revelation , Sam's phone buzzed. It was a WhatsApp picture message from Alex; a selfie of the group of boys. Sam held up her phone to Zoe. Zoe's stomach lurched as she saw the blue eyes. She didn't know what it was with Pete, she just felt such a strong connection to him. Perhaps it was because he had been the first man to show her any interest after Ryan. That was probably it.

Sam typed back quickly and the phone buzzed again almost instantly. Sam pulled Zoe by her side he wants a selfie of us now'. The girls smiled into Sam's phone. Sam was gifted at taking flattering selfies, she always got the angle just right. Within seconds she had pinged it off to Alex and the almost instant vibration of Sam's phone told Zoe that Alex was happy to have received it. 'Alex says Pete wants to know if you are with Dan' Sam glanced up from her phone to Zoe as she read the message. 'What's it to him, with his beautiful petite blonde date the other night!' Zoe's voice was borderline shrill as she responded. Sam laughed 'I'm gonna say we are having a drink as a four...'. Zoe shrugged to give the impression that Sam could say whatever she wanted and it wouldn't bother Zoe, but her heart was pounding again. She didn't know what it was with Pete Saunders, but he was well and truly under her skin.

By 1am Zoe had consumed all the cocktails she could take and was ready to head back to the hotel. Sensing her unrest, Dan said 'Sam says we are in the same hotel so we can all walk back together'. Then in a private gesture, he leant across to Zoe and whispered into her ear, 'why don't you come back to my room? Zoe, if I don't take you to bed soon I'm going to explode'. Zoe's heartbeat raced. She had never had anyone tell her so explicitly that they wanted to have sex with her. As her and Ryan had been together since they were so young, it had been a journey of discovery rather than passion. Sex with Ryan was always lovely, but since meeting Dan she was getting the strong Impression that 'lovely' was average and she was soon to find out what adult passion and intensity really was. The thought of it was making her hot with desire.

Having whispered her plans to Sam on the walk back, Zoe and Dan headed straight to his room as soon as they got back to the hotel. The second the door shut behind them, Dan was kissing her hard. He slid his hands up and down her body, skimming the fabric of her dress and brushing her thighs at the hemline. Zoe let out a moan. She had been thinking of his kiss all night and now she was with him, it felt amazing. His touch was electric.

Zoe reached her hands to the back of his head and tangled her fingers in his hair. She wanted him so much. Whilst he continued to kiss her, Dan gently steered her to the double bed and lowered her onto it. The bed linen was white and crisp with newly laundered freshness. The mattress was soft and they sank deep into the bed, kissing passionately. By this point Zoe was writhing with anticipation. Dan undressed them both, skilfully and swiftly, he left her heels on and stroked the length of her legs. His hands were everywhere and the intensity of his touch was amazing, she had never felt this level of passion, or the sense of longing and urgency all in one.

Dan was breathing more heavily and it turned Zoe on even more. He continued to kiss her passionately, touching her so sensually that it almost sent her over the edge. His kisses became deeper and slower as she squirmed beside him, the need for him was agonising until at last, Dan pulled her underneath him, lowering himself on top of her, and finally, Zoe let go and allowed herself to be truly lost in the moment.

*****

Zoe woke a little before 7am after a restless alcohol induced sleep. She looked over at Dan, who was asleep on his back snoring. He didn't quite look like the hunk that had taken her to bed, but she guessed she looked pretty different herself. She recalled someone telling her about something Rita Hayworth had famously said 'they go to bed with Gilda, but wake up with me'. Zoe looked at Dan again and mused that it didn't just apply to women.

She eased herself off the side of the bed, grabbed her clutch bag and headed into the bathroom. Her head was pounding. Too many cocktails and not enough sleep. Zoe had never been a big drinker and had always struggled to keep up with Sam on nights out, but since August and the fateful night she met Pete, she seemed to have had far too many cocktails. 'Maybe' she thought, 'I'm self medicating and it is part of the process of grieving for Ryan'.

Zoe sat in the bathroom wondering what happened next. She had never, ever, had to extract herself from a man's hotel room before and she wasn't really clear on the etiquette involved. She decided on freshening herself up and then waking Dan to say goodbye before retreating to the sanctuary of hers and Sam's room. Zoe looked in the mirror at her pale skin and smudged panda eyes. She looked pretty rough around the edges. She opened her clutch back and retrieved her wipes and powder. Since Ryan had left, Zoe had learned to carry wipes with her, as she was prone to crying and smudging her mascara. She was grateful to be able to tidy up her eyes now, wiping the black smeared rings carefully away and leaving the remaining mascara in place on her lashes. She snuck some of Dan's toothpaste from its tube and used her finger as a toothbrush. Finally she applied a layer of powder. She still looked pale and far from the polished version of herself that had left the hotel last night, but she was passable and that would have to do!

She crept back into the room and as quietly as she could, slid herself back into her bra and knickers that were easily located on the floor next to the bed. Dan awoke and frowned. 'Were you going to leave?' He asked 'without saying goodbye?'. Zoe began to respond but Dan tugged her onto the bed and kissed her hard. It seemed his questions were rhetorical and Zoe didn't need to explain herself or her inexperience at hotel room departures. Dan pulled her back under the covers and leant over her to kiss her. His morning breath mingled with her minty kiss and made her think again of Gilda and Rita. She ran her fingers through his hair, soft now that the hair product had rubbed away on his pillow. He reached behind her and unhooked her bra and in moments her underwear was back on the floor. Dan reached for his wallet and Zoe knew that he wasn't wasting time on foreplay this time. Within minutes Dan was lying on his back once more and Zoe was feeling a little disappointed at the speed at which Dan had climaxed, and at how little attention he had paid to her enjoyment compared to the night before.

When Zoe slipped her underwear back on this time, she was desperate to leave Dan behind her and get back to the safety of her room and best friend, Sam. As she slid her sandals back on, Dan lingered in a towel, scrolling his phone, ready to get in the shower as soon as she left. As she fastened her ankle straps, she took a sneaky sideways glance at him as he stood scrolling through his phone. He was athletic and very attractive, both in and out of his clothes and there was no doubt she still felt her heart rate pick up every time their eyes met, but for some reason, the previous night had left her feeling a little dirty and used. Zoe had only ever slept with Ryan before and had never ever had a one night stand. She knew Sam, who was far more experienced in the bedroom department, would say that technically it wasn't a one night stand. But Zoe felt a sense of embarrassment in having shared a passionate night with Dan, and this morning's 'quickie' had made her feel a little sick in her stomach.

She stood up and fixed her biggest smile on her face. Dan came towards her, throwing his phone on the crumpled bed. As he stood in front of her, he wrapped one arm behind her back and kissed her neck softly. 'You are sexy as fuck Zoe' he said, kissing her square in the mouth. 'Can I see you again soon?'. 'Sure', Zoe said noncommittally as she disentangled herself from Dan's arms and backed away to the door. He followed her and kissed her once more on the cheek, before reaching around her to open the door and let her out.

Zoe walked as quickly as she could to the lift and jumped in as soon as the doors opened. She was back at their room within minutes and closed the door behind her with a heavy sigh. Sam looked up from the dressing table, where she was applying her make up. 'Good morning you little minx' Sam laughed before seeing Zoe's face and stopping abruptly.

Once Zoe had filled Sam in on the events of the previous night and that morning, Sam hugged her tight and stroked her hair. Before going into a full Samantha monologue, not even stopping to draw breath. 'Oh Zo. Poor you, feeling like that. It is because it is the first man since Ryan, that's all. It sounds like you had an amazing time last night anyway. Shame about this morning, but all men are like that sometimes. You have no reason to be down on yourself. You're a grown woman and you have broken the chain from Ryan. I understand you are feeling a bit of an anti-climax, no pun intended, but I am happy that you have been with someone else and you are moving on from Ryan. If Dan isn't for you, then let's put it down to experience, but you have started to move on and that's the main thing. Plenty more fish in the sea Zoe'.

'Like who?' Zoe responded. She hadn't got Sam's confidence, and if this was the way that sex with another man made her feel, then she wasn't sure she wanted to head out fishing anytime soon anyway.

'Well', started Sam 'there's sexy Mr Saunders, isn't there'. Zoe looked at Sam with eyebrows raised. 'Sexy Mr Saunders who called me up the day after we met to tell me he wasn't interested, told your boyfriend you were snogging Mark, pretty much threw me out of his car after collecting us from the airport and who now has a petite blonde girlfriend? That Mr Saunders?' Zoe replied.

'Well when you put it like that' Sam laughed 'but there is something about him Zoe. I spoke to Alex when I got back to the room and he said that Pete had gone in a foul mood when Alex told him we had bumped into Dan and Mark. Alex said he was jealous'.

'Well, I doubt it, and as much as I feel a connection to Pete, he is so moody, I'm not sure he would be a good person to invest energy in anyway' Zoe responded.

Sam thought for a moment before speaking 'I hear you loud and clear! But Alex says he isn't usually moody, that he is genuinely great and he doesn't know where this dark brooding side of Pete is coming from'.

'Maybe trouble with Katya' Zoe offered in response before heading off to the shower in order to close the topic down completely. Whilst she lathered her hair, Zoe thought of Sam's comments, could it be true that Pete was jealous? It just didn't seem to fit with the girlfriend and the cold front she had got from him ever since the night they met. But there was that night in the The Swan. What was it he had said to her? She tried to recall but had been so upset to find out he had shared her ridiculous behaviour with Matt, but he had definitely said something along the lines of him thinking she could have meant something to him.

Zoe rinsed the shampoo and reached for her conditioner, pausing to replay the moment in her head again. 'Could have', she pondered. He must have meant if she hadn't run away and if he hadn't hooked up with Katya. Zoe rinsed the conditioner from her hair and shut the water off. It was past anyway, and she needed to move forwards. But not with Ryan, and not with Dan. Maybe she just needed to be alone. The thought filled her with dread, but also gave her some comfort that she wouldn't need to have anymore one night stands with hot pilots or otherwise.

*****

As Sam and Zoe walked out of the train station at Lintfield, Alex's black Audi Q3 swung into the carpark. Sam's eyes lit up and she rushed over to the driver's door, where Alex was opening his window. They kissed and said a few words before Sam turned and shouted for Zoe to get in the car for a lift. Zoe politely declined, she wanted to walk. Her head was feeling distinctly fuzzy and she knew she needed some fresh air. She had a small pink case on wheels but no other luggage and so would be able to make the walk home in 15 minutes if she wanted to, but thought a leisurely walk would suit her today. As Alex put Sam's case into the car, Sam gave Zoe a hug and promised to message later that day. Zoe smiled and waved them farewell, happy for some solitude to properly process the events of the last 24 hours.

She stopped at Costa and bought her usual skinny chai latte, opting to take out and sit on a bench in Lintfield's beautiful town park to enjoy the early November sunshine. It was mild for the time of year, but the Christmas decorations were already up in the shops and now Halloween had passed, the Christmas Playlists had been added to every stores sound system. Zoe loved Christmas much more than your average person. She loved the build up, the Christmas lights, jumpers, films, food and parties and she loved spending the actual day at her parents house, sleeping in her old bedroom and waking up to her dad's bacon butties on Boxing Day. She loved the sales afterwards and then the New Year's Eve parties.

This year schools broke up late for the holiday, meaning Christmas Day was the first Sunday of the two week holiday. Whilst it didn't leave much prep time, it did mean that she would see New Year in and then still have a week off work. Prep time wasn't really an issue for Zoe, as she was always well organised and things were different this year anyway. She wouldn't need to shop for Ryan or his family, something that Zoe was thankful for.

In recent years Ryan had left her to do more and more of the gift shopping and arrangements, even though she was the one with more job responsibilities. He had come to expect that Zoe would do the food shop for when his family visited between Christmas and New Year, do the cooking and buy gifts for all of his family. Zoe had felt taken for granted and now she thought, she had no need to! She felt pleased to have identified something that was a positive about Ryan leaving. It had taken her over three months, but it was there. A feeling that in the smallest, tiniest way, she might be better off without him. Well, for the festive season at least.

As Zoe finished her latte and stood up to head home, she recognised a petite blonde figure bounding down the path towards the bench she was sitting on. The look of glee on Katya's face suggested that she was meeting someone she was passionate about. Zoe's stomach lurched as she realised that somewhere behind her, Pete was waiting open armed for his beautiful girlfriend. Zoe almost winced as Katya moved past her and she turned to watch them embrace, but to her relief, and horror, Katya was embracing a tall dark haired and dark skinned man. They were speaking in a language that Zoe thought was Italian and hugging. Perhaps they're related Zoe thought, just as they began to kiss passionately. Zoe stood glued to the spot for what seemed like an eternity, before gathering her senses and quickly setting off for home.

On the walk home all she could think about was Katya and that man. They definitely weren't related. She felt angry that Katya was cheating on Pete. Although he had been blunt with her, she knew from Sam that Pete's friends adored him. He had been kind to her when they met hadn't he? And sent her wine. He was clearly a good person underneath the hostility he had shown her. Whatever had passed since she had met him, he definitely deserved more than being cheated on. Zoe didn't know what to do. She couldn't tell him herself, she just didn't have that sort of relationship with him. But if she told Sam to tell Alex, then it might cause Pete embarrassment with his friends that he would have preferred to avoid. Zoe didn't know what to do, but her heart hurt with the thought of the pain that Pete would feel.

It was late afternoon by the time Zoe arrived home and the sky was already darkening. The walk home had cleared her fuzzy head, but hadn't presented her with any solutions for the Katya situation. She lay on her bed thinking about the situation. Perhaps it wasn't her place to say anything and Katya would realise the error of her ways. Zoe covered her face with her hands. She hated being in this position. But she realised that the feelings she had weren't just out of human decency, they were because she still had feelings for Pete and despite there being no prospect of a rerun of that night in August, for some reason, her feelings grew stronger with every interaction that related to him.

*****

Zoe awoke suddenly at 6pm, it was fully dark outside and she could see the tops of the street lamps from her bedroom window. She must have fallen asleep.  She sat up and rubbed her eyes to try to dispel the groggy feeling she decided to run a bath and consider the Pete situation some more. But as she slid into the bubbles, her mind wandered to the night before, not back to Pete. Dan had been fantastic company, she had had a great time until this morning, when she had felt used by him. But now she was in the bath and reflecting, she wasn't sure she'd have been up to much more after all the cocktails, maybe Dan had felt the same. Perhaps she should have told him no, but it wasn't that she hadn't wanted to have sex with him.

Zoe was so new to it all, she just didn't know what she was doing, but at that moment determined she would follow her head more and be brave in every moment to do what she felt. And if it felt good, she would have no regrets. 'No regrets' she said aloud just as her phone buzzed on the floor beside the tub. Zoe reaches down, drying her fingers in the plush cream bath sheet before picking up her phone.

It was a WhatsApp message from Dan. 'Had a fantastic night with you. You are so sexy. What are you doing?'. Zoe smiled. He did make her feel good when he told her how sexy she was, and she was pleased that the feeling was mutual about sharing a fantastic night. What was wrong with a little flirting and safe sex anyway? She was old enough and had some catching up to do in the experience stakes.

Zoe smiled to herself and typed back immediately 'Just soaking in a hot bubbly bath' she followed her sentence with a winking face emoji. She saw Dan was online and the double blue ticks showed he had read it immediately. 'Be there in 5!' The response came back, also with a winking face. Zoe sent back three crying with laughter emojis and set her phone back on the floor as she pulled herself out of the bath and wrapped herself in the soft cream towel. She had piled her hair on top of her head in a bun that made her resemble a pineapple, to avoid getting it wet again. Drying and straightening Zoe's hair took a long time, it was so thick and the length didn't help. She patted herself down, applied her summer glow moisturiser and then wrapped herself in her old soft grey towelling robe. It was battered and frayed through years of wear, but it was still Zoe's favourite. Her mom had tried to replace it numerous times, and now a rainbow array of towelling robes hung in the back of her bathroom door unused as she continued to favour her old grey robe.

It was 7pm when Zoe headed downstairs to answer an unexpected knock at the door. Anticipating that it would be door to door sales or charity collectors, she headed to the door with her robe pulled tight and her hair still piled high. She swung the door open to find Dan standing in her door step, bottle of wine in hand. He was wearing dark black skinny jeans, a dark shirt and white Nike air max trainers. He looked dreamy. He smiled and said 'you weren't expecting me?' Looking up at Zoe's hair and then down her body, taking in her grey robe and bare feet. Zoe was dumbstruck. 'No, I thought your text was a joke' she managed to string her words together, whilst self consciously pulling her robe around her. 'Well 5 minutes was a bit of a stretch from the city centre, but here I am 40 minutes late. Shall I go or are you going to invite me in? Kinda cold out here with no coat'.

Zoe stood back and gestured for Dan to come in and led him into the lounge. 'How do you know where I live?' She asked. She felt unnerved that he had just turned up on her doorstep. But she felt a little excited too. 'You told me the street name in Madrid, and I knew what car you have from last night, thought I'd take a chance. Thank god you live on a small cul de sac, could have been like a scene from love actually if not!'. Zoe knew this was a bit weird, but Dan's relaxed manner put her at ease. Zoe glanced down at herself and said 'I'll just go change'. 'Don't' Dan's response was urgent as he stepped closer to her.

He put his hand on the back of her neck and kissed her softly. Zoe stepped back, not sure whether she was freaked out or elated. Whichever it was, it had set her pulse racing. Dan held up the bottle of wine and Zoe took the opportunity to head through the lounge-diner of her small three bed detached, into the kitchen to get glasses. She took the time to loose her hair down and combed it roughly with her fingers. She looked at her reflection in the mirror and thought how different she must seem with out her make up and heels. When she returned to the lounge, Dan was sitting in the sofa, with the ankle of his right foot resting on his left knee. He looked sexy and confident.

'I had such a great time last night' he stated. Zoe smiled and picked the wine up from the floor beside him, feeling self-conscious that her robe might part and show her nakedness. She poured the wine on the side table at the other end of the sofa and passed Dan a glass. He looked at her inquisitively. 'Are you annoyed with me?' He asked. 'No!' Zoe responded immediately. 'It is just a shock, you turning up like this. I kind of didn't expect to see you again after this morning'. Dan's face reddened 'I'm sorry Zoe, not my finest
performance. I could tell you were disappointed this morning and kind of wanted to make it up to you. If you'll let me'. It was Zoe's turn to blush now. But at least he knew he hadn't made her feel good this morning. She bit her lip, trying to decide how to respond. She *really* fancied Dan, and he was good company, but she knew it was a fling and didn't want to get attached only to be hurt again.  She also kept thinking of Pete. Maybe if Katya was moving on, Zoe would be in with a chance. Zoe internally reprimanded herself for getting her hopes up and went back to chewing her lip and gazing at her wine. 'You chewing your lip like that is not helping me' Dan laughed. Zoe glanced up and looked into his smiling face. 'Let me take you to bed Zoe' he murmured with desire in his eyes. Zoe wasn't sure what came over her, but stood up holding her wine glass and led the way out of the lounge and up the stairs. Dan followed, grabbing the bottle of wine on his way.

It was 1am when Dan left. In the hours since his arrival he had definitely 'made it up' to Zoe. She was exhausted and had to be up for work in five and a half hours. She lay back in her bed and closed her eyes, but despite being exhausted, sleep wouldn't come to her.

She ran through the last few hours in her head. It had been amazing, but again, she felt a little empty as soon as Dan had left.

Perhaps she just wasn't suited to flings. Her mind raced and she thought of Ryan, the ease of being with him. Knowing exactly what he would do next, being completely comfortable in her own skin when she was with him. She missed the ease of it, she missed the simplicity.

Her final thoughts before she drifted to sleep were of Pete and Katya. She was no closer to deciding what to do. She thought perhaps she should leave it alone, but there was a part of her, a part that did not make her proud, that wanted Pete to leave Katya, because it was him that Zoe wanted. Not Dan and not Ryan. Moody, brooding, sparkly eyed Pete with his blue eyes and dazzling white smile. Zoe's sleep was restless and she woke more exhausted and confused than ever.

# CHAPTER 9: HAPPY BIRTHDAY SAM!

The next two weeks passed quickly, as Zoe worked hard in school and helped Sam with her party preparations in the evenings. Sam's party was to be held in the function room of a local golf club. In the summer, when they had booked the venue, the terrace views over the undulating golf course had been breathtaking. They had realised at the time that it would be too dark to appreciate the views when it actually came to Sam's mid-November celebrations, but they had concluded that the terrace space would be a bonus anyway for people to spill out of the warm event suite and away from the DJ for those wanting a quieter time.

Sam had chosen a rose gold colour scheme with amazing floral centre pieces and metallic balloons. She had hired a floral wall backdrop for photos, where party would be spelled out in rose gold helium. The obligatory '30' number balloons would highlight Sam's age next to a gift table by the entrance to the suite. The DJ already had a list of Sam's girlfriends favourite songs, and Zoe was looking forward to a night with her friends, dancing and letting her hair down.

Dan's text arrived the day before the party. 'So, Sam invited Mark to her party and said I could be his plus one. I was kind of hoping to get a plus one of my own ;-)'. Instead of feeling a flutter of excitement, Zoe's heart sank at the thought of entertaining Dan all evening. They had exchanged a few messages since the night he had arrived on her doorstep, but other than that contact had been limited and Zoe had felt relieved.

Even though her affair with Dan had been completely consensual, something about it had left her feeling uneasy and used, and she was certain that she didn't want to revisit it. She considered the message for a moment and then responded frankly. 'Dan! It will be fantastic to see you, but I am not going to be leaving the party as anyone's plus one. I'm looking forward to a night of drinks and dancing..... see you in the dance floor!'. Dan responded instantly 'I hear you Zoe, will wear my dancing shoes and be the perfect gentleman'.

Zoe smiled at the response, maybe her mom was right and honesty was always the best policy. Maybe she should tell Pete what she had witnessed two weeks earlier.... she still hadn't done a thing with what she had seen and the incident still crept into her thoughts with churning regularity. The night before Sam's party, Zoe opted for a solo pamper evening, with a long soak in the bath and preening for the following day. She had an early night and went to bed with a sense of anticipation of the day that would follow for her beautiful best friend.

The following day, Zoe awoke with the same anticipation and excitement for her friend. Sam had been fortunate enough for her birthday to fall on a Saturday, meaning that her party was actually on her 30th. They had originally had a whole day of celebrations planned, but since Alex's arrival in late August, they had made some adjustments to make sure Sam got to spend time with him too. Zoe really didn't mind. Alex and Sam were perfect for each other and Zoe was truly happy for her friend. Sam was at Alex's now and he was going to be doing the whole breakfast in bed thing, then Zoe would meet Sam in town for lunch at The lemon Grove.

Zoe had already arranged for there to be balloons and banners around their table and for a Chocolate cake with candles to arrive at the end of the meal. Sam didn't know that Leyla, Tam and

Lou would also be at lunch. The three of them had clubbed together to buy Sam a luxury spa weekend for two. Zoe knew that it would be Alex that got to go with Sam, but was happy that Sam would get to enjoy a weekend of relaxation.

Zoe had arranged with Alex for flowers to be deliver to Sam that morning. She had also bought her friend a beautiful white gold necklace with a diamond heart pendant. Sam loved white gold, and diamonds (which girl doesn't), and they had seen this particular necklace in a boutique jewellery store in Lintfield back in July. At £400 it was far more than Zoe would have ever considered spending on a birthday gift, but Sam had been such a support through everything since Ryan left that Zoe really wanted to get her something special. Zoe's new job had meant a big pay rise, and she hadn't exactly been spending much. As she put the neatly wrapped gift, with rose gold bow into her handbag, she really hoped that Sam would love it. Her friend meant so much to her and Zoe wanted her to have the perfect day.

When they arrived at the restaurant, Sam was overwhelmed to see all her friends at the table, with balloons, banners and gifts. Leyla presented a diamanté tiara with '30' in the centre of it, along with a pale pink sash with rose gold writing on it proclaiming that Sam was indeed the birthday girl. Sam laughed and eagerly put both on. 'You've got to wear them tonight too' Leyla laughed and Sam nodded her head enthusiastically.

They ate their first two courses happily chattering and reminiscing about girls nights out they had enjoyed together, touching on their need for a girls night soon to prep their annual New Year's Eve karaoke effort. Every year the girls went to The Sun for new year celebrations and the karaoke session was always the main event, followed by a live band or singer after midnight until the early hours . Each year the five girls prepped a song to sing during the karaoke. Lou had an amazing voice and covered for the tone deaf others. They girls discussed some potential songs for new year whilst finishing off their main courses.

When the chocolate cake arrived, the whole restaurant sang to a Sam and she blew out her candles through tears of happiness. Zoe's heart was bursting for her friend. Tam declared it was present time and handed over the envelope on behalf of herself, Leyla and Lou. Sam opened it and shrieked with excitement. She jumped up and hugged each friend in turn. She turned to Zoe. 'Thank you again for my amazing bouquet Zo, it barely fit through the door!'. Zoe smiled back at her best friend 'I have something else for you Sam', she reached into her bag and handed the neatly wrapped parcel to her friend 'Sam, thank you for looking after me so well. You truly are the best friend a girl could wish for and I am so thankful to have you in my life'. Sam burst into tears and hugged her friend. 'Are you going to open it then?' Tam asked in her usual forthright style. Sam nodded and laughed through her tears.

As she unpeeled the paper, Zoe felt nervous of what Sam would think. They had never really gone in for big gifts. Sam opened the hinged lid and her mouth fell open. 'Zoe, this is too much. It is so very beautiful and I love it. Thank you'. The girls hugged and more laughter was shared. Zoe looked at her friend and felt sheer joy at the happiness she could see in her friends face.

*****

There was a buzz of excitement as the girls parted company at 2.30pm, each going their separate way to get ready for Sam's big party. Zoe and Sam hung back to check everything was in order and to discuss their outfits once more, before Zoe headed to her mini manicure appointment. She didn't really go in for gel or acrylic tips, but loved to have her nails painted with high gloss gel colours. Growing up, Zoe had never managed to keep nail polish on her nails for more than a few hours before the edges were chipped and tatty and so indestructible gel polishes really made her feel a bit special . Zoe chose a deep red for her nails to go with her dark coloured dress.

She had ordered her dress for Sam's party online and was really happy with it. It was a tight mid-thigh black dress, with long sleeves and a high neck. It was embellished all over with fine bronze sparkles that formed zigzags around the dress. Zoe had always loved buying dresses for Sam's birthdays over the years as the Christmas stock was always in, and Zoe loved all things sparkly.

For Sam's big night, she had tanned her legs and would be wearing her best shoes. Zoe had bought them a few years ago as a real treat to herself, as the price tag was near £500. They were black patent Christian Louboutin court shoes with their trademark red sole. Zoe loved them and always felt so special wearing them. Tonight would be no exception. She showered and conditioned her hair with a treatment mask and then moisturised all over. She was determined to look and feel fantastic tonight, not to please or attract any man, just to feel good in herself.

Zoe took her time straightening her thick dark hair. Her hair was naturally wavy, but she had always worn it straight since her late teens. Today she sectioned her hair into thin pieces to make sure that it was perfectly straight. She applied her make up with the same care and when she was ready, she stood in front of her full length hall mirror to assess how she looked. She was delighted with what she saw.

Zoe had never been thin, and hadn't got the willpower to starve herself. She enjoyed food far too much, but as with most women, she viewed losing a few pounds as an achievement and the fact that she was an easy size 12 at the moment gave her more confidence than her usual 12-14 figure. She knew she was meant to be 'happy with the skin she was in' and all that other body confidence stuff, but the truth was, she was as much a victim of women's representation in the media as the next girl and being a few pounds thinner for Zoe meant being a little more confident and happy in her skin.

The taxi picked her up at 7pm. The party didn't start until half past, but she had told Sam she would get there at ten past so that she was there when people began arriving. As she entered, Zoe couldn't believe how fantastic the room looked. Zoe smiled as she saw Sam standing by a table in the corner where Sam's family were all sitting, Sam was proudly wearing her tiara and sash. Zoe waved and Sam came towards her looking stunning.

Sam was wearing a floral off the shoulder midi dress that really accentuated her womanly shape. Her hair was curled in perfect loose curls that fell onto her tanned shoulders. The friends hugged. 'Alex is so lucky' Zoe told her friend as she stood back to admire Sam's beauty. Sam blushed a little and said 'I don't know about that!' She continued 'tonight he meets my family.... eeek!'. Zoe smiled and squeezed her friends arm for reassurance. Zoe headed to greet Sam's family and asked if anyone needed a drink before heading to the bar to buy Sam a gin and tonic and get herself a nerve settling Sauvy B. Zoe had butterflies for her friend!

A large group of Sam's work friends and their plus ones were next to arrive, followed by some more of Sam's family and some of Sam's old school friends. Tam, Lou and Leyla arrived shortly after and Zoe settled into a group with them, sipping wine and chatting about each other's outfits and other chitchat.

Sam's work friends were primarily women and were loud and excitable. Sam had always told Zoe they were hysterical and she could see what Sam meant. They stood in a large group of about fifteen, with ages ranging from twenty to mid-fifties. Every so often a loud eruption of laughter would break out from the group and fill the room, drowning even the DJ out. Zoe smiled, they clearly knew how to have a good time!

Zoe saw Mark and Dan arrive, and waved across at them, but she didn't leave her group of girlfriends. She didn't want to give Dan the impression that she would be spending the evening with him. Tonight was about Sam and her friends and she was determined not to get lured into Dan's enticing trap again.

It was only 8.30pm when the DJ played the first of the girls requests, and one of the group's favourite songs to dance to on a night out. Sam practically ran to the group and dragged them to the dance floor. The group of friends were all happy to dance perfectly sober, but as it was they were all well into their second drink and the alcohol bolstered their confidence.

They were in a circle dancing and singing loudly and off-key when Alex arrived with Jake and Jaiden. They stood in the doorway of the function room and Zoe's heart skipped a beat and then felt heavy as she noted Pete wasn't with them. The disappointment was only momentary, as Pete and Matt appeared in the doorway behind the trio, seconds later. Sam was already moving towards Alex, beaming and Zoe was frozen to the spot. She locked eyes with Pete and he smiled at her, his sparkling blues eyes captivating even from this distance.

The next song began playing and the spell was broken as Leyla stepped in front of Zoe whilst leaving the dance floor. Tam, Lou and Leyla were chatting and laughing loudly but Zoe couldn't focus on what they were saying. She followed them off the dance floor on autopilot, but her head was a million miles away. She still wanted him. Despite all the stormy moments, Dan, Katya, she still just wanted Pete. She would have to tell him about Katya tonight. It was the right thing to do, but might ruin any chance she had with him. She realised she was in a complete mind racing trance, when her thoughts were abruptly interrupted by a male voice.

'Sauvignon blanc?', there was a glass of wine being held in front of her. She looked who was holding it and met those azure blue eyes. Her heart was pounding so hard she thought it might escape her chest altogether. She couldn't find any words, and felt conscious that she was just standing and staring into his eyes, but she didn't seem to be able to unlock her own gaze.

Thankfully the realisation that she was rooted to the spot and staring made her uncomfortable enough to smile an embarrassed smile. Pete smiled back as he bent down and kissed her lightly on the cheek. Unsure how, Zoe managed to take the wine from him without dropping it and took a sip of the cool liquid. 'Hi Zoe' he said, flashing that sparkling smile again. 'Hi Pete, thank you', she managed to almost exhale his name, still captivated by those eyes. The spell was finally broken as Alex and Sam joined their duo. Pete wished Sam a happy birthday and handed her an envelope he retrieved from his back pocket. 'Thank you, Pete' Sam exclaimed, opening the envelope there and then. Her eyes widened as she read out the gift of a wine tasting and food experience for two in a vineyard on the South Coast. She threw her arms around him, shocking him a little and kissed him on the cheek to show her appreciation.

Sam looked at Alex and then at Zoe. Zoe knew that Sam was gearing herself up for the big introductions. 'Wish us luck' she said, taking Alex's hand and steering him towards her mum and dad, leaving Zoe and Pete alone once more. For the first time since she had met him, Zoe sensed that Pete felt uneasy and as he spoke, his words seemed awkward 'how have you been?' Zoe smiled at him and responded that she was well. She told him about her day celebrating Sam's birthday, and he chatted back, the uneasiness he had seemed to evaporate. She was pleased to feel as relaxed talking to him as on the first night they had met. Before she had ruined it by running away.

The meeting between Alex and Sam's parents went well and they were soon back to report their progress. Sam was beaming and the girls headed to the ladies for Sam to fully update Zoe. When they got back, Pete was in conversation with Jake and Jaiden. Zoe caught his eye and he smiled again. Zoe glanced at the bar and saw Alex standing next to Mark and Dan. Leyla, Tam and Lou we're back on the dance floor along with most of Sam's work colleagues. Sam's old school friends and their partners had taken two of the large tables near the dance floor and seemed to be smiling and laughing and the remaining tables were full of other friends and family of Sam's. Zoe found herself grinning. The party was perfect and turning out just how Sam had intended.

She turned to find her friend in the mass of people and frowned. Sam and Alex were now standing near the entrance and Alex's face looked angry. He was gesticulating and Sam looked upset. Zoe's heart sank. What was happening. As she began to make her way towards the couple, Alex stormed out of the room and Sam looked around desperately for her friend. Zoe was by her side in seconds. Sam was crying now. Zoe pulled her around the side of the bar, away from prying eyes.

Sam was gasping and struggling to speak, but Zoe ascertained that Mark had told Alex that he had arranged to meet Sam on that Saturday night in Birmingham and that Alex had taken her flexibility with the truth as evidence that she had been unfaithful.

Adrenaline flooded Zoe's veins as she tried to analyse her options. Should she get Mark to say Alex had misunderstood and that their encounter was one of chance? Should she try to speak to Alex? She hoped Alex hadn't left already. Zoe hadn't noticed Pete follow his friend out, but she saw him re-enter the suite now, eyes scanning the bar area until he locked eyes with Zoe and signalled her to join him. Zoe grabbed Leyla who was just returning from the ladies and instructed her to take care of Sam. 'I'll be back as soon as I can'.

Zoe was by Pete's side in a moment. He was frowning. 'Is it true?' His eyes burned into Zoe's, as though he was looking to extract the truth by telepathy. 'Is what true?' Zoe asked, trying to measure what Alex had told his friend. 'Has she been unfaithful to Alex with that Mark?'. Zoe was shocked and her wide eyes responded before she formed her response 'God, no!' Zoe knew her voice was shrill but didn't care if it meant defending her friend. 'Sam loves Alex' Zoe continued. 'She would never cheat on him. Her and Mark are just friends. They just talk, that's all. Sam would never be unfaithful. We hate infidelity'.

Pete's eyes searched Zoe's face. 'Ok. I will go and speak to Alex'. Zoe frowned 'wait Pete, why didn't Alex believe Sam, but you believe me?'. He exhaled slowly 'Alex is just in a mess out there Zo. He is head over heels for Sam. I don't think he is emotionally rational at the moment. And, I believe you because I trust you, and your face gives you away completely. You would be a crap poker player' he laughed. He squeezed her hand and then he was gone.

Zoe returned to Sam who had stopped crying, but was now sitting forlornly on a bar stool at the end of the bar. Zoe stood holding Sam's hand and kept glancing toward the door. She hoped Alex and Pete hadn't left. She hoped that Alex and Sam would make it up and that the party could be redeemed for the birthday girl.

After what seemed an eternity, Pete appeared in the doorway and signalled for Zoe to bring Sam onto the terrace, then he headed back out the door. Sam was wobbly as she stood, and Zoe realised the depth of her friends feelings. She had never seen Sam so upset and felt a sense of panic in case this couldn't all be worked out.

As they exited the building, Zoe scanned the terrace, Pete and Alex were standing about ten metres to their left, facing each other and talking in low voices. Pete had a reassuring grip in his friends right shoulder. Sam gripped Zoe's hand and Zoe sensed the panic rising in her friend. Sam clearly though that Alex was going to end it there and then.

Zoe began moving towards Alex and Pete but Sam was a stiff weight at her side. 'Come on Sam,' Zoe whispered gently to her friend. 'We will be ok'. As they got within five meters of the boys, Alex turned and saw them approaching. He broke away from Pete and was hugging Sam in an instant. 'I'm sorry I accused you' Alex declared as Sam sobbed 'I'm sorry I wasn't totally honest' and then they were kissing, Zoe and Pete awkward onlookers. They caught each other's eyes and giggled. 'Crisis averted' Pete smiled, just as Leyla shouted Zoe's name from the building entrance. Zoe turned and headed back into the suite with a wide grin in her face, telling Leyla that all was ok as they headed to the dance floor.

It was a while later that Zoe spotted Sam, Alex and Pete re-enter the room. She tracked Pete as he headed across the room towards the bar. As she followed him with her eyes, she noticed that Dan was getting very friendly with a young woman that had arrived with one of Sam's work colleagues. Zoe caught Sam's eye and signalled towards Dan with a look of incredulity on her face. Sams eyes widened and she mouthed OMG back at Zoe. Zoe shook her head a little, but stopped as she noticed Pete watching her. It wasn't that Zoe wanted to revisit her brief fling with Dan, it just seemed a bit of a cheek to hit on a girl at Sam's party.

Zoe began to walk towards Sam to share her feelings about Dan's behaviour. As she walked behind Dan, she noticed Pete was now next to Dan at the bar. She saw Pete say something to Dan as they stood side by side, Dan with his back against the bar and Pete facing the bar to get served. She couldn't hear what it was, but she looked up and spotted that Sam was focussed on the interaction between the two men also. Dan smirked in response to whatever Pete had said, and turned his body towards Pete, putting his hand on Pete's upper arm as he said something in return.

Zoe had arrived at Sam's side as she saw Pete's left hand rise to the centre of Dan's chest and the subsequent shove that completely threw Dan off balance, causing the girl he was chatting to to catch him and steady him. Again Dan spoke, with flashes of anger in his eyes. Pete seemed to square up to him, but Zoe didn't see his mouth open to speak. Dan turned his back on Pete and spoke to Mark who had also been chatting to one of Sam's work group. After a few moments of conversation, both men headed towards Sam and Zoe, who were standing wide eyed and rooted to the spot somewhere between the room entrance and the bar.

It was Dan that spoke to Zoe, as Mark wished Sam happy birthday again and tentatively hugged her. 'We're heading off Zoe' Dan said 'your boyfriend is feeling particularly protective of you'. Zoe frowned, completely confused by the sentence. 'What?'... Dan gestured toward the bar and Pete with a nod of his head 'That guy, he says I am disrespecting you and that I needed to consider how to treat you. I told him he didn't know anything about us and that I hadn't got a clue who he was. Seems that really pissed him off. Anyway Zo, it has been good to see you, but we are going. I don't wanna cause you or Sam any trouble. We are flying in the morning anyway so it seems a good time to head off'.

Zoe felt so confused. She just nodded, Dan and mark headed out the door, their two new lady friends in tow. Sam shrugged and headed back to Alex and Zoe followed them out, not to see them off, or to gaze wistfully at Dan, just because she needed some air. Tonight was turning out to be more eventful than she had imagined. She sat herself on one of the rattan sofas and sank into the textured cushion exhaling deeply.

She leant back and closed her eyes, letting the cool air penetrate her skin and her lungs. She sat perfectly still like that for a couple of minutes until she felt the sofa hollow as someone sat alongside her. She sat up and opened her eyes in one fluid motion, to see Pete sliding a glass of white wine across in front of her. His head was close to hers and they locked eyes. There was a moment when Zoe thought he was going to kiss her. Her heart sang. She really wanted him to kiss her. But he sat back in his chair quickly, away from her lips and as he reclined, the chance of any intimacy between them receded.

'I know it isn't really my business or place to comment Zoe, but you deserve better than that indiscreet joker.' His voice was calm and even, and he looked out into the night as he spoke, not even glancing toward where Zoe sat looking at him. In profile he was possibly even more handsome. His jawline was square and strong and from this angle she could see the creases in the corners of his smiling eyes. He looked distant, as if he was speaking on auto pilot. Zoe frowned. She didn't really know what to say, so many times she had caused offence with this beautiful man and she didn't want to do anything that would make him move away. She wanted to stay next to him, looking at his face, smelling his aftershave, as long as possible. But she knew she had to speak. She took a deep breath.

'Thank you for saying that I deserve more Pete. But there is nothing between Dan and I. We had a very brief moment in time together, but it is passed and he hasn't wronged me tonight. It was Sam who invited him and Mark'. Pete turned his head to look at her as though considering what to say, but Zoe hadn't finished. 'I liked you stepping in and defending me Pete, but I don't think I'm the kind of girl that needs that sort of look-ing after....'. She took a deep breath and continued 'Pete, I need to tell you this, and I'm sorry for the hurt that it might cause you.' Zoe knew she had to say it all now. 'A couple of weeks ago, I saw Katya in the park kissing another man. It wasn't family from the way they were kissing. I'm sorry I left it so long to tell you. I didn't know what to do. I couldn't discuss it with Sam in case she told Alex and caused you any embarrassment and I just wasn't sure how I could tell you over a message, it seemed cold. I'm sorry'.

Pete was looking straight ahead into the darkness again. Zoe could see the slight frown across his brow and her stomach turned that he might be annoyed with her. It seemed an age be-fore he opened his mouth to speak. He spoke slowly, as though

he hadn't quite constructed his sentence, and was still considering it as he spoke 'I'm a little taken aback Zoe. Not quite sure
what to say'. Zoe gulped as Pete adjusted his positioning to face
her. 'That would be Katya's fiancé, Lucas. Katya and I are not,
have never been, an item. I tried to tell you in The Swan but
you said you didn't care. Her dad owns a number of vineyards
in Italy. That is where she is from. She comes over occasionally
and I tend to look after her.' He gave a wry smile. 'Katya isn't as
independent as you Zoe, and does need some looking after.'

Pete glanced down and took hold of Zoe's hand in his. She gasped
involuntarily, but he didn't seem to hear. He continued to stare
at her hand as he went on 'I'm really touched that you tried
to protect my feelings and that you decided not to confide in
Sam to spare me any embarrassment.' He let out a short laugh
'maybe you're not the sort of girl that needs looking after, but
it looks like you decided that I'm the sort of guy that does'. He
looked up into her eyes and Zoe swallowed hard.

'Zoe, I think we have misunderstood each other since we met
and I guess now is a good time to clear things up. I was really
sorry to upset you that first night. Sam has told me without
going into much detail that you have had a tough time and
I really never intended to upset you like that.' Zoe wondered
what Sam had told him. 'Pete', she started tentatively 'I'm so
sorry I ran away from you that night when you had been so
lovely. It was my first night out in months, my first night since
Ryan..... I.... it was just so confusing and I'm sorry'.

Pete smiled at her 'you don't have to be sorry Zoe. I was too forward. I really liked you and felt bad for upsetting you like that
and then not coming after you. I should have checked you were
ok. After that night I kept thinking of you, and when it emerged
that Alex and Sam were a thing, I kind of decided that I would
try to talk it through with you and see if we could maybe go on
a date. But then you met Dan and I heard what he said in the car
on the way back from the airport, I guessed the night we met

was more to do with me, since you were ok with him.  It made me jealous. I'm sorry for the way I spoke to you that night. I was meant to be apologising for the night we met and ended up biting your head off'.

Zoe smiled at Pete. She was so relieved to be clearing the air and to hear that he had really liked her was music to her ears. 'The thing is Zoe, you are really complicated and it is hard to know what is going on in your life. There was the picture of you back with.... is it Ryan? Then Alex said that girl had been hammering on your door, then at The Swan you couldn't get away from me fast enough again, then you were back with the Pilot.  I have been struggling to get a measure on where I stand,or where I might fit.'

Zoe tried to process everything that Pete was saying. She could see it from his point of view. Her life hadn't been straightforward recently. 'I really enjoyed that first night we met Pete, but was so embarrassed at how I behaved and when we were at The Swan, Mark called me Zoe the runaway and it just brought all the embarrassment back to the surface.' Pete looked cross 'I will have a word with Mark' he scowled 'and whoever told him'. He was still holding her hand, and she placed her free hand onto his forearm. 'Please don't' she whispered. She knew what she wanted to say now, but her chest was pounding and her mouth was dry.

'Pete, could we, maybe forget what has happened, and have a fresh start'. Zoe wanted to say more, to tell him that she thought about him all the time, that he made her heart pound like no one ever had before and that she wished more than anything she hadn't run away that night, but her words failed her and she fell silent.  Pete squeezed her hand before releasing it. Zoe felt instantly sadder and lonelier once her hand wasn't in his. But Pete was smiling ' Ok he said, I'm going to forget it all, except for the part where I watched you dance to maniac and Aha, and possibly the part where you were messaging me from the bath' his eyes twinkled and Zoe felt heat rise to her cheeks. Thank goodness it was dark.

Pete smiled once more as he stood up. She didn't want him to go, but he was already glancing towards the building entrance. Zoe stood and faced him. 'We better get back' he said 'Zoe, do you want to go for lunch with me tomorrow?'. Zoe knew she was grinning the second he said it. She couldn't help it 'yes, I would' she responded and with that they headed back to the party in silence and headed back to their respective friendship groups. Both smiling and both hopeful at what the next day might bring.

The rest of Zoe's evening was spent on the dance floor with her friends. She felt so excited by the conversation with Pete. The air was clear and they were still on good terms. Zoe was happy to have chance to see him again tomorrow and wondered where they would go and what they would speak about.

Sam was having a fantastic night and was flitting around the tables enjoying time with all her guests. Alex was frequently by her side, or at the bar with Pete and their group. Zoe looked in Pete's direction frequently and his mood seemed light and happy too. Each time their eyes met, he smiled and she beamed back. She felt excited at what might be and couldn't wait until the following day.

As the end of the night was approaching, Zoe headed around each table to take pictures so that Sam had some photos of the evening. When she got Pete's group, they stood as a group, arms around each other's shoulders. Jake was first to break the pose and extract Zoe's camera from her hand. 'Bet you're not in a single pic yet Zoe, get in the group'. Zoe nestled herself in between Jaiden and Pete and each put their arms around her. As Jaiden broke away, Pete kept his arm around Zoe and indicated for Jake to take a shot of just the two of them. Pete said something about a first night keepsake and Zoe looked up at him. When Jake returned the camera, As she reviewed her pictures, the shot of her and Pete showed Pete grinning at the camera, arm tightly squeezing Zoe's shoulder and eyes sparkling. Zoe was seemingly gazing up at him adoringly, eyes wide and face beaming. She smiled to herself. It was the perfect shot and she knew she would look at it a thousand times before she saw Pete again tomorrow.

The DJ was close to ending his session when he played Mr Brightside. Sam and Zoe loved the song and they piled into the dance floor with what seemed the whole function room. Zoe danced alongside Pete and Sam and Alex, singing and laughing loudly. This had been the best night and she couldn't wait to see what happened next!

# CHAPTER 10: GETTING TO KNOW YOU

The Facebook message was already there waiting for her when Zoe awoke at 9am. 'Hi Zoe, let me know if you still fancy lunch today. P x'. The message had been sent at 5.30am. Zoe had got into bed around 1am, having stayed behind to help Sam and her family bundle gifts and balloons into various cars and taxis. Pete was probably in bed earlier than her, but still, being up and sending messages at 5.30am seemed a bit extreme. Zoe clicked reply 'Yes! Can't wait xx'. As soon as she clicked send she realised that Pete had probably sent her message and then gone back to sleep. She immediately typed again.'Sorry if I woke you up'. She could see immediately that Pete was typing. 'You didn't, I don't sleep much :-). Pick you up from yours at 12.30. P x'. Beneath his message he had sent her a business card to his mobile phone number. She saved it immediately and opened WhatsApp. She clicked on his name and saw a different profile picture to the one on Facebook. This picture was in black and white and as she clicked on it, it took her breath away. Pete was looking downwards to his left, and laughing, his long eyelashes were dark and pronounced against his cheeks in the black and white filter. He looked like a movie star or model. Wow. He was so handsome and so out of her league. The thought unsettled her. She'd probably end up getting hurt by all this. Pete could do so much better. She thought back to the night before. She had been tipsy and couldn't remember all the things she had said or done. She remembered hugging him goodbye and Pete laughing and having to detach her from him. He wasn't drunk. Actually,

Zoe thought, Pete wasn't really ever drunk and now she thought about it, she had seen him drinking soft drinks last night. Perhaps he had been driving.

Zoe jumped into the shower and was in her skinny jeans and favourite slogan t-shirt, ready to head out by 9.30am. She had a stack of Sam's presents piled in her hallway and had promised to drop them around to Sam first thing. She loaded her car and then climbed into 'Bibi', her little silver Renault Clio. Zoe had never been into cars. If it got her from A to B, she was happy. Lots of her new colleagues had much nicer cars than hers and she had wondered whether she should buy something bigger now that she was an Assistant Headteacher, but the truth was that she was happy with her little car that she was confident driving, and that she wasn't into status cars at all.

Sam was still on a high from the night before, she had really had the best time, except for the small set back with Alex, but it seemed that was all forgotten now anyway. Sam was still in her dressing gown, but had clearly been up a while. The living room was full of gifts and balloons that Zoe had to clamber over to follow Sam to the kitchen. Armed with a cup of tea each, the girls headed back to the lounge and Sam started opening her gifts. Alex had gone to play golf and so it was just the two of them and Zoe really enjoyed the intimacy of this time together. As Sam opened bottles of champagne and gin, gift vouchers and jewellery, Zoe kept a note of who had gifted what so that Sam could send her thank you texts later. Sam had received so many gifts. 'I'm so lucky!' She kept exclaiming time and time again, but Zoe knew it wasn't luck. Sam was a good friend to everyone and her warmth made people feel special. It was no wonder she had received so many gifts.

Zoe and Sam chatted whilst Sam worked her way through over fifty gifts. Zoe filled her in on the progress with Pete and talked about their plan to go for lunch. Sam was happy for her friend but strangely advised Zoe to be 'good to him'. Zoe assumed that her protectiveness towards Pete was because of Alex's love for his best friend. Zoe laughed, a little uncomfortable at Sam being on the wrong side 'I will, if he is good to me' she laughed light heartedly but felt a little concerned that if things didn't go well with Pete, Sam's loyalty to Alex would make things difficult.

It was 11.30am when Zoe left Sam's house. She applied her make up carefully and re-straightened her hair. Pulling on her black skinny jeans and her grey slouch top that fitted tightly around her hips, but hung from her shoulders, she considered her reflection. She didn't really know what to wear out for a lunch date, and as she had no idea where Pete was planning on taking her, she didn't know if she had chosen well with her outfit. As she packed her black over the shoulder bag, she wondered what they would talk about and as she put her cards and cash into the inner pocket, she wondered if it would be awkward when they came to pay. Should she offer to pay in total, or would they split the bill? Or should she assume he would pay? He seemed quite old fashioned, but should Zoe just accept that, even though she was used to being financially independent. She wondered how much he earned. Zoe's salary was healthy and with Ryan she had often ended up paying far more than her fair share as she earned more and he pointed it out frequently. Pete didn't seem like that, but then again, what did she really know of Pete?

Zoe had pulled on her ankle boots and was sat in her lounge waiting by 12.10pm. Her tummy fluttered and gurgled as she waited. She hadn't had breakfast due to the nerves, and now the cup of tea Sam had made seemed to be on a wash cycle in her stomach. She was hungry, but felt it would be impossible to eat in front of him. Zoe stood up and paced a little to disperse some of the nervous energy.

Pete pulled up outside her house at 12.27pm. His black Audi TT gleaming. The two occasions that Zoe had seen his car, it had been sparkling. She looked towards her little car and the dullness of its silver stood out. She committed in her head to take Bibi through the car wash as soon as possible.

Pete beeped his horn and looked toward the house. Zoe had assumed he would come to the door and now fumbled to slip on her waist length quilted Barbour jacket and open the front door whilst he waited. As she set the alarm and locked the door, she could feel his eyes on her which made her fumble more. Turning her key slowly, she took a deep breath and muttered 'come on Zoe, you can do this' to herself in way of a pep talk.

She slid into his passenger seat with a pumping heart and was welcomed by that trademark white smile and blue eye combination. Zoe managed to mutter a 'hi' before they pulled away and Pete turned the car at the end of her cul de sac. Pete picked up his phone and glanced over to Zoe 'something 80's?' He asked. 'Oh, I do love 80's music, but I love lots of different styles. I love indie as that was the music my parents listened to when I was a little girl, I love pop. I love the carpenters and ABBA; my Nan used to play them all the time, and my grandad, you'll be pleased to hear, loved the Beatles. I'm really happy listening to anything Pete'. Pete grinned 'I am very pleased to hear that your grandad had such good taste, but let's go for this', he selected an album in his Iphone and Oasis's Wonderwall burst from the speakers. Zoe smiled. This song had played on so many Sunday mornings in her house as a young girl. Pete began to sing and Zoe was struck by his tuneful but husky singing voice. This man had it all. But could she have him?

Pete drove along the lanes away from Lintfield and kept driving for 35 minutes. Zoe had been expecting to go somewhere local, so was surprised that he had chosen somewhere at this distance without asking. She liked it though. Ryan and her ate out a lot but had set places they liked to eat. More of their comfortable routine. But if they tried to go somewhere new it would often end up in twenty minutes of suggestions, each shooting down the others, before ending up in a usual spot in town anyway. For the last couple of years they really hadn't even bothered to try new places.

Pete pulled into the car park of a pub that looked like a traditional country pub called The Briar Rose. Zoe wasn't really sure quite where they were, but it was very picturesque and as a Disney fan she approved of the name because of its link to the timeless animation 'Sleeping Beauty'. The pub was brown brick, with leaded windows and window boxes. It looked out onto a quaint little village green and a series of terraced cottages lined up like soldiers on the other side of the green. The air was crisp for November, but the sun was bright and the sky clear blue. As Zoe climbed out of the car she savoured the cool air on her face and took a moment to take in her surroundings and companion once more.

Pete smiled at her and signalled for her to go ahead of him. She headed to the entrance where Pete stepped in front and held the door open for him. His manners were old fashioned. She hoped that it didn't mean his views about women were too.

Zoe stepped into the pub and took in her surroundings. It was a really cosy, country pub, open fires and arm chairs, along with older gents propping up the bar nursing pints of amber brown liquid. Pete turned to Zoe 'How about the table over there by the fire?' She followed his gaze to the secluded alcove and nodded her head. 'You go and grab it, I'll get the drinks. White wine?'. Zoe nodded and smiled and then headed straight to the table, grabbing her phone to quickly message Sam to say all was well.

When Pete returned to the table, he placed a white wine in front of her and sat down opposite. She noticed he put a coke in front of himself. 'I'm really sorry I never thought that you were driving last night Pete and now you are today too. I could have picked you up today'. Pete smiled and shook his head. 'It's not a problem Zoe. I wasn't driving last night. I just don't drink much socially. My job involves a fair bit of drinking so I try to give my liver weekends off' he laughed as he spoke and she pictured his WhatsApp profile picture. He just mesmerised her. Zoe's heart was beating faster than usual. Again. She felt on edge and alive whenever she was with him. She had never felt like this about anyone, but she also felt an insecurity she had never experienced before either. He seemed so out of her league and she knew she didn't have the interesting life that he did. She got the feeling that she would end up nursing her broken heart again really soon.

'What are you thinking?' His voice was low and soft as it cut into her thoughts. She smiled shyly as she said cryptically 'not much, just about blue eyes and broken hearts'. Pete's smile faded momentarily and then was back. 'Let's decide what we're eating and then you can tell me about your new job. I don't really know what an Assistant Headteacher does, so I'm ready to find out about the other side of your life Zoe'.

Zoe chose five bean chilli with rice and nachos, even though it was Sunday and most people in the pub were working their way through enormous plates of roast beef and Yorkshire puddings with all the trimmings. Whilst Zoe would happily eat a roast dinner, it had never really been her meal of choice and she would often choose a vegetarian option rather than eat meat. Pete selected a gourmet burger that was enormous when it arrived.

They ate slowly whilst Zoe told Pete about her career and what it was actually like being a secondary school teacher. Pete listened intently, appearing genuinely interested in her and her job. She touched on her time at her previous school and the fact that she was grateful to leave as Ryan's new partner still worked their. Pete's face was gentle and soft as he spoke 'I'm sorry he broke your heart Zoe. You deserve to always be happy'. Zoe felt a lump in her throat as his piercing eyes seemed to look into her soul. She managed a smile and a jumbled sentence 'Well, you can't have a rainbow without a little rain. Anyway, I'm sure you have a far more interesting life. Your turn to tell me about your job.'

Pete took the hint immediately that the topic of her broken heart was off limits. He told her about his education and how he had studied business at Liverpool university, but that his part time work in a local, independent wine merchants had actually set his career course. He talked about his time in Liverpool with obvious fondness and touched on his love of the Beatles more than once. He was easy to talk to and had a dry sense of humour that Zoe loved. He didn't seem like the same guy that had snapped her head off on the phone in Madrid or after the airport drop off.

By the time their plates were cleared, it was 2.30pm and they had been talking for nearly an hour and a half. Zoe hadn't seen any sign of the Pete that had been so distanced and down right arsey in the past, but she still remembered clearly how he had gone from civil to awful on that night he drove them back from the airport. He seemed so complex, such a mystery.

As the waitress brought their coffees to the table, Pete told Zoe about the busy week of tastings he had ahead of him. 'Out drinking on school nights' Zoe laughed 'cardinal sin for us teachers'. Pete smiled 'like I said, comes with the job but it does mean I don't drink much socially. To be honest, my dad was a bit of a desperately depressed drunk, so it kind of suits that I don't get like that.'

Zoe looked at his face, he didn't seem emotional about the matter, but it must have affected him to influence his behaviour in that way. 'I'm sorry to hear that Pete'.

'Don't be, he was a good dad. He didn't drink much at all when we were younger, but it changed when I was a teenager. He just used to get himself in a right state and it was tough for me and my brothers. I just don't like the thought of ever being like that with people I love.' He paused and gave a half smile. 'Don't get me wrong, I have been wasted in my time, usually when I am pissed off or upset, but I don't think I'm a desperate drunk or an angry drunk, well, I never have been yet. But let's just say I am happy to see my world and social life clearly, without the fog of the grog'. He laughed and so did Zoe and then he added quietly 'it means I can look after the people I care about too'. Zoe smiled at him with genuine admiration. Pete was as lovely as she remembered from that first night they met. She chose to ignore the sulky and abrupt Pete she had encountered since and focus on the incredibly handsome, gentle man sitting across the table from her.

\*\*\*\*\*

It was 4pm when Pete pulled up by the curb outside Zoe's house. They had driven home in companionable silence, listening to Pete's music on shuffle. He had sung some of the songs and Zoe had thought again how melodic and lyrical his voice was. He really was a dark horse, but definitely a dark horse she wanted in her life. Zoe knew that Pete Saunders was truly going to be in her head and heart this week and she reflected, hopefully for a long time to come.

As soon as he had stopped his car by the pavement, he immediately jumped out from his side and moved around to open Zoe's door. She climbed out and smiled up at him. 'Thanks for a fantastic time Pete, and thanks for paying. My treat next time?' Her voice was quiet and tentative as she held her breath to see how he would react to the request for a re-run.

He smiled from the other side of the passenger door. 'Definitely, I'll choose somewhere pricey for us to go, Assistant Head-teacher'. He winked and Zoe giggled. She was just relieved he was up for another date. He could book a Michelin three star restaurant as far as she was concerned. If it took a months salary for a few more hours one on one with Pete, she would happily pay it.

Zoe stepped out from behind her door and Pete closed it. She headed onto the driveway and turned, ready to ask if Pete wanted to come in, but to her disappointment, he was already getting back into the drivers seat. He wound his window down and smiled the glorious dazzling smile she was growing to adore. 'Have a good week Zoe. I'll message you'. With that, he started his engine and reversed out of her small road.

Zoe stood still watching him drive away and then remained still, watching the route he had driven, for several minutes. She was confused. She had been hoping for, well, expecting, some display of affection after the wonderful hours they had just spent together. But nothing. Not a peck on a cheek, a brush or squeeze of a hand, a hug and certainly no kissing. Zoe felt that the wind had been knocked from her sails.

She headed back into the loneliness of her house and flopped onto the sofa. He didn't like her did he? She had been thinking all was going fantastically as they chatted, and he had clearly been waiting to get away from her. Zoe felt her face redden with the embarrassment of misreading the situation so badly, but no tears fell. She was getting hard to the heartbreak she told herself. She doubted she would hear from Pete during the week and so set about readying herself for work and the parts of her life she could control.

Sam text later in the evening to ask how it had gone. Zoe was soaking in the bath and had already decided to be sparse with the facts with Sam. She didn't want Sam to be in an awkward position if Alex asked, and didn't feel up to another of Sam's 'plenty more fish' pep talks. Zoe typed that she had enjoyed the afternoon and then lied, saying she was working now, prepping for the week. Zoe knew Sam would respect this and leave her alone. Zoe sunk lower in her bath and turned her music up, thinking of Pete Saunders beautiful face and how, for a moment, that afternoon, she had felt like the stars were aligning for her once again.

*****

Monday passed slowly. Zoe taught her groups slightly robotically as she kept running through the afternoon she had enjoyed with Pete. She didn't feel upset, just bemused, but she was still enjoying the memories of his face, laughter and singing voice. She rushed from lesson to lesson and lesson to duty all day and finally at 4.30pm, following a training session she had run for the entire teaching staff, she headed back to her office. She sat down at her laptop and spent thirty minutes going through the sixty odd emails she had received since checking that morning and then at 5.15pm, pulled her bag out of her desk drawer and headed to her car.

As she walked down the steps to the car park she pulled her phone out to check if she had any messages. To her surprise, there was a message from Pete that he had sent at 11am. Zoe hadn't expected to hear from him so soon, well, she hadn't expected to hear from him ever and so the WhatsApp notification sent the blood surging through her veins. She fumbled to open her car and flopped backwards onto the drivers seat, feet still planted firmly on the concrete of the carpark.

'Hi Zo, just wanted to say that I had a great time getting to know you yesterday. I know we both have busy weeks, but how about dinner on Wednesday. I know it is a school night, so I promise to have you home in bed by 10 ;-)'

Zoe gasped. What? He wanted to out again! And was that an innuendo about getting her home to bed? Zoe had a busy week this week with two late work days on Tuesday and Thursday. She knew going out on Wednesday would make her 13 hour day on Tuesday and parents evening the following day hard, but she also knew she was going to say yes and go out with Pete anyway. Definitely. She began texting back, but decided to consider what she wrote first. Her next instinct was to call Sam, but she knew she shouldn't discuss Pete in depth with her until she was clear where she stood. Sam and Alex were so close, Zoe wasn't entirely sure how much of what she said to Sam got back to Alex, and she definitely didn't want anything she said going via Alex to Pete. As she slid into her car she decided to ponder her reply and for now she did as she did every day when she drove home and called her lovely mom.

Zoe's mom was everything a mom should be. Caring, proud, encouraging and loving. She always listened to Zoe, but Zoe hadn't told her about Pete or Dan. Her parents had both loved Ryan like a son, and seeing him treat Zoe the way he had, had taken its toll on them as well as their daughter. Since the end of August, Zoe had made an effort to paint her life positively to her parents as they both worried about her. This evening, she chatted to her mom about work and Sam and then talked about her mom's friends and how they were all doing.

Zoe arrived home at 5.45pm. She loved the fact her new commute was fifteen minutes shorted than her old one. Once she was home, she headed straight upstairs and slid out of her suit with the same sense of relief she always had when returning home. Pulling on her loungewear, she flopped onto her bed and reopened WhatsApp.

'Hi Pete, sorry for the slow reply, busy day. I really enjoyed yesterday too. Wednesday sounds good. Shall I drive?'.

Zoe saw the ticks appear to say the message was delivered, and watched as they turned instantly blue. Pete was online. Zoe hoped he had been checking his phone to see if she had messaged back, but told herself it was more likely coincidence than Pete checking his phone continually for seven hours since 11am. Zoe clicked her screen lock button and lay her phone next to her . She couldn't sit and wait online to see if he replied. Her phone lit up silently beside her almost immediately, indicating an incoming call... from Pete! Zoe's phone was always on silent because of her job. She rarely remembered to switch it to sound or vibrate after work or on the weekends which meant she often missed incoming calls or texts. She made a mental note to make sure she changed this habit in case Pete called her more frequently in future.

She picked up the phone as though it might explode and gently slid the screen to answer. 'Hello?' She heard her voice squeak and felt the embarrassment creep up her neck.

'Hi Zo. It's good to hear your voice. I was worried you were ignoring me all day'. Zoe responded quickly 'of course not, I rarely check my phone at work. I would never ignore you'.

She could almost hear his sparkling white grin 'glad to hear it' he said. Pete explained he would already be in town on Wednesday due to a late work meeting. They arranged to meet in The Swan at 7pm and then Pete said goodbye. The call was warm and friendly, but it was also brief and to the point. It didn't seem like he wanted to chat with her at all. Zoe felt disappointment as she headed down the stairs to spend the evening alone on the sofa.

\*\*\*\*\*

By the time Wednesday arrived, Zoe had been over the telephone conversation in her head thousands of times, and again had convinced herself that Pete really wasn't interested. But then why had he messaged her and suggested meeting up again. Once more Zoe found herself confused by Pete Saunders. She left work at 4pm. An earlier finish than she usually allowed herself. The late November sky was turning dark grey already and she couldn't believe how quickly autumn was turning to winter. She headed home and set about her usual comforting preparation schedule for going out. A soak in the bath followed by moisturiser, hair and make up.

She opened her underwear drawer and selected a matching red bra and knicker set. It was better to be prepared she thought and then giggled to herself 'wishful thinking Zoe'. This evening Zoe selected thick black tights with a deep red tunic and her burgundy suede ankle boots. She loved dresses and boots in winter and often went without her skinnies for months on end once December arrived. She had already decided that she would drive and only have one drink. She had a busy day at work the following day, and was already feeling tired. She slipped into her car, Bibi, just before 7pm and headed to The Swan car park, just a five minute drive from her house.

When she walked in, she spotted Pete straight away at the bar. Today he was in a deep blue suit with brown brogues and a crisp white Ralph Lauren shirt. The suit complimented his colouring and his eyes perfectly. Zoe stood in the doorway for a moment and just looked at him. She knew she was falling deeper. Every time she saw him, she thought he was more amazing than the time before. Her heart skipped a beat with the nervous prospect that it may get broken again by the blonde haired, dashing wine merchant in-front of her.

Zoe took a deep breath and headed towards the bar just as Pete turned and spotted her. He smiled and Zoe thought his face showed genuine warmth and even affection. She really hoped so anyway.

They sat at a table next to where Matt had called her 'runaway Zoe' the last time she had been in The Swan. She recalled the cold interaction with
Pete and decided it would be best to avoid mentioning that evening. As they studied the menus, Zoe glanced occasionally at Pete. He looked a little tired compared to usual. 'Stressful week?' Zoe enquired. Pete looked surprised she had noticed, but openly told her about some issues with contracts with growers in Italy. He had to fly out on Friday morning for a week and a half and would be home the first week of December. Zoe smiled and listened, but inside she was disappointed he had to go away. She wondered if he would be visiting Katya and if she was really

completely committed to her fiancé.

Zoe and Pete both ate more quickly than they had the previous Sunday. They were both fatigued from late nights and didn't have as much energy for endless conversation. They spoke about work and about Sam, and then Pete asked a little about how things had ended with Ryan. Zoe explained how it had come completely out of the blue and that she had assumed she would be with Ryan forever. Pete sat quietly and after some time, spoke softly.

'So you still have feelings for him?'
Zoe was caught completely off guard by the question. She hadn't been expecting to talk about Ryan, let alone be asked about her feelings for him. Zoe stuttered. 'I.... umm... I haven't really thought about it like that..... I mean, it's kind of irrelevant what I feel.... isn't it?.....I suppose it's..... it's complicated'. Pete looked down at his plate and didn't speak. An eternity seemed to pass before he looked her in the eye again. 'I'm sorry Zoe. I shouldn't have asked you such a personal question'. Zoe's heart sank. Oh no. She could feel him withdrawing from her again. What should she do?

Finally she spoke 'how about you Pete? Anyone ever broken your heart in two?'. Pete slowly shook his head. 'Not really. I mean, I've been hurt a few times, but nothing of the same magnitude. I've never really felt strongly enough for someone to be able to break my heart. I guess I've always kept my distance and protected my heart. Kind of a self-preservation thing.'

He was looking into her eyes as he was speaking and she held his gaze as she responded. 'That's sad Pete, not to have ever loved deeply. Ryan broke my heart into a million pieces and then I'm sure stamped up and down on the shattered remnants, but I don't regret the love we had. I just regret how badly it ended. Being heartbroken. It's.... it's a bad place to be'. Pete didn't respond, or look away. He continued to hold her gaze and reached out and gave her hand a squeeze. She smiled 'enough! Let's not talk about really depressing things anymore!' Pete smiled, let go of her hand and passed her the dessert menu. He had never let anyone into his heart then. But he was already in hers. Zoe had the sick feeling again that she was going to end up with her heart broken twice in a year, and despite all the history that her and Ryan had, she felt like the heartache she would feel from Pete would be bigger and harder to swallow. Maybe she needed to follow Pete's lead and take some steps to save herself from any future heart ache.

As promised, Zoe was home and in bed by ten. Sadly she was alone and disheartened again. They had chatted over dessert about how well Sam and Alex got on, and talked about their different friends and then Pete had walked Zoe out to her car, held the door open and.... nothing. Again. She had actually leant in this time, and kissed him on the cheek, but he hadn't reciprocated in any way.

Zoe lay in bed feeling as confused about Pete Saunders as ever. But she was starting to suspect that somehow, between that sublime first kiss outside Afters all those months ago, and this cold November evening, she had managed to manoeuvre herself firmly into the friend zone of the most desirable man on the planet! Zoe growled at herself in frustration and rolled onto her stomach, screaming silently into her pillow.

Pete text Zoe on Friday morning. A brief message saying he was in departures and would be busy in Italy, but that he would message as soon as he was home and that they should go out again. Zoe messaged back something non descript about enjoying himself and staying out of trouble before putting her phone away, on silent, in her bag for the rest of the day, where it spent much of its time for the next week and a half.

# CHAPTER 11: THIS IS LADIES NIGHT

The first Saturday in December was always 'ladies night', when Sam, Zoe, Tam, Leyla and Lou would spend the afternoon, evening and night together, catching up, watching chick flicks (one of which always had to be a festive film to mark the beginning of December) and choosing and practicing their New Year's Eve karaoke song.

This year, the first weekend was already days into Zoe's favourite month of the year and she was already feeling festive. Zoe had chosen her 'Gin-gle bells' festive slogan jumper, a short black skirt with thick tights and her favourite Mulberry knee high boots. The girls had chosen to meet for tapas and cocktails in town at 3pm and following an afternoon of friendship and laughter, they headed back to Zoe's to snuggle up and watch some quality girly films.

Zoe loved the way they always kick started their festive season this way. The girls always took their PJs and sheet face masks to one of their houses and pampered whilst drinking, watching films and singing. It was like a slumber party, but without the slumber. The girls all liked to get a decent nights sleep in their own beds!

This year, as they were at Zoe's house, she had the responsibility of choosing the films. Her festive film hadn't been an easy choice between Love Actually and The Holiday. She loved both of them massively, but for very different reasons. The holiday was a tear-fest and love actually had such a great sound track. But both of them had an element of infidelity, which since Ryan's early summer departure, Zoe had found hard to stomach. She had decided to choose love actually. Although the heart ache of Emma Thomson's character was more intense than Kate Winslets in The Holiday, there were far more light hearted parts that the girls could enjoy together. Zoe didn't want to get too emotional and ruin the night. The second film she had chosen was of course Dirty Dancing. The girls had been expecting Zoe to choose it, but as they all really loved it, they were happy. Besides, the dancing would get them in the mood for some tipsy karaoke practise.

As the final credits of Love Actually rolled at 11pm, Zoe topped up everyone's Prosecco. They were into bottle three now, but were all happy drunk and having a great time. Zoe loved her friends. They didn't spend enough time as a five, but always made sure they had at least four girls nights in a year. Sam's phone was ringing and she took it into the hallway to answer. When she came back she returned to her seat with a loved up expression on her face that immediately prompted a mass of teasing from the other girls. Sam didn't mind. It was clear that her and Alex were in love and the girls were all happy for her. Sam smirked and giggled at the comments about hats for weddings for a few minutes and then spoke.

'I think we're all clear where I stand on Alex, but maybe we should all be wondering why Pete has been texting Alex to try to get me to dish the dirt on her feelings for that absolute arse Ryan'. Sam pointed at Zoe with a flourish. The girls fell silent and looked to Zoe. Zoe sighed and shrugged.

'I don't know. I really like him, but somehow he ended up asking me if I still have feelings for Ryan and I couldn't answer. Ryan was my best friend and partner for nearly a decade and I can't just erase or forget it. Pete told me he doesn't let people into his heart. I really like him, but he is so guarded. I'm scared he is going to hurt me. He seems out of my league.' Zoe looked at the sympathetic faces around the room and it was Leyla that broke the silence first.

'You have to do what is right for you Zoe. If you feel you need to protect yourself, then do it, but if you want to go all in, we will be here to pick up the pieces if you need us to. There is not a man on this planet that is out of your league'. A series of approving sounds immediately backed up Leyla's stance.

Zoe smiled and looked from face to face. 'You are all so amazing. I really appreciate the sentiment Leyla and I know that you would pick me up again, but I think it is clear that Pete only thinks of me as a friend and that is that.' Zoe picked up her glass of Prosecco, raising a toast 'to heartbreak and spinsters' she cheered and her laughing friends raised their glasses chanting back to her 'to heartbreak and spinsters'.

As the opening credits played for Dirty Dancing, Lou declared that 'Be my baby' by The Ronettes would be their New Years karaoke song and the girls all agreed that it was a great choice and made a change from their usual song themes. The previous year it had been 'It's raining men' and the year before 'I need a hero'. They were all happy to try a more subtle song.

'Besides Lou said, Leyla can sing it to Jake and Zoe can sing it to Pete'. Leyla blushed and Zoe tutted as the girls erupted into laughter and then settled down to watch the film.

It was 2am by the time taxis were called. After watching The Ronettes on YouTube a few times, the girls had coordinated their song with matching finger clicks, hip bumps and swaying from side to side. The copious amounts of Prosecco had led them all to believe it was a fantastic vocal and choreographic performance. Zoe crawled into bed at 2.30am with the song well and truly planted in her head as an ear worm.

The girls messaged throughout the week about their song and

sent each other video clips of themselves practising. It brightened Zoe's days, as she was feeling lonely with Pete away and showing her no interest, and Christmas approaching. She kept thinking about the things her and Ryan would have been doing.

The next Saturday she headed to Tesco to buy herself a whole load of pink and purple Christmas decorations. Zoe loved girly colours, and Ryan had always insisted on traditional red and gold. Zoe didn't mind, she loved the traditional Christmas colours, but as she was on her own, she figured she should go all out and have exactly what she wanted. She opted for pastel pink and white on a traditional green tree and spent the remainder of the afternoon putting it up. Zoe loved dressing the tree. She always poured herself a glass of baileys and played her favourite Christmas playlist.

Decorating the house was a welcome distraction as Zoe knew today was the day that Pete arrived home. According to Sam his visit had been extended by a few days and stretched to two weeks. Zoe hadn't heard from him at all which was all the confirmation that she needed that he wasn't interested in any more than friendship with her. It made her heart heavy, but she had resigned herself to the idea that it was better to have a slightly heavy heart now than a completely broken one in a couple of months.

# CHAPTER 12: GOING BACKWARDS

Zoe had just placed the angel on the top of the tree when the door knocked. She glanced at her watch. It was 3pm. She didn't know who would be calling, so quickly checked her reflection on the way to the door. Zoe was wearing her favourite black knitted dress and had tied her hair in a messy side bun before heading out that morning. Her makeup was plain, but presentable and she looked well rested compared to how she had looked a few months back.

She swung the door open to find Ryan standing on the door step, his backpack on his shoulder and the suitcase that he had packed all those months ago beside him. Zoe had long since moved the rest of his stuff into the garage, but he had never come to collect it.

'Hi Zoe, I'm home.' He looked sheepish as he spoke but had obviously practised his line to get the confidence level right. Zoe was gobsmacked and she was aware her mouth was gaping. As she tried to form some words, out of the corner of her eye she spotted a black car swing into her road. She glanced up. It was Pete whose eyes were already fixed on the scene before him. It was excruciating waiting for him to turn his car around and pull-up at the curb.

Zoe still hadn't uttered a word in response to Ryan when Pete jumped out of his car and walked towards them with an outstretched hand. 'Hi, you must be Ryan'.

Ryan eyed Pete suspiciously and then spoke with confidence that surprised Zoe. 'I am. Who are you?'

Pete looked calm. Zoe couldn't speak. She felt like she was watching a disaster unfold before her. She was rigid. It was like she imagined an out of body experience would be, how could they have arrived at the exact same moment. Coincidence didn't seem to cover it at all. Pete's voice jolted her back to the moment.

'I'm Pete. I'm a friend of Zoe's'. Pete seemed so relaxed and calm as he spoke. Zoe's heart plummeted. A friend. That was that confirmed then. Pete glanced at Ryan's suitcase. Ryan's face showed recognition of the name Pete and he spoke confidently once more as he looked directly at Pete.

'Zoe and I have had some time apart. I'm just coming home'. Pete nodded, no emotion on his face whatsoever. He glanced at Zoe for the briefest of moments.

'You must have a lot to catch up on. I'll leave you to it. Really happy for you both.' Just as quickly as he had arrived, he turned to leave. He got to his car door before Zoe found the strength to move her legs. She ran to the car as Pete slid smoothly into the leather seat. 'Pete, wait' it was little more than a gasp but the words were out. Pete froze with his right leg still on the pavement. He looked at Zoe and then across to Ryan who was lifting his suitcase into the house. 'I can't Zoe. You still care for him and you need to go and sort things out. I'm sorry I interrupted you. You and I, it clearly just wasn't meant to be. I had hoped it was, but fate is not on our side Zo.' Pete looked into her eyes one last time. She couldn't read his expression as he slid his right leg into the car and closed the door. She couldn't breathe, let alone speak but wanted to tell him to stop, tell him to let her get her thoughts together.

She was so confused and couldn't comprehend what was happening, but it felt like she had no control over it. Pete started his engine and pulled away from the curb. And with that he was gone. Zoe stood in utter dismay but still couldn't find the breath or energy to call after him, cry or even move from the spot she was stood on. She remained still until Ryan came out and guided her back into the house.

Zoe wasn't sure how long she had sat on the sofa gazing into space but was suddenly conscious that Ryan was standing in front of her holding a steaming cup of tea out towards her. He had always made the best tea and always knew exactly when she needed a cup. Zoe had missed having someone to make tea for her.

She took the tea tentatively and blew across the top of the mug as Ryan sat beside her on the sofa. He looked straight ahead of him towards the fireplace as he spoke.

'Who is he Zoe?' His question was direct and Zoe felt obligated to respond, but as she tried to form her sentence, she realised that she didn't have the answer to the question Ryan was actually asking, nor did she want to share any details with Ryan. They had yet to discuss his unexpected return and Zoe didn't want to fuel any difficult conversation with details of her feelings for Pete.

'His name is Pete. He is a friend. His best mate and Sam are a couple. They're serious'. Zoe kept her sentences short so as not to betray her genuine feelings for Pete. Ryan spoke again.

'That's great news for Sam. I'm so happy for her. To be honest I could tell there is nothing between you and that Pete. He was super casual about me being here. I guess I will see more of him if Sam is settling down. Good that things were so amicable'.

Zoe couldn't think straight. She couldn't even begin to tackle Ryan and his actions with her head so foggy over Pete's reaction and him telling her to sort things with Ryan. She felt stupid for thinking that someone like him could even consider someone like her. She stood up, feeling the redness of humiliation creep upwards along her neck.'I'm going for a bath'. She picked up her tea and left the room before he had chance to respond, she locked herself in the bathroom and put her headphones in. She needed time to reflect and time to consider her next steps.

After an hour of solitude, Zoe's hands were wrinkled and coldness of the long since cool bath water seemed to have seeped into her body. She left the bathroom reluctantly and headed across the landing. She noticed Ryan had already made the bed in the spare room. Her stomach turned but she felt relieved at the same time. How had he assumed he was staying? But also, thank goodness he hadn't assumed he was moving back into their bed.

She put on her loungewear not comfortable to throw on just her dressing gown, and headed down the stairs with a sense of trepidation. Ryan had been cooking. The smell hit her immediately. She found her memory transporting her back to all the nights he had cooked and they had sat hands joined across the table, talking about their futures. She remembered the excitement of all that was to come and the security of having someone that was always there. She hated the solitude she had endured since the summer, but also hated the heartache he had caused. She remembered the feeling when he left. The utter loss and desolation and flopped back onto the sofa, head in hands. What was happening, she still was nowhere near comprehending the afternoon.

Her phone buzzed with an incoming call , it was Sam. 'Is it true? Has that absolute prick moved back in?'. Zoe didn't know what to say, but she knew she didn't have the energy. 'Sam, yes, he is here. I can't talk now, I'm sorry Sam.' Zoe hung up with a feeling of immense guilt. After all that Sam had done for her, she deserved an explanation. But there wasn't one was there, Zoe didn't have an explanation to give. She would have to speak to him to find out what on earth he was thinking and then, she would need to consider her own stance and feelings based on what he said.

Reluctantly, fifteen minutes later, Zoe took her place opposite Ryan at the dining room table. She hadn't sat at it since he left and felt uncomfortable returning to their normal seats, but knew she needed to get everything out in the open in order to make sensible choices and move on, however hard that might be.

Ryan had cooked steak. It was his signature dish. Zoe was confused, he must have brought it with him in his rucksack, knowing he would cook for her. The thought of it annoyed Zoe beyond measure. It seemed Ryan sensed her annoyance and took a deep breath as though he was ready to begin a monologue immediately.

As he prepared to speak he looked directly at her, searching her face for her reaction, but Zoe was determined that on this occasion she wouldn't show her feelings. She couldn't let Ryan walk in here and get any sense of the hurt and devastation that he had left behind all those months ago before summer. As he began speaking Zoe turned her head so that she could focus on the twinkling of her Christmas tree lights, they had a calming effect on her and she knew she would need all her strength to remain calm in the next few minutes. She couldn't bear to look him in the eye, not with so much anger welling up inside of her. She was ready for Ryan to begin his defence, how she had forced him away, how she hadn't met his needs. Whatever he was going to say she wouldn't give him the pleasure of reacting overtly emotionally. Ryan began speaking and Zoe steeled herself, but Ryan's words were unexpected. He spoke softly and his voice was full of emotion. She glanced at him and saw the tears welling in his eyes and the pleading expression on his face.

'Zoe. I'm so sorry. I beg you to forgive me and take me back. I love you. I have always loved you and I made a catastrophic mistake that I have regretted every day since I took the decision'.

Zoe looked into his face. The man she had loved so whole heartedly for the last twelve years. It was the face that she loved, the face that she had laughed and cried with. The man who had shared all her firsts. Her Ryan.

But he had done the worst thing possible. He had left her for another woman. How could she ever forgive him for that. It wasn't the sort of thing you could just return home from was it? She wasn't sure she could ever forgive him. But then, coming home to a cold dark house over the last few weeks hadn't been her idea of festive or cosy. She had felt the solitude more heavily recently than she had throughout the early autumn. The last couple of weeks, with the exception of the girls night in, Zoe had felt alone and vulnerable more than ever before. Not in the same heartbroken way of the summer. Just in a weary resigned to being alone sort of way. She didn't think she wanted that for herself. But did she want Ryan back? She wasn't sure.

Zoe realised that Ryan was still speaking. He was crying. She had no idea what he had been saying, but he was as emotional as she had ever seen him. This was the man that she would have been prepared to marry six months ago. Surely, after twelve years of happiness she had to give him a second chance. She knew things had changed over the last few months, but had she changed so much that what she wanted six months ago was history? She wasn't sure and needed to find out for definite.

'Ok', she began firmly, exactly as she meant to go on. 'You can come home, but there are a number of ground rules'. Ryan's face was flooded with relief as he nodded his head enthusiastically. Zoe picked up her wine and took a long sip, wondering if she had just displayed a monumental error of judgement.

# CHAPTER 13: 'TIS THE SEASON

It was the final weekend before schools broke up and Sam and Zoe had walked into town to do some Christmas shopping. It was getting less often that they had impromptu meet-ups since Alex had arrived on the scene and Zoe was excited to have a few hours of devoted Sam time.

'So how is it going?' Sam asked as they strolled towards the top end of the town. Zoe paused whilst she considered her response. 'It's ok, it's only been a week. And hardly that to be honest. I had two late nights at work with the Christmas fayre and a governor's meeting and Ryan had to work late on one of the nights I was home. So we haven't really spent much time together. The nights we were both home were fine. Ryan cooked, we ate together as usual and then sat and watched TV. It's the end of term and you know us teachers.... so you know, I'm really tired and turn in pretty early. Ryan stays up later than me and turns in when I'm already asleep'.

'Still to separate beds?' Sam asked. They had been friends long enough not to beat about the bush but Zoe wished she hadn't asked such a direct and personal question so early in their morning together. 'Like I said Sam, it's only been a week. I don't want to rush back into anything'. Sam nodded. She seemed satisfied with the response, but the truth was that Zoe really wasn't keen on sharing a bed with Ryan any time soon. She had without question rekindled some of her feelings for him since his return. He was still very much the Ryan she had adored in many ways, and whilst she probably didn't love him now, she definitely had a sense of longstanding affection towards him. But that was where it currently ended. At affection. She just didn't fancy him anymore, not in the slightest. She could imagine going to bed with him and it being ok, but after the passion with Dan and the absolute yearning she had discovered for Pete, she just didn't think 'ok' was going to meet her needs at all.

On top of that was the anger she felt towards him for leaving her in the first place. He had apologised plenty in the week he'd been back. But an apology didn't make it right. She knew she would always think back to how he was unfaithful then dumped her for someone else, and she didn't see how she could ever love him again after he hurt her so badly and showed so little respect and compassion towards her. If she was absolutely honest with herself, Zoe knew this was a massive road block in the path to any future happiness with Ryan. She couldn't spend the rest of her life with someone that she felt affection for but not love could she? Not just to avoid being lonely.

Zoe glanced over to Sam. Her friend smiled at her, took her hand and squeezed it. 'It's ok Zoe. It will all be ok'. Zoe smiled back but had to swallow hard to get rid of the lump in her throat. She hadn't been truthful with Sam for such a long time. Since Pete and Alex had arrived. Zoe knew she could trust Sam, but didn't want to ever make things awkward or put Sam in a difficult position that made things hard for her and Alex. He genuinely seemed perfect for Sam and Zoe wanted their relationship to be unhindered by being middle-men for Zoe and Pete's relationship. Zoe laughed inwardly. What relationship. There was nothing with Pete anymore, not that there ever had been really. She decided that when they had a coffee break later, she would tell Sam the truth about her feelings for Pete and how things hadn't worked out how she wanted at all. She would trust Sam with it all and hope that it didn't make Sam feel awkward.

The first stop off of the day was at the department store make up counters. Zoe and Sam both treated themselves to new makeup for their Christmas nights out. They had never socialised together much around Christmas, both usually heading off to their respective work parties and having a girls group Christmas meal just before Christmas. This year they hadn't even arranged a meal, as they all broke up so close to Christmas Day.

One year when they were younger, Sam and Zoe had gone on a big Christmas eve night out and had both regretted it massively. Christmas Day had been ruined for both of them and they had vowed never to stay out past 11pm on Christmas Eve ever again! New Years Eve had always been their festive season celebration when they really let their hair down. This year would be a little different. Sam and Alex would be together, Leyla and Jake seemed to be developing a fledgling relationship and then she guessed Ryan would be with her. He had always gone out separately with his own mates, but this year had made a point of saying he wanted to be by her side all holiday.

After a little more window shopping and a couple of cosmetic gift purchases for Sam's family, the girls decided it was time for refreshment. They had already spotted that one of the quirkier, old fashioned pubs was serving mulled wine and decided to head in by the open fire to sample the festive drink.

Zoe saw him as soon as she walked in. He was sat in the corner by the window, at a high table with another man. The winter sun was low and shone through the window, reflecting off his blonde hair and making it shine. He had a black thick knit jumper on with blue jeans and black Chelsea boots. He looked as sublime as he ever had. Zoe's stomach turned, her heart pounded and her blood rushed through her veins. She still wanted him more than she had ever wanted another human being. Sam followed her gaze just as he looked in their direction.

'Petey!' Sam was on her way towards him, arms outstretched. Zoe stood rooted to the spot as her best friend kissed him on the cheek and summoned her over. Pete smiled at Zoe warmly. 'Hi Zoe'. His words were warm, accompanied with smiling eyes that wrinkled at the corners. Zoe couldn't help but gaze into his eyes as she smiled back at him, moving closer to the table.

'This is my big brother, Paul'. Pete looked from the girls to the man sitting beside him. The resemblance was clear, but it was obvious that Paul was the elder brother. Sam smiled and said hello before declaring that she must dash to the ladies and leaving Zoe high and dry standing before Pete and Paul.

'This is Zoe', Pete concluded the introductions. Paul's smile was warm and welcoming just like his younger brother's. They shared the same laughter lines and square jaw, but Paul's smile didn't stun like his younger brothers could.

'Ahhhh.' Paul's eyes lit up. 'The infamous Zoe'. Zoe glanced nervously at Pete but the younger of the men was smiling at his brother as he continued to speak. 'I've heard a lot about you Zoe'.

Zoe frowned 'really? I can't imagine what! Unless Pete has shared the events of the night we met'. Zoe was laughing, but she also wanted to test Pete. Had he told his brother about her running away? Had he told all his friends? Paul frowned as he responded 'No, unfortunately the tale of your meeting isn't something Pete has gone into detail about. I'm sure I would be very interested to hear it, but as you no doubt know, my younger brother is a model gentleman and would never kiss and tell'.

Zoe laughed properly now. She realised what Paul said was absolutely true. Pete had always behaved in such a gentile way. He really was a gentleman. Sam was back from the ladies and headed to the bar. Zoe smiled at Paul and then at Pete. 'It was really good to meet you Paul, and good to see you too Pete. Have a good day'. Zoe turned and headed to the bar where Sam was just collecting her change, wondering, if it wasn't about the night they met, just what Pete had told his brother. The girls headed around the corner and found a quiet alcove to sit in. Zoe looked at Sam and took a deep breath.

'Sam, I haven't been entirely honest with you about Pete' Zoe glanced around to check he hadn't appeared around the corner, before telling Sam about everything that had happened between her and Pete from their first meeting in August up to the previous weekend, when he had encountered Ryan returning home. Sam sat and listened intently, occasionally taking a sip of her mulled wine, but never interrupting.

'The thing is Sam, I have really strong feelings towards him. Every time I see him, he just takes my breath away. I know nothing is going to happen between us, he has made it clear that we are just friends, but I wanted so much more. I think I might still want more Sam'.

Sam hugged her friend tightly and finally spoke. 'I knew you liked him Zo, but wow! It sounds like you both have a real connection to Me. Maybe you can't see it, but Alex always says that Pete is different around you. He says when you are mentioned Pete acts extra interested, or seems jealous if another man is mentioned. Perhaps it could be more. But Zoe, you'll never know the way things currently stand. You cannot continue with Ryan if this is how you feel about another man. You just can't'.

'I know Sam.' Zoe felt relief at being able to speak openly with Sam 'the thing is, despite what you say, I know for certain that Pete doesn't see me like I see him. He made it clear when we went on our two non-contact dates'. Sam giggled and Zoe gave a look of mock despair before continuing. 'I can't not give Ryan another chance because I am lusting after a man I will never have. I need to be realistic Sam. We don't all end up with the Adonis we spot across the cellar bar do we?!' Sam laughed again. 'That's very true. I am a very lucky girl, but you can't blame me for wanting the same for my BFF can you?!'

Zoe smiled and finished her mulled wine. She had come clean with Sam and now, perhaps it was time to come clean with Ryan. But not before Christmas and the New Year. That would just be cruel, and whatever Ryan had done to her, it wasn't in Zoe's nature to be uncaring. She would see the festive season out, and then assess her feelings. That would be best for every-one.

# CHAPTER 14: MERRY CHRISTMAS

The week running up to Christmas was a busy one for Zoe. The annual Christmas show was running at school Tuesday and Wednesday night, meaning front of house duties and 11pm finishes. By the time school finished on Friday afternoon she was exhausted. Zoe knew she had to go to the staff party that evening, at least to show her face and headed home from school at 4pm to reluctantly get ready.

Ryan also had his Christmas work party that night , and for some reason it was in the back of Zoe's mind that Kate would be there, her and Ryan had plenty of mutual acquaintances and Zoe wouldn't put it past her. Although Zoe had no idea how Kate and Ryan had parted, given Kate's door hammering that weekend in the summer, Zoe couldn't see she would let him go easily. She hadn't mentioned it to Ryan, but it was nagging away at her, although not in the way she expected. Zoe sat straightening her hair, and thought back to early summer when her whole world had crumbled around her.

When she had first found out about Ryan and Kate's affair, she had been jealous beyond all reason. She had thought all manner of territorial thoughts about how she would handle the man eater that had taken her Ryan. But tonight, she was wondering if it might be a good thing if Kate wooed Ryan back. After all, Zoe had pretty much decided that there wasn't a future for her and Ryan after talking to Sam the weekend before. Perhaps Kate luring him back would be the best thing for everyone.

Zoe shook her head. How had she landed herself in this new mess? She had let him come back with no resistance whatsoever, straight off the back of disappointment over Pete, and now here she was living as house mates, with a man who kept saying he loved her, who she would have done anything for six months ago, but now couldn't really bear the thought of him touching her. 'Oh Zoe.' She spoke to her reflection in her make up mirror. 'What are you doing? And what are you going to do next?'

She slid into the dress that she had worn for Sam's party, she still loved the cut with high neck, long sleeves and mid thigh length. She slid her feet into her Laboutins and headed downstairs. Ryan was still on the sofa, watching reruns of some show where people auctioned off unclaimed storage units.

He looked up and jumped out of his seat. 'Zoe! You look amazing'. He stepped forward and put his hands on her waist, leaning in to kiss her square on the lips. Zoe stepped back as she removed his hands. 'We are not in that place yet Ryan'. Her voice had a tinge of disdain that she hadn't intended. Ryan's face betrayed a flare of annoyance before he spoke calmly. 'When will we be in that place Zoe?'. He looked at her intently as he waited for her answer.

It annoyed Zoe that he thought he had the right to ask the question. After all, it was him that had gone off screwing another woman, ruining the life that she had considered perfect. Her face was hard as she replied 'when I say we are.' She held his gaze for a moment, her face not softening at all, and then she turned and headed straight out the front door to the staff party. Her pulse was raised as she climbed into her car. She felt angry. Angry that Ryan had dared to hold her, angry that he felt he could ask when they would be physical again, but most of all, she was angry at herself for landing herself in this mess that she undoubtedly had to sort out, sooner rather than later.

Zoe didn't want to be at the staff party for long. As a member of the leadership team, she knew staff wouldn't let their hair down with her there, but neither did she want to go home too soon. Not until Ryan had definitely gone out anyway. As she sat in the corner sipping her wine with her colleagues, she decided to ask Ryan how his evening was going, to get a sense of her best window for getting home and to sleep before he came home.

Ryan had definitely been trying to accelerate things between them in the last week, with his physical contact, hints and his blatant questioning that evening. Zoe was worried that he would try something on tonight, when he got home drunk from his staff party and she really did not want that battle in the early hours. Not that she thought Ryan would ever force himself on her or act against her will, just that she could already picture the hurt puppy eyes he would give. She knew them well, in a previous life they would have hurt her heart and she would have moved mountains to make things better for him, her love. But now, since his return, they just infuriated her, beyond all reason. She didn't know why, she just knew that she had a completely different view on Ryan's needs since he had returned.

'Sorry we argued. Hope you have a fab night'. She text him, lightheartedly to test the water. Her heart sank as she spotted two immediate blue ticks and an instant response being typed. 'Decided to stay home'. The reply made Zoe's stomach turn. Firstly, he wasn't going out, secondly, he was calling the house 'home' again and thirdly there was no chance of a) him hooking back up with Kate or b) her sneaking in under the radar. Zoe felt angry. At him and at herself. She placed her phone face down on the table and considered her options. She could stay here, or go home and face the uncomfortable music. She chose option three and picked up her phone, typing out a WhatsApp detailing her predicament to Leyla and the sat and waited.

Zoe always found it easy to be honest with Leyla. She was down to earth and never felt the need to say what she would do under the same circumstances or give unwanted advice, she would always just listen and naturally coach Zoe to find her own answers to her problems. Zoe had shared all of her feelings and experiences associated with Pete with Leyla along the way and Leyla true to form had listened but never judged or advised. Tonight Leyla text back swiftly and was immediately willing to support and council her friend. Over a bottle of Chablis of course!

Zoe parked her car around the corner from her cul de sac and without alerting Ryan, caught a taxi straight to town to meet Leyla. Town was packed with people celebrating breaking up from work, but Zoe and Leyla were undeterred as they headed to The Sun. The pub was always packed at the weekend, but since its refurb, had plenty of seating, standing and outdoor space, that meant it was a good option for a catch up. Zoe and Leyla often chose it when they wanted to talk, not dance. It also had a decent selection of wines and Leyla was a bit of a wine snob. They loved that the pub was quirky with its wine offer. It didn't have ice buckets for the expensive wines, instead they had PVC wine gift bags packed with ice, that could be easily transported around the pub.

The girls sat on two tall bar stools at the bar and sipped the cool Provence rose that Leyla had ordered. It was crisp and dry and Zoe held it on her tongue to savour the flavour. Leyla had a glow and chirpiness about her that Zoe hadn't seen in a while.

'So Ley, what's new with you? I can tell, there is someone or something in the world floating your boat at the moment!'. Leyla smiled at the question, as though she had been expecting it. She took her time, taking the wine from the ice bag, pouring it slowly into their glasses and placing it back, carefully nestling it into the remaining ice, before turning to Zoe with a smug smile.

'Well,' Leyla exclaimed, milking the suspense and creating a sense of drama. 'I may have been seeing someone, just a little, you know, early days and all'. Zoe half smiled half pouted as she teased Leyla into giving more detail. Leyla was clearly anxious to oblige. 'He is very handsome. One of the fantastic five, and has the most incredible auburn hair!'.

'Jake?! I knew it!' Zoe couldn't hide her pleasure at the prospect of Leyla and Jake becoming a proper item, after their weeks of flirtation.  Although they had only spoken at length once, Zoe could tell he was down to earth and a decent human. Leyla grinned and nodded. Zoe shrieked with laughter and took another massive gulp of wine, 'fantastic!' She told her friend and genuinely meant it, though at the back of her mind worried that with Alex and Sam, Jake and Leyla, Zoe might become a lone outsider of the group, or worse still, be forced to socialise agonisingly with Pete, yearning for him but not able to be with him. Zoe didn't relish the prospect, but then if her two best mates were happy, she wouldn't have much to complain about would she?!

\*\*\*\*\*

It was 2am when, after a fabulous night of girly fun with Leyla, Zoe finally stumbled through the front door of her house.  She was trying her absolute best to be quiet, but failing miserably.  She needn't have bothered though as she stepped into the lounge to find Ryan sitting on the sofa, waiting up for her. Bleary eyed,  but perfectly sober, wearing an expression of disdain mixed with panic and weariness.

'Where have you been?' His voice was calm, but Zoe could sense his agitation.  She was in no mood for an inquisition and was way beyond any sort of conversation. Zoe was well on the way to being extremely drunk. It wasn't very often she indulged beyond the point of tipsy, well she hadn't before Ryan's summer departure, but tonight she and Leyla had followed the wine with cocktails and dancing, soaking up the excitement of the festive season and singing along with classics from Slade and The Pogues.  The outcome was that she was standing in front of

Ryan, head spinning and trying to focus on her response.

'Out, with Leyla.' She tried to stop but couldn't. 'Not that it is anything to do with you.'. He raised his eyebrows, presumably to make her remorseful but actually causing her to feel real annoyance..

'Were you with him?'. His expression was intense. Zoe's alcohol infused brain didn't follow. 'Who?' She asked, not making any effort to conceal her annoyance . 'Pete'. He spoke the name boldly, as though he knew all about her history with Pete, but she couldn't see how he would. She felt angry that he had dared mention Pete's name. She was also saddened by the fact that whilst Ryan stood there thinking she could have been out with a Pete, she knew there was no chance. Zoe had never been an unfaithful person, and the fact Ryan suspected she could have been should have been insulting, but instead she found herself wishing he was right and that she had been with Pete instead of Leyla.

She stared at Ryan, momentarily hating him for leaving her in the first place, but then arriving back in her life at the exact moment in time Pete had returned from Italy, meaning she would never actually know what he had come to say that Saturday afternoon. Long moments passed, neither Ryan or Zoe averting their gaze from the other . 'No'. she finally admitted, spitting the word out, not wanting to give Ryan a response that would ease his suffering, when she had lived through so much pain because of him.

She watched his gaze turn from anger to relief and spun on her heel to bed. Rage burning inside her from him daring to mention Pete's name but even more from his relief that she hadn't seen him, when she was desperately wishing she had the chance to spend just another moment in Pete's company.

She shut the bedroom door loudly behind her and stripped her clothes quickly and angrily, discarding them in a pile on the floor. As she fell into bed, she closed her eyes and the room span around her. The last thing Zoe thought was that the room wasn't the only thing spinning, her life was too. It was definitely time for Zoe to take hold and get her life back in order. But for now she needed to sleep. And she did.

The sound of the front door knocking awoke Zoe around 9am on Christmas Eve. Her head was pounding and she felt sick with the hangover from the night before. She remembered the angry words shared with Ryan and sighed a weary sigh. This hadn't been the start to the Christmas holiday she had hoped for. She peeled open her eyes, they were heavy from the previous night's make up that she had failed to remove. She slowly sat up, taking a moment on the edge of the bed before she was able to stand and head to the bathroom. Zoe brushed her teeth and cleansed her face, hoping to improve the way she felt. It was no use and she was in no mood to humour Ryan downstairs. She decided to head back to bed with two paracetamol and a glass of water and face the day when she felt better equipped to deal with Ryan.

When she resurfaced around 10am, she felt very slightly better but still wasn't really ready to face Ryan. Instead, she spent long moments with her head under the shower faucet, trying to wash the alcohol induced fog from her brain. As she headed out of the bathroom she glanced down the stairs to see a beautiful Christmas bouquet on the hall table. The door knock at 9am she realised, must have been a delivery. She headed down the stairs in her robe and looked at the bouquet. It was full of lush red roses, red freesia and winter greenery. Spread throughout there were festive baubles and pine cones. It was beautiful. She parted the flowers, trying to look for a card amongst the stunning foliage.

'There isn't one' Ryan was standing in the lounge doorway, holding a cup of tea out towards Zoe. She sheepishly took it and smiled. He continued to talk 'they arrived at 9am for you, but no card. Look Zoe, I'm sorry about getting all jealous last night,

I know I have no right. I don't want to fight. Shall we call a truce and enjoy the next few days? I know how much you love Christmas'.

Zoe was relieved. She didn't have the energy for an argument and her head still throbbed despite the paracetamol. She nodded and smiled, moving past him into the lounge. She knew it was this inability to tackle the problem head on that had landed her here with Ryan back home in the first place, but today, whilst she felt so rough, was not the time to address the current situation.

The rest of the day passed in the sad blur that only a hangover can induce. Zoe finished wrapping some gifts and messaged her friends some festive memes and greetings. She chatted to Sam briefly and filled her in on the events of the night before. Sam was sympathetic but had a clear view about what Zoe needed to do and wasn't overly chuffed at Zoe's decision to delay tackling the matter with Ryan until after Christmas and New Year. 'Clearly Ryan has some understanding about where your heart is Zoe. All you need to do is tell him and you'll have done something about it.'. Zoe knew her friend was right. She just felt trapped and didn't really know how she had landed herself back in this position. Throughout the day she spent long moments gazing at the picture of her and Pete from Sam's party. Pete's eyes shining at the camera and her gazing up at him, a grin as broad as the Grand Canyon. Jake had perfectly captured her feelings in that one moment and Zoe knew that there would be no chance of anyone ever catching her looking at Ryan in the same way.

*****

Christmas Day was a calm and peaceful one, though Zoe carried a tinge of sadness throughout. Her and Ryan sat at the tree, opening gifts, as they had for so many years before. Zoe had bought Ryan a North Face T-shirt she had seen him looking at. She had felt awkward about what to get him, but had concluded that he had only been back in her life two weeks, and that a T-shirt was more than he should expect after the way he had treated her. She wasn't expecting a gift off him at all. He opened his gift and seemed touched that Zoe had known what he wanted.

Zoe opened her gift from her girl group. Each year they did secret Santa and just bought one gift to a higher value than buying gifts for all the girls. She didn't know who had bought her gift this year, but it was beautiful. It was a silver bangle with a small infinity shape sculpted at the centre. On the infinity sign 'Have the courage to follow your heart' was engraved in a beautiful italic script. Whichever of her friends had bought it, knew she was in the wrong place in her life at the moment. A lump rose in her throat as she slid the bangle over her wrist. She was still thinking about how well her friends knew her and how well cared for she was when Ryan's voice, saying her name, interrupted her reflection.

He was holding out a small gift and smiling. The box was perhaps 5cm cubed. It fit easily in his palm. Oh God. Zoe felt sick. In that moment she thought of all the conversations with Sam last spring about how and when Ryan would propose. It was all she had wanted. And now, here he was, tiny box in hand and she actually thought she was going to throw up.

She took the box, and tried to conceal the shaking in her hand. As she opened it, he was talking. But all she could hear was the blood pounding in her ears. She slowly unpeeled the foil paper, trying to plan what she would say to him. She wasn't a cruel person, she didn't want to hurt him, especially not on Christmas morning. She had taken him back almost by accident, and she knew it wasn't going to work, but she didn't want to cause him the same pain he had caused her.

The box was navy with a small gold clasp. Her hands were really trembling now and for all the wrong reasons. She felt herself draw a deep breath and her body tense. As she pressed the clasp and the box opened she felt relief flood her whole body as she saw two beautiful diamond stud earrings. She gasped with relief. 'Thank you! They are beautiful. Far too generous, but very beautiful'. The relief that the package hadn't been a ring, flooded Zoe and she hugged Ryan with genuine gratitude. He held her tight and leaned in for a kiss and parted her lips with his mouth. Zoe tried to kiss him back, but she didn't want him. The kiss felt dull and wet and sloppy, not how Zoe remembered kissing Ryan at all. She pulled her head back but he still tried to continue. Zoe felt a bit sick as she turned her head sideways to escape his advances. She knew it was wrong to accept the earrings and pretend all was ok, when she felt such disinterest in him, but she was determined to get through Christmas and New Year before asking him to leave again. It seemed only fair.

Zoe took her time getting ready and then Ryan drove them to Zoe's mom and dad's house for dinner. Her parents had always loved Ryan, but since he had broken her heart, they had found it difficult to come to terms with his homecoming. Her mom had begged her not to pursue the reunion from the first day he had returned. How Zoe had wished she had listened.

The dinner was delicious as always, her mom was a fantastic traditional home cook, and Christmas dinner was always an absolute feast. Her parents were warm and pleasant with Ryan, and he was clearly trying too hard to re-establish himself in their good books. After dinner they opened their gifts and to her surprise, Ryan had bought her parents gifts separate to the ones she had purchased. Her parents were polite and thankful for the books Ryan had gifted them, but Zoe could tell their hearts were no longer with Ryan, just as their daughters wasn't either.

Zoe's mom fetched a bag of gifts for Zoe. Her parents always spoiled her at Christmas and this year was no exception. Zoe opened the gifts slowly, enjoying the thought and love that had gone into each one. Amongst the gifts was a beautiful silver locket with a picture of her Nan and grandad inside that made her tearful, and a pink Dirty Dancing slogan T-shirt with 'Nobody puts Zoe in a corner', that made Zoe laugh out loud.

By the time Zoe and Ryan arrived home, it was 10pm and Zoe headed straight to bed. Apart from the unfortunate kissing incident in the morning, the day had been a really good one. She had laughed and shared a happy day with her mom, dad and Ryan. Whatever happened next, she would be ending things with Ryan on better terms than when he had left her for Kate. The idea brought Zoe some comfort, or at least she tried to convince herself it did.

The following day Ryan headed to his parents up North for a few days, giving Zoe some quality time alone with her parents and in her house. Back in the summer she never imagined it being the case, but she relished the solitude and took advantage of being able to lounge about in her dressing gown, take long baths and play her music too loud.

*****

Zoe headed sale shopping the day that Ryan was due to come home in order to extend the solitude for as long as possible. New Year's Eve was quickly approaching and Zoe had to find something to wear to The Sun's annual New Year's Eve karaoke party. Alex and Jake were definitely going to be there, which made Zoe hope that she would at least get to glimpse Pete at some stage during the evening. She knew whatever potential there had been between them had long since dissolved with Ryan's return home, but she wanted to look her best anyway.

By the time she boarded the train home she had purchased a black shirt dress and new stiletto sandals. The shirt dress hung to mid thigh and buttoned all the way up the front. It had a tie belt at the waist that pulled it in neatly and Zoe felt it flattered her curvy hips, boobs and bum. The sandals were medium pink and had a single ankle strap with a delicate gold buckle fastening. The single strap across the toes had a matching gold buckle. The heels were narrow and high and had Zoe felt fantastic as she had stood in front of the store mirror.

As she arrived home, she spotted Ryan's car was home and her heart sank a little. She knew she had to end the relationship in the next few days but it was not a prospect she relished in the slightest. She opened the front door quietly, unsure whether she wanted to sneak in and straight upstairs or not. She could hear Ryan's music coming from the kitchen and knew he was cooking. She was grateful as she hadn't eaten lunch and was starving, but her stomach turned at the thought of another meal sitting across the table from Ryan.

She shouted out a greeting and headed upstairs. Hanging her new dress up, she detached the labels and carried them downstairs to put in the bin. The bin bag was overflowing and so she headed out with the torch to put the bin bag into the black wheelie bin. As she lifted the bag into the bin, something caught her eye. She shone the torch into the bin and retrieved a small gift card. The sort that comes with a flower delivery. The card had been printed by the florist and simply read 'Wishing you a magical Christmas time, Pete x'.

Zoe's heart soared that he had sent the flowers and then she realised that Ryan had deliberately thrown the card out so that she wouldn't know. She decided to wait until sitting at the table to challenge him about his deceit.

Zoe headed straight back through the kitchen to the lounge and picked up her phone. She tried typing a number of messages before settling on a simple thank you 'Pete, thank you so much for the flowers. They are so beautiful. I'm so sorry, the card was misplaced. I love them. I hope you had a great Christmas'.

Zoe clicked send and moments later the ticks turned blue. She sat waiting, but Pete went straight back offline. He wasn't going to respond! Zoe was gutted. Perhaps he was annoyed with her, or maybe she should have asked a question in her message to force a response. Perhaps he was out, maybe with a woman. Zoe's heart sank. She hadn't spoken to him for a few weeks now, well, not properly. She had no idea what was going on in his life at the moment, but the fact he hadn't responded definitely wasn't a positive sign.

As she sat opposite Ryan, she couldn't help but keep glancing at her phone. She knew it was a long shot, but hoped Pete had just been busy at the moment he received her message, and would return her text at some point during the evening. Ryan had clearly noticed her persistent phone checking but took his time to comment.

'Expecting a message?' He was casual as he ate another mouthful of the moussaka he had cooked. 'Well,' Zoe began. 'I'm feeling a little bad that it took me so long to thank Pete for the flowers, with the card being thrown away and all, I was hoping he wasn't upset by my apparent rudeness.'. Ryan reddened slightly before speaking. 'I was just trying to protect us Zoe, we don't need that guy confusing things for us as we grow stronger.'

Zoe was incensed but also anxious that he believed they were growing stronger when she was biding her time to end the relationship. 'We didn't need that woman either Ryan, but I didn't get a say in that. Don't ever sensor my life for your benefit.' In that moment Zoe thought of a thousand things she had wanted to say to Ryan since his infidelity, but she didn't have the energy or inclination. She picked up her phone and headed to her bedroom to wait for Pete's reply. It never came.

# CHAPTER 15: HAPPY NEW YEAR

New Year's Eve was always about friendship for Zoe. It was the festive night that she spent with her girls, dressed up and having fun. She couldn't wait. She knew this year was going to be a little different. Sam and Alex were so committed now, that she knew she wouldn't get much time with Sam, but she was pleased that Sam had chosen to bring Alex so that they could still all be together. Jake and Leyla seemed to be building a more serious relationship too, not with the same intensity that Sam and Alex had launched into their affair, but there was definitely a mutual like and it seemed to be going well. Leyla was happy and Zoe was happy for her friend.

Zoe took her time applying her make up. She chose dark smokey eyes, with long lash extensions she'd had applied earlier in the day. She had tanned her legs the day before and now applied a shimmering moisturiser to add a little sparkle for the occasion. Zoe straightened her hair carefully, her appointment with her stylist Lucy just prior to Christmas had resulted in an all over deep red hair colour that Zoe loved. As she looked at herself in the mirror, she could see the change that had happened since the summer. She was slightly thinner, her hair and skin were glowing with her new found independence and she exuded confidence. Something that Zoe would never have believed possible in August.

Zoe thought back to the day that Sam had told her to give it six months, when she had felt that there was no way past the pain and utter desolation. It had only been four and a half months, but she knew now that she was going to be fine. That she would be well and truly recovered from Ryan by the sixth month mark in February, even though technically she was currently back in a relationship with him. She thought about how she had longed to have Ryan home back in August and remembered how her Nan had always often used the quote 'Be careful what you wish for', Zoe truly understood what the saying meant for the first time ever.

Ryan would be joining Zoe at tonight's party, and in exchange she had to drop in to see his friends before heading to The Sun. Zoe didn't really mind visiting his friends, she loved and missed them, especially James, and knew she would enjoy seeing them although she would rather be heading straight to The Sun to meet her girls. She was less keen on the idea of Ryan joining her night out and didn't really know how it would go. She wasn't keen on investing time introducing Ryan to Alex and his friends. After all, what was the point, she knew that things with Ryan were fizzling out at a rapid rate and was just trying to get through the festive season before letting him down gently.

Although he knew her girlfriends, Ryan hadn't spent much time with them since his return. Zoe thought that he must have sensed how annoyed they would all be with him, and was surprised he had asked to come tonight, he never would have done previously . Since he had returned he seemed to have a new found insecurity, just as Zoe had truly found her confidence. She was frustrated by the prospect of spending her night babysitting Ryan when he could easily have gone out with his friends instead of her. She wondered if he had figured Pete might be there and was actually going to make sure she behaved.

As she headed down the stairs, ready to head out for the celebrations, Ryan stood in the hallway and his eyes widened as he looked up towards her. 'What?' Zoe's tone was unintentionally short and she softened her voice 'is there something wrong?'.

Ryan shook his head and sighed. 'No Zoe. Nothing is wrong. You just look incredible. I should never ever have left you, but whilst I was away, something drastic happened and somehow you changed from a pretty girl to an amazingly attractive woman. Sometimes it feels like you are a different person.'

Zoe remained on the step half way down the stairs and looked at this man, that she had once loved, that she now had so little respect for. She tilted her head slightly as she spoke 'I am a different person Ryan. You crushed me. Completely. And I had to pick myself back up with the help of my amazing friends. I have learned a lot about myself and am proud of how I have grown. You let me down massively and I picked myself up Ryan.'

She continued down the stairs before he had chance to respond. She could tell Ryan felt crestfallen by her response to what he clearly intended to be a compliment. Checking her reflection once more she turned and asked 'ready?' Ryan nodded silently and they headed out the door and into the taxi waiting outside.

As they walked into The Feathers, James shouted them over to the social group that Zoe had been a part of for so many years. She hugged James and waved hello to the other members of the party. The next hour passed enjoyably with Zoe remembering how she had belonged when she was in the group and how Ryan had taken more than himself from her life. James sat down beside her with a glass of white wine for her and a pint of lager for himself, he smiled and wrapped his arm around her shoulder. 'You look amazing Zoe. I was so pleased when Ryan told me you were back together but I can tell it's not going to last. I can see how far apart you have grown, even if Ryan can't. But promise me we can still be friends.' Zoe was surprised by his insight and forthright manner, but hugged him back and looked into his eyes. 'You're right Jamie. I have grown beyond what we had and I don't think it will last, but please don't say anything. I need to let him down gently.... of course we will always be friends'. James smiled and hugged Zoe and picked up his glass in a celebratory toast. 'To you Zoe. Here's to the happiest of New Years. You deserve it.'

\*\*\*\*\*

It was 9.30pm by the time Ryan and Zoe entered The Sun. Zoe spotted Sam by the long bar as soon as she entered, she began weaving her way towards her best friend with Ryan in tow behind her. As she got closer, she spotted Alex next to Sam and Leyla and Jake standing just to the side. They were huddled at the end of the bar, filling the space next to the glass collecting section, but just close enough to the service part of the bar to buy drinks without having to move far. Zoe could see Tam and Lou standing behind Layla with Jaiden, and Matt was nearby talking to a girl Zoe didn't know, presumably his long term girlfriend she had heard mentioned previously. Just as she reached Sam, the man leaning on the bar behind Alex turned around and Zoe locked eyes with him. The one and only Pete Saunders.

Once more the wind was taken out of Zoe's sails as she realised how hard the night ahead would be. What was it about this man? He completely owned her, without a shadow of a doubt and she couldn't do anything about it. She searched the area around him to see if he had a girl with him, and felt relieved that he appeared to be alone. She smiled at him awkwardly and he nodded his head in greeting, glancing over her shoulder to Ryan and then swiftly averting his eyes. He leaned in and spoke to Alex and they both took a step away from the group. Sam grabbed Zoe by the shoulders and kissed her 'Zoe! You look amazing!' Sam moved in to give Ryan a kiss too. She was even friendlier than usual and Zoe guessed she had started on the gin a few hours earlier. Zoe chatted to Sam but was distracted by the feeling of Pete being close to her. She tried to subtly glance sideways at him but Ryan stepped into the space between them deviously ensuring her view was blocked.

Leyla headed towards Zoe and hugged her tightly. 'You look absolutely stunning Zoe. You're like a new woman.' and then she whispered in her friends ear 'apart from the old boyfriend but that should be easily sorted!'. Zoe quickly looked up at Ryan to check if he had heard, but he was laughing with Sam, Lou and Tam, who all appeared to have forgiven him for his summer indiscretions rather more quickly than Zoe had hoped.

Leyla turned and spoke loudly to the group in her usual charismatic manner. 'Thank goodness Zoe got here in time for the singing! Our girl group just wouldn't be the same without her hip bumping and finger clicking'. The girls all laughed. It was well known that Zoe's singing wasn't the best and that she primarily brought coordinated backing moves to their karaoke efforts. Zoe laughed too and did a few hip bumps for her audience. She saw Ryan's face drop as she laughed with her friends and sensed that the night ahead was going to be more difficult than fun.

Ryan continued to manoeuvre himself into her view point of Pete as they headed to the bar and returned to the group. Zoe could only catch glimpses of Pete as he laughed and chatted to his friends until Zoe spotted him heading to the toilets. She waited a few minutes and then made her excuses to head across the bar herself. As planned, as she approached the ladies, Pete was on his way back from the gents. He stopped dead when he saw her and Zoe weaved her way to stand right in front of him.

'Zoe, I don't think your boyfriend wants me talking to you'. He was looking awkwardly over her shoulder back towards where Ryan was. Zoe frowned, Pete's voice was a little off. Zoe shrugged 'so what, I wanted to say thank you for the flowers and say sorry for not texting sooner. I think Ryan threw the card away on purpose'. Zoe was testing the water to see his response, but It was Pete's turn to just shrug. He stumbled a little and Zoe realised he was well under the influence. 'You've been drinking?' Her question was more of a statement. Pete shrugged again and said 'what's it to you Zoe?'. The sharpness in his voice hurt her. She wanted to tell him it mattered but suddenly Ryan was by her side and Pete was walking away.

'Everything ok?' Ryan acted concerned but Zoe knew he was there to break up the party. 'Leyla told me to get you to come back'. Zoe scowled at Ryan and turned to immediately head back towards Leyla. She was about to give Leyla a piece of her mind about sending Ryan after her when Leyla made a shushing signal to the group.

The previous karaoke act was just finishing and the host for the evening announced a Beatles fivesome. Leyla shrieked as Alex, Jaiden and Matt headed towards the low stage set up for the evenings entertainment. Zoe saw Jake pulling a slightly drunk looking Pete away from the bar and they headed up too.

Zoe stood still on the spot as the host announced that the next group would be singing two Beatles songs. Finally she got to stare at a Pete for at least six minutes, completely guilt free. Excitement tingled across her skin as she smiled warmly at Sam who was clearly the proud and doting girlfriend, grinning from Alex to Zoe and back again.

The quintet began by singing Hey Jude and they were amazing. The whole pub was singing with them in no time. Zoe focussed on Pete and she could hear his smooth and lyrical tones above the others. Even though he had been drinking, his voice stood out as something beautiful to Zoe. She could feel her heart pounding and wondered if this was what true love really felt like. As they finished their first song, Pete's eyes searched her out in the room and focussed on Zoe whilst the host announced their second performance. Pete's eyes were slightly dulled by the alcohol and his face seemed different, but she saw him smile at her ever so slightly as their second song 'We can work it out' was announced. Zoe's breath caught. Had she told him this was her favourite song? She thought she had. Had he remembered? Had he chosen it for her? Ryan was talking in her ear, but all she could hear was her own thoughts. Was this his way of showing he cared for her? Was there actually there a chance that Pete still wanted her? The thought made the hairs on the back of her neck stand up.

As they finished the second song, the crowd applauded loudly. Zoe joined in and a reserved Ryan clapped begrudgingly alongside her. 'They were fantastic!' Sam was all but shrieking in Zoe's ear. Zoe grinned at her best friend, 'they really were Sam. They were amazing'.

As the boys rejoined the group there was much merriment. Everyone was getting tipsy and the boys shock performance had raised everyone's spirits massively. Ryan was still right by Zoe's side, talking to Tamasyn, as Zoe's eyes searched the bar for Pete. Where had he gone? She spotted him leaning over at the bar and placing an order with a pretty young barmaid. They were chatting and laughing as the girl appeared to pour a whiskey for Pete. Zoe felt jealous as they flirted and realised that she didn't know that Pete was a whiskey drinker; maybe she didn't know all that much about him at all.

Ryan had finished his conversation with Tam and was back hip to hip with Zoe in his territorial position that was beginning to wind her up. He slid his arm around her waist and kissed her shoulder in an overt display of affection. Zoe faked a smile as she took a deep gulp of white wine. Her head was beginning to spin, but for once she relished the thought of being so drunk she couldn't remember the evening.

For the second time that night Leyla seemed to be bursting with excitement. Zoe mentally tuned back into what the host was saying and heard him announce the first of two dirty dancing tracks. Zoe waited to be called to the platform, but to everyone's surprise it was Jake and Leyla that headed towards the host, hand in hand. What followed could only be described as a comedy cover of Dirty Dancing's hit song, 'I've had the time of my life'.  Leyla and Jake sang their hearts out to each other and completed sections of the routine in a poorly rehearsed rendition. They seemed perfectly suited.  Everyone in the pub was laughing and cheering them on, Zoe felt so proud of Leyla's ability to get people onside and made a pact to tell her friend more often about all the qualities she admired so much.

Leyla and Jake concluded their turn on the karaoke, arms around each other and gazing affectionately into each other's eyes. Zoe was laughing hard and shaking her head. Leyla was always the one to bring a surprise and she hadn't disappointed. As Leyla returned, the girls all gravitated towards her and they found themselves in a group hug. In that moment, Zoe felt incredibly grateful to have such a fantastic group of friends to share her life with.

It was approaching quarter to midnight when Zoe became aware that they had just been announced for their turn at performing. She usually didn't care and enjoyed the annual stint singing and making a fool of herself with her friends, but tonight she suddenly felt self conscious.

She followed the girls onto the stage at the back of the group and looked into the crowd.  She saw Alex beaming at Sam, and Jake winking at Leyla. She saw Ryan speaking to a random bloke next to him and pointing at Zoe. Marking his territory again she thought crossly. And then her eyes found who she was really looking for. He was leaning back against the bar, alone, slightly separated from the group. His one arm was crossed tightly across his chest and the other rested a tumbler of whiskey on it. He seemed to be hugging himself tightly, almost protectively. He looked drunk and he looked vulnerable. In that moment, Zoe wanted to leave the stage and go to him. To kiss his face and hold him tight and tell him that he was everything she wanted in the world.

As the percussion intro of their song began, Zoe locked eyes with Pete, and resolved not to look away until he did. He held her gaze as the intro played out. The girls began their choreographed hip bumps, finger clicks and step taps to a series of whistles and heckles and launched into their song with wine infused confidence. Zoe held Pete's gaze as long as she practically could as Lou led the group in their song, 'Be My Baby' by the Ronettes.

'The night we met I knew I needed you so. And if I had the chance I'd never let you go'. As Zoe sang she felt the emotion of the last four and a half months hit her full force. The words caught in her throat as she realised they had intense meaning for her. She had felt like that the night she had met Pete, but she had stupidly run away because she thought she still loved Ryan. If only she hadn't run out on him. As she sang the words 'you know I will adore you 'til eternity', tears pricked the back of her eyes. Was she going to feel like this about Pete forever, even though she couldn't have him. She suddenly grasped the meaning of unrequited love and it hurt her heart.

Zoe blinked hard and forced a smile. What was she doing, getting emotional on a stage in front of a pub full of people. She quickly glanced to her girls and they were all smiling as they sang. Zoe looked back towards Pete. He was still completely focussed on her but now he was smiling, a kind and compassionate smile that reminded her of the night they had sat outside at Sam's party.

As the girls completed their song, there were loud yelps and whistles from Alex and his friends. The host announced a thirty minute break before the live band, as the New Year approached and Zoe couldn't help smiling as the girl group headed back to the bar hand in hand. But as she got closer to the group she noticed Pete had moved away. She looked around but couldn't see him. Instead, Zoe saw that Ryan's face was as dark as the clouds before thunder. She knew she was in for a rough ride now, but it had been worth it for those few moments looking into Pete's gorgeous face and having him smile back at her.

Ryan grabbed the top of Zoe's arm tightly and pulled her away from the group. Zoe yelped slightly but Ryan didn't let go. Who did he think he was?!

'What were you doing Zoe? Staring at him all through the song? It was humiliating' Ryan was seething and all but spat his words at Zoe. She pulled against him, trying to loosen his grip on her arm but he held it tighter still. 'Let go Ryan!' She used her spare hand to pull her arm away from him and he finally let go looking uncomfortable and embarrassed that he had been so physical with her.

'What was I doing Ryan? What was I doing?' She was glaring now, her anger reaching a crescendo. Her voice had moved up an octave, but she knew she couldn't stop herself from giving him a piece of her mind now, not now he had started it, so publicly and physically. 'I was looking at him because it is him a want. Not you! You left me for another woman and then just turned up back at home? Expecting me to welcome you in with open arms?' She was beyond emotional but couldn't stop. 'Well guess what Ryan. I didn't really want to and I definitely can't do it anymore. Because I don't love you Ryan!' She registered the hurt on his face, the sadness in his eyes, but still didn't stop. 'Newsflash Ryan! Whilst you were away screwing your other woman, I fell out of love with you and moved on. Your infidelity broke me but then I met someone that I want. Like really, really want. More than I have ever wanted you. I was looking at him because I meant it all for him. Not you Ryan. Not you anymore.' Zoe suddenly heard herself and stopped.

Realising she had said far more than she ever should have. She had been deliberately hurtful which she never wanted to be. Ryan stood silent for a moment and then turned and walked towards the exit. 'Shit!' Zoe knew she had gone way too far. It was like someone had pulled the stopper out of all the anguish and pain he had caused her, and once the contents had started spilling, she couldn't get them to stop. She turned to find her friends to tell them that she was leaving and was immediately met with four pairs of eyes on her and four mouths wide with shock. Sam, Alex, Leyla and Jake had seen and heard it all. They were silent as they stared. Sam stepped forward and hugged her friend. 'Do you want me to come?' Sam asked as she already knew that Zoe was leaving. 'No, it's fine'. Zoe replied over her shoulder as she headed out the pub to catch up to Ryan. She might not want him romantically, but she had been a complete bitch and needed to put things right.

\*\*\*\*\*

They sat in silence all the taxi journey home and entered their house just before midnight. They stood standing facing each other in the lounge as Zoe spoke. 'I never should have spoken to you like that. I am sorry'. Ryan looked in her eyes. 'No, you shouldn't, but I shouldn't have grabbed you either. I think it was probably just the wine Zoe, helping you to say what you have wanted to for such a long time. I know I hurt you in the worst possible way, and I know you fancy that Pete, but i still want us to work it out together. Look, it is clear there is nothing going on between you and him, it is just attraction, he wouldn't fight for you Zoe. He didn't say a thing when I came home. I'm sure you think that he could love you, but not like I do Zoe. I know all your quirks and embarrassing habits. I'm the one you're meant to be with. We can get past this. I know we can'.

Zoe shook her head 'how can you say that Ryan? If we were meant to be, you wouldn't have left me.' He seemed to have lost his self respect somewhere along the way. Zoe didn't know why Ryan had returned to her, she had never asked, but now she realised that whatever his time with Kate had been, it hadn't had a positive effect on him and he was scarred in some way.

'Ryan, I meant what I said about not loving you, about not

wanting you'. Her voice was soft with compassion, the way she should have broken the news in the first place. 'I know you don't at the moment Zoe, but I also really think that you could fall for me again. It is only a few months ago since we were planning our future. You can't have changed that much. It will take time for you to forgive me but I'm willing to wait and earn your forgiveness. Please give us a chance' his voice was pleading and the hurt on his face wrenched her heart.

Zoe thought about Ryan's words. He was right that a few months ago she was ready to marry him. Could she love him again? She knew she couldn't, but it was so hard standing in front of him, watching his heart breaking and being the one responsible.

She was suddenly conscious of fireworks in the distance. It was midnight and the new year was here. As she stood rooted to the spot, trying to work out what to say next, her phone buzzed in her hand. She lifted it and saw a message off Pete. Another followed immediately.

'Happy New Year Zoe xx'

'Keeping with the Dirty Dancing Theme....'

A third message arrived and Zoe recognised the text immediately. It was the lyrics of the song 'Hungry Eyes' from Dirty Dancing, sung by Eric Carmen. Zoe knew the song by heart, but she stood in silence in front of Ryan as she scanned the lyrics.

I've been meaning to tell you
I've got this feelin' that won't subside
I look at you and I fantasise
You're mine tonight
Now I've got you in my sights
With these hungry eyes
One look at you and I can't disguise
I've got hungry eyes
I feel the magic between you and I

I want to hold you so hear me out
I want to show you what love's all about
Darling tonight
Now I've got you in my sights
With these hungry eyes
One look at you and I can't disguise
I've got hungry eyes
I feel the magic between you and I
With these hungry eyes
Now I've got you in my sights
With these hungry eyes
Now did I take you by surprise
I need you to see
This love was meant to be.

She looked up from her phone into the eyes of the man she had once loved.

'I'm truly sorry Ryan. It's over. For good.'

\*\*\*

As Zoe climbed into bed she reread the messages from Pete. She could see he was online and started typing a response. Her heart was pounding as she told Pete how much she wanted him. She reread her message, and looked at the word 'online' showing her that Pete was there, on the other end of the message. She typed again, reread the message again and then deleted it immediately. She was tired and emotional and had drank too much wine. It wasn't the time to be messaging her innermost thoughts and feelings to Pete. It when she had just crushed Ryan. She opted for two kisses to show that she had seen his message and was thinking of him 'XX'. She would message him in the morning, when she was clearer headed.

As Zoe drifted off to sleep she sang the song in her head over and over and realised that he had missed of the final two choruses that were how the song finished. Pete had chosen to finish his message with the words 'I need you to see, this love was meant to be'. Was it intentional? Zoe went to sleep fantasising that Pete wanted her, that this was his declaration and that they would be together. That would make it a very happy new year indeed.

# CHAPTER 16: I'M STILL STANDING

Zoe was awoken just after seven by the wind and rain. There was an almighty storm and the wind was howling across the roof. All had seemed calm last night, but today turmoil, Zoe thought how the weather was reflecting her life. She lay quietly and listened for a few minutes before getting up and peeking through the curtain. It was still dark but she could see that Ryan's car had already gone. Her stomach turned. She had expected him to leave today, but not before they'd had the chance to speak again. She headed to the spare room. The bed was made and his suitcase gone. She wondered when he had left and if he was safe, but realised she hadn't seen him drink much last night. She had been the one in the alcohol induced rage, not him. He was just jealous, plain and simple.

The thought of Ryan's jealousy reminded Zoe of Pete's text and she dashed back into her room and scooped her phone up. The message she had sent was there with two ticks showing it had been received and read, but the previous message with the lyrics was missing and in its place the words 'this message was deleted'. Zoe slumped down into the side of her bed, her fantasies of a relationship with Pete expiring just as the message had.

The app told her that he had last been online at 5.30am. He had clearly regretted drunkenly sending the message and his sober self had deleted it. Zoe swung her legs back onto the bed and snuggled back down into the duvet. Wind howling, rain pouring, boyfriend gone again and love interest disinterested in her.

It didn't seem like the best start to the year, but at least she was warm in bed, alone in her house and ready to start moving forwards properly. Zoe exhaled and felt a sense of calm flow over her as she closed her eyes and listened to the rain against the window.

The next time Zoe got out of bed it was gone ten. In the three hours since waking, she had sent New Years texts to her friends and family and told her mom and dad and closest friends that she was fine but that Ryan had left and their relationship over forever. She had bought some new skinny jeans online and wasted at least half an hour trawling Facebook. And then, after employing all of those distraction techniques, she had listened to 'Hungry Eyes' on repeat at least ten times.

As Christmas had fallen on a Sunday, so did New Year's Day. Zoe took it as the perfect opportunity to have a duvet day. She showered, to wash away all traces of the previous night, got dressed into clean Pyjamas and then dragged her duvet downstairs, on to the sofa. She made herself a pot of tea and settled down to a day of chick flicks... starting of course with dirty dancing.

The day passed peacefully and Zoe enjoyed the solitude more than she expected. Ryan called later in the evening to amicably discuss collecting the rest of his things later in the month when he had found a rental, and they discussed briefly the fact that he would not try to claim any part of the house despite him having contributed financially for a number of years. Zoe's salary would enable her to cover the mortgage repayments on her own comfortably with her new job, and she was ready to be independent of Ryan. Ryan sounded positive too, as though a weight had been lifted for both of them. Zoe went to bed feeling positive about the fresh start even if she had repeatedly checked her phone for a message from Pete throughout the day.

The following day, Zoe opted for another day of solitude, getting her preparation done for the term ahead. She knew if she worked the full day she would be able to relax for the remainder of the holiday and not worry about any looming deadlines. Still all day she checked her phone periodically, every incoming WhatsApp message sending her heart racing, but despite him being online, Pete never messaged. Zoe resigned herself to the fact that the drunk message he had sent on New Year's Eve had been meaningless, perhaps even a little cruel, poking fun out of her love of Dirty Dancing. Whilst disappointed, Zoe felt philosophical about the whole thing. The absence of alcohol helped her rationalise that what would be would be, and as things stood, she was ok back on her own.

Tuesday morning Zoe called Sam. She was missing her friend and felt she hardly spoke to her at the moment. Sam was busy as always and so Zoe suggested a drink that evening. Sam hesitated 'I'm sorry Zoe, I have a party at Alex's parents' house. I would have loved to though.' Zoe responded 'no problem' but gave away a little too much disappointment in her voice. 'Just a minute' Sam had gone before Zoe had chance to respond. She was clearly covering her phone with her hand, as Zoe could hear muffled voices. Sam returned 'how about we go out for a cheeky Prosecco at seven? Alex will pick me up at nine to head to his parents house'. Zoe smiled into the phone 'Great! See you for a quick drink at 7'.

As Zoe got dressed, she was grateful for next day delivery. She slid into her new indigo blue skinnies and put on her tight fit pink slogan T-shirt that her mom had given her for Christmas. She laughed as she read the slogan 'Nobody puts Zoe in the corner.' She added her new pink stiletto heels and looked at her reflection. Her skinnies showed off her curved thighs, hips and bottom and her T-shirt was tight over her chest. Zoe thought about Ryan's comment about her transformation, and understood what he had seen. She didn't look like the same person from six months ago. Her hair, make up and shape all contributed to the illusion of a confident young woman and Zoe felt pleased. She had definitely grown in both confidence and independence and it was time to show the world who she was. Starting with a chilled out Prosecco with Sam!

The girls entered The Sun together at 7pm. It was really quiet, which suited Zoe fine for a drink and a catch up. They headed to the bar and ordered a bottle of Prosecco. Zoe looked around, recalling the events of New Year's Eve and thought about how her life had changed so much again since just two days ago. She glanced over to where the make shift stage was still set up from the karaoke event, and looked back to the section of bar where Pete had leant watching the girls singing. She remembered how he had been drinking whiskey, it was no wonder he had deleted the message he sent when he was drunk.

The girls settled on a leather sofa in the front of the pub, chatting and sipping their Prosecco happily together. Zoe told Sam about what had happened with Ryan after they got home on New Year's Eve and about the text from Pete. She went on to tell Sam about the next morning, Ryan being gone and the message being deleted. Sam listened intently before commenting. 'You know I don't usually talk to Alex about you Zoe, but he said that Pete was really anxious about going out with you and Ryan there together. Alex really had to convince him to come out and not stay home alone. Alex says he has never seen Pete like this and that he must really like you.'

Zoe thought about Sam's words before responding. 'Sam, you have no idea how much I want that to be true, but I just don't see how it can be, he is just so confusing'. Sam squeezed Zoe's arm. 'Well Zoe, there is definitely something there. What about him choosing your favourite Beatles song? He chose them both and the lyrics to Hey Jude are pretty intense too..... and what about the way he looked at you when we were singing. I know it seems unlikely with the way he is but it must have looked like something to Ryan too for him to react like that! Alex and I can't quite fathom it, but Al is convinced Pete is really hung up on you. He said Pete never gets drunk but that he said he needed it to get through the night. It must mean something Zoe!'.

Although Zoe's pulse rate accelerated at the suggestion, she shrugged 'I don't know Sam and maybe I never will. I just don't think I can spend my life regretting that one night in August and live every day hoping for a re-run. I need to move on now for my own self esteem, even though every part of me wants to cling to some hope that Pete might want me'.

As Zoe finished speaking, she picked up the bottle of Prosecco out of the ice bucket to top up their glasses. It was empty. Zoe looked at her watch. It was only just after half past seven, they had got through the first bottle ridiculously quickly. 'Another?' Zoe asked Sam.

Sam smiled and nodded 'yes, but let's go somewhere with some music'. As they stepped into the cool air, the fizzy wine made its way to Zoe's head and she stumbled. Sam frowned 'you did have tea didn't you Zoe?' Zoe laughed and quoted one of their university sayings 'eating is cheating!'. Sam laughed and shook her head 'not when you're our age Zoe! Let's get you some food'. Zoe shook her head back at Sam, 'No thanks, let's go get some more fizz! Celebrate me being me!'. The girls linked arms as they headed into Afters.

Cal was in his DJ booth and waved as the girls entered. It was equally as quiet in Afters, but the music made the atmosphere more enjoyable than The Sun. Zoe and Sam ordered another bottle of fizz and headed to a table with bar stools near the dance floor. As they drank they chatted about Jake and Leyla and how things were developing between the two, they talked about Zoe's Christmas gift off Ryan and how it had given Zoe the final evidence that she didn't want to be with him. Zoe talked about how Ryan and she had both changed so much, but Ryan in a less positive way. As they chatted, Zoe noticed Sam had slowed down her drinking, but Zoe was enjoying herself. She was celebrating the New Year as she should have done New Year's Eve.

At 8.45pm Zoe persuaded Sam to have a quick dance and Cal put on a few 80's tracks. They were the only people on the dance floor. Zoe was pretty drunk as she had drank most of the second bottle of Prosecco and hadn't eaten since midday. She still had her champagne flute in hand as she sang and danced with Sam laughing beside her. Sam headed to the ladies and Zoe headed to the bar to get herself a cocktail. She knew Sam would try to stop her drinking any more, so took the opportunity of ordering two whilst Sam was in the ladies.

When Sam returned, she had Alex in tow. 'Come on Zoe, we will drop you home' Sam tried to guide her off the dance floor but Zoe wasn't ready to go home. 'No thanks Sam, I'm gonna stay and finish my drinks and then I will get a taxi'. Zoe saw that Sam's expression was one of worry. Alex had a go at persuading Zoe that a lift would be better, but Zoe was certain she wasn't leaving. Sam and Alex stood to the side of the dance floor whilst Zoe continued to dance.

Cal asked Zoe what she was celebrating. 'Freedom and independence' she exclaimed and then followed up with 'and surviving a broken heart'. Cal smiled and began mixing 'I will survive' as the next song. Sam and Alex were still standing near the dance floor ten minutes later as Zoe danced to the classic Elton John song 'I'm still standing'. Zoe was really feeling the meaning in her drunken state and dancing as expressively as her heels would allow. The bar was still quiet and a few of the other customers glanced her way occasionally, but generally Zoe was just able to just be herself.

Sam arrived by her side once more and Zoe heard her say words along the lines of them having to leave, but knowing she would get home safe now. Zoe hugged Sam tightly and continued to dance to Elton's chorus that Zoe's drunk brain was now thinking could have been written for her.

She watched as Sam and Alex paused near a pillar by the entrance and then turned her back to the door, necked the last of her second cocktail and continued dancing through the lengthy instrumental section of the song. Now she was feeling really drunk and the room was starting to spin but Zoe felt reinvigorated from all the hurt of the last few months. She knew she was starting to stumble but couldn't really think clearly what she should do about it and so just carried on dancing.

She felt a tap on her shoulder and as she turned, saw the blue eyes of her dreams. She wondered if she was imagining it and the distraction caused her to sway off her heel, slightly stumbling to one side. He caught her and bent down a little so that his face was close to hers. His eyes smiling next to her. His hand was gently holding her left elbow to support her as he spoke 'Hi there lovely lady. Shall we get you home?' Zoe let him wrap one arm around her back as he led her outside the bar. His car was there, parked illegally right out the front of the bar. He slid her into the seat and reached across her to fasten her seatbelt. Zoe inhaled his aftershave and thought about what she would say when he climbed in next to her, but her eyes were heavy and the leather comfortable. She rested her eyes and thought of Pete coming to save her.

*****

It was 2am when Zoe awoke. Her mouth was dry and her head was pounding. She was in her bed, but had no idea how she had got there. She remembered Sam telling her to come and get a lift, and telling Sam she would get a taxi. She remembered ordering two noxious cocktails and vaguely recalled dancing solo, but everything was just a blur and beyond that point she couldn't remember anything.

She lifted her head from the pillow and noticed she was still clothed in her skinnies and T-shirt, but her sandals were missing. She reached for her phone and shone it on her bedside table. Thankfully there was a glass of water and she gulped it thirstily. She reached into the bottom drawer of her bedside table and pulled out one of her baggy T-shirt's. She lay back down as she slid off her jeans and pulled at her T-shirt. Her head was spinning and the water hitting her stomach had made her feel a little queasy. Zoe regretted the cocktails.

As she pulled her baggy T-shirt down over her stomach, she heard soft music from downstairs. Oh no, Sam must have brought her home and stayed with her instead of going to Alex's family party. Zoe stood up slowly. She was still drunk. She struggled to walk straight to the bedroom door to try to listen. Perhaps Sam had just left the TV on by accident.

As she got to her bedroom doorway, she noticed a soft glow of light from the box bedroom next to hers that she used as an office. The room was just about big enough to fit a single bed, but Zoe had a desk, bookcase and bucket chair in there instead, so that she had somewhere dedicated to completing her school work.

As she stepped into the entry of the small room she realised the sound was a mans voice. It was quiet singing. As she stood in the doorway she froze. Pete was sitting in the bucket chair in the corner, his legs flung over the side and his back leaning against the other side. He had headphones in and was scrolling his phone. The soft light highlighted his face and Zoe stood, just looking at him. As she admired him she vaguely recalled getting into his car. He must have brought her home instead of Sam and Alex. Zoe felt relieved that she hadn't ruined Sam's night, but also embarrassed that she had been in such a state she needed bringing home. So much for being independent.

Pete's soft melodic voice cut into her thoughts as he sang along to whatever was playing on his phone. He hadn't noticed she was there. She remained frozen, listening to him. The song he was singing was soft and beautiful. She had never heard it before but tried her hardest to memorise the lyrics so that she could listen to it when he had gone. Zoe's heart sank at the thought of him going, but realised that her head was well adjusted to the fact that he never stayed, he was never in her life for more than a fleeting moment at a time and so she should savour those moments when they came along. Just like this one now.

The lyrics seemed sad and Pete's gentle voice added a layer of melancholy to them. Zoe listened as the verse repeated 'Once there was a way, to get back homeward, once there was a way to get back home. Sleep pretty darling do not cry, and I will sing a lullaby'.

Zoe swayed and grasped the doorframe to stop the room from spinning. Pete must have seen her out of the corner of his eye. He looked up and smiled tenderly at her as he removed his headphones and swung himself up to a sitting position. 'That song was beautiful' Zoe's voice was almost a whisper. She couldn't bring herself to speak any louder, lest she break the spell of the moment. She wanted to be able to stand in the doorway watching him forever.

'Hey sleepyhead. How are you doing?' He smiled again. His smile was warm and she wanted to go to him and kiss him. Instead she held the door frame more tightly to stop herself from swaying and responded to his question. 'I feel awful. I'm sorry, I don't really remember....' her voice trailed off as she had no idea what had happened and didn't want to suggest anything about how she had ended up in her own bed.

'Sam called me. Her and Alex were late, but she wanted to know you would get home safe. I was just going to drop you off, but then you fell asleep in the car. I helped you get into the house, but then you begged me not to leave you.'

'Oh my god' Zoe was blushing in the dark, what had she said to him? 'I'm so sorry Pete. I feel so embarrassed'.

Pete laughed a wholesome laugh and said 'well if you are embarrassed at that, I had better not tell you that you serenaded me with 'all by myself"

Zoe cringed inwardly and outwardly. She put her face in her hands and he laughed again. 'Don't worry Zo. It was all very endearing! I will spare you the embarrassment of any more details' he laughed again as he teased her.

Zoe was trying her best to remember what she might have said, but she had no recollection at all. She wondered if she had declared her undying love at any time, surely he would tell her if she had. 'Maybe you can tell me another time' she concluded. Feeling a little braver she asked 'have you been to sleep?' Pete shook his head. 'I'm fine Zoe, I don't sleep much anyway. Troubled soul or something' he shrugged and Zoe didn't know what to say in response. She just rested her head against the door frame to try to steady the woozy feeling creeping up through her stomach and head.

'The song was Golden Slumbers by the Beatles. One of my favourite songs of all time. I'm glad you liked it'. He was still smiling warmly at her.

'I enjoyed it very much' she smiled back 'If you are tired and you want to sleep, you can sleep on my bed next to me' she ventured. He looked at her and his expression wasn't one that Zoe was familiar with. 'Thanks Zoe, but I'll pass, I'm guessing the bed isn't cold yet from Ryan and Dan before him'.

Zoe took a moment to process what he had said. The meaning of his words penetrated her mind and she felt like he had kicked her in the stomach. She couldn't believe he had been so cruel. In that single sentence he had told her all she needed to know about what he thought of her. Her hopes of him being more than a friend came crashing around her once more and the sadness that engulfed her was instant and hot with anger.

Her hand moved to cover her mouth as she tried her hardest to stop the tears coming, but they were there already. As she all but ran back to the safety of her bed to get away from him, she heard him scrabble to his feet and softly call her name 'Zoe, I'm sorry', but Zoe was already sobbing into her pillow, finally understanding why Pete had placed her in the friendship zone and her heart breaking a little in her new knowledge of how Pete Saunders saw Zoe's life.

*****

It was nearing 8am when she woke the next time. Her eyes opened to look at the ceiling above her and the memories of her 2am exchange with Pete flooded immediately back. She rolled onto her side to check the time on her phone and was surprised to see Pete lying on the floor in the space between her bed and the room's inbuilt wardrobes. His head was resting on the cushion off the bucket chair from her office and his eyes were fixed on the ceiling with his hands resting on his abdomen. He spoke without looking at her. 'I'm sorry for saying something so unkind. I don't know why I said it. It isn't even close to what I think' He pushed himself up and turned to sit back against the wardrobe door. His knees bent up and feet apart. He hung his head into the palms of his hands, elbows resting in his knees. 'I wanted to come and lie near you because you were so upset I hope you don't mind, you went to sleep pretty quickly, but I just needed to know you were ok. I'm sorry'

Zoe pushed herself up to sit on the side of her bed, legs dangling with her toes just touching the floor. She pulled her duvet over her thighs in a gesture of modesty as Pete lifted his head to meet her eyes.

'Of course I don't mind you lying there. You could have lay on the bed if you hadn't jumped to the conclusion that I am so easy and unworthy'. Pete opened his mouth to speak, but Zoe raised her hand to stop him. 'Not that I have to explain myself to you, but Ryan hasn't slept in this room at all since last July. And for your information Pete, I have only slept with two men my entire life. You were cruel saying what you did and you didn't even get your facts straight first. I'm really sorry that you have such a low opinion of me, especially when my opinion of you is such a high one. I cried because you hurt my feelings. A lot.'

Pete's expression was one of remorse and hurt. 'I'm so sorry Zoe. I don't know what happens when I am with you, I just get jealous and say things I'm really not proud of. It's not me. Or at least it isn't usually me. I don't even think you are easy, I just really try to protect myself and save myself from getting hurt. When it comes to you I just get so jealous and seem to react by saying hurtful things that I really don't mean. Please forgive me.'

Zoe frowned 'jealous?' The word was a confused acknowledgment of what he had said. He held her gaze and shrugged slightly 'Yes. Jealous. Of Dan and of Ryan'

'But you made it clear after Sam's party that you didn't want me, that we were just friends. Why would you be jealous?' She paused momentarily 'Look Pete, I'm not a game player, and I would never deliberately try to make someone jealous or do anything else that would hurt them on purpose. Especially not you.' She took a deep breath before finishing her sentence 'If I was lucky enough to have someone like you I would never ever hurt them.'

Pete shook his head slightly, seemingly a little confused by what she was saying. 'Someone like me, or actually me? …. Zoe, I'm sorry, I'm not very good at this….. I erm… I really wanted to….erm…. I figured on those dates that I couldn't risk scaring you off again by being too forward. I already made that mistake the first night we met.'

Zoe considered what he was saying. Her heart was beating faster as she hoped that he was telling her he liked her. She thought back to December 'But when Ryan turned up, you just left' she was speaking slowly. She couldn't work out what had happened.

'Zoe, I thought you still cared for him and that it was what you would have wanted. Look…. like I said, I'm not much good at this.' He paused, a pained expression on his face and then he continued 'I've always gone out of my way to save myself having a broken heart. I guess that I was trying to find excuses to separate myself from you, worried that I would get hurt.'

Zoe waited for him to continue, hoping he would explain the need to protect himself from her. She didn't wait long as he sighed and continued speaking almost immediately. 'My mom left my dad when I was fourteen. Paul was 17 and Luke, my younger brother was just 8. It completely crushed my dad. I mean completely crushed him' he paused as he remembered the time in his life he had always talked about the least. 'My mom was a really committed Christian. She went to church every Sunday without fail, gave us biblical Christian names, helped those in need, she was a pillar of the community, a model wife and mother. It was just massively unexpected. There was no other man, she didn't have any grand plans. She just didn't love my dad. It turned out she had never been 100% certain. She said she just couldn't wait another ten years until Luke was grown'.

Zoe could see the pain in his eyes as he spoke. 'I'm so sorry that your family went through that Pete.' Her voice was gentle. She wanted to go to him, but didn't know how he would react.

He continued speaking softly and slowly as he recollected his feelings. 'My dad had always thought she was his soul mate and suddenly it turned out he had been living a lie. He hit the drink. Hard and for a long time. He's sober now, but won't ever be the man he once was…. Paul ended up taking care of us as we continued to grow. My younger brother Luke, he turned into a bit of a wild one, he's ok now, travelling the world, but it could have gone either way with him..... for me, it felt like my mom had been stringing my dad along for eighteen years! I decided I would NEVER lead anyone on or let anyone lead me on and I vowed never to say anything that I didn't truly mean, I guess it is just habit now. I also vowed to protect my heart at all costs so that I never ended up in the state my dad did. Paul calls it my self-preservation mode.'

He stopped talking momentarily and looked into Zoe's eyes with a gaze so penetrating that she was sure he could see right into her soul.

'Like I said Zoe, I'm not very good at this, but if I ever gave you the impression I wasn't interested..... if I ever made you feel unwanted.... I'm sorry... I just, well, I've never wanted to be with anyone like I want to be with you and I have been trying to save myself from any hurt or pain. New Year's Eve though, it hurt.'

'Where did you go?' Zoe asked, her voice quiet and gentle 'after we had done our song, you seemed to disappear'.

'I left. I knew it was gonna be a hard night Zo, but it was harder than I imagined. I chose the songs we sang for you and it kind of got me emotional. I don't know. I was drunk and I just couldn't watch you with him anymore. I didn't want to do anything stupid. I just went home'.

Zoe nodded. 'And the text? Why did you send me those lyrics and then delete them?'

He paused and frowned before speaking again 'well, it's not the first time I've tried to tell you how I feel through music.... you know Hey Jude, and wonderwall in the car; I guess it was a bit too subtle...... Anyway I listened to the Dirty Dancing soundtrack a few times after you told me it was your favourite film. That song Zoe, it says everything I wanted to say to you. I guess the whiskey helped me copy and paste it? Then when I woke up, Alex had left me a voicemail to see where I'd gone, and he said about you and Ryan fighting. I thought you would think I knew and that I was trying to put pressure on you to leave him. I didn't want you to think I was playing games. I saw you typing a response to me and I got my hopes up that you felt the same, but then when your message came it was just two kisses. You cannot imagine how much those two small kisses stressed me out and with Alex's voicemail too I went back into self-preservation mode. Turns out it is easier than declaring your feelings mode!'

He laughed a wry laugh and then continued. 'Look Zoe, I'm sorry if you ever felt that I wasn't interested in you. The truth is, I have never wanted anyone more. I'm yours Zoe. Completely yours. I have been since the first time I saw you in The Cellars'.

Zoe was sure her heart would burst through her top it was pounding so hard. She realised she was actually grinning at him as she tried to respond.

'Pete, I'm no good at this either, but you have no idea how much I have longed to hear you say that. I'm so sorry I ran from you on that night in August, I've been yours ever since then too. When Ryan came back, he never actually moved back in with me. My heart was already elsewhere. I tried to respond New Year's Eve, but I had just told Ryan to leave and it didn't feel the right time to share my feelings with you. I'm so glad you sent me those lyrics'

They were both smiling at each other now. The silence was comfortable and Zoe heard the cathedral clock chime 8am. Pete glanced at his watch and jumped to his feet 'oh shit, I have an 8.30am Skype meeting. I need to go and get a shower. I can't believe I have to leave. How about we agree to have a fresh start?'

Zoe smiled 'yes, that sounds good, but a fresh start where we already know we're into each other? No more self-preservation or friend zones!'

His smile said it all as he beamed at her 'Deal! I actually have tastings tonight and tomorrow night. How about Friday night?'

'Great' Zoe began but then frowned 'Oh, I'm meant to be eating with Sam, but I will rearrange'. Pete shook his head 'No, don't, I know You don't get to see her so much now. How about lunch Saturday?' Zoe grinned 'it's a date'.

Pete stepped forward and kissed her cheek 'it's a date' he repeated before heading down the stairs and out of the front door.

Zoe shrieked in excitement. He was hers!!! He was actually hers and she was determined not to screw it up this time!

# CHAPTER 17: A FRESH START

As Zoe got ready for her girls night out with Sam, she couldn't help wishing she had rearranged so that she could be seeing Pete instead. The last two days had dragged since he had left. He had text her a few times, arranging times for Saturday, saying he couldn't wait but other than that there hadn't been any renewal of the sentiments he had shared Tuesday morning and she was panicking that he was regretting his candour and about to go back on his word.

He was all that Zoe had thought about since their heart to heart. She was so desperate to spend time with him now that she finally knew how he felt. She wanted to feel his lips on hers, look into his eyes at close range and run her fingers through that golden hair. Zoe sighed. She would just have to wait one more day. It wasn't that she didn't want to see Sam, she did, it was just that she desperately wanted to be with Pete as soon as possible.

She finished applying her makeup and slid into the green dress she had bought for the night out in Birmingham with Sam, Dan and Mark. She had forgotten how much she loved the dress and now that her hair had a red tone to it, it suited her colouring even more.

Zoe headed out the door walking to their usual bench with her heels in her hand. As she walked into town she began to properly look forward to the evening. Sam had booked The Lemon Grove as the girls hadn't eaten there since Sam's birthday. The last time they had been there as a two on a girls night out was the night she met Pete. Zoe smiled at the thought. What a lot had happened since then. Another smile formed on Zoe's lips as she remembered Pete's declaration of being hers and Sam spotted it from a distance. 'What are you grinning at?' Sam called down the street as Zoe approached her. Zoe hadn't given Sam all the details of her heart to heart with Pete, and was looking forward to filling her friend in over drinks.

The girls chatted as they ate and Sam giggled with excitement as Zoe told her that he had said he was hers since the first time they met. Zoe grinned with excitement too and the girls made a toast to fresh beginnings for Zoe and continued happiness for Sam.

Zoe suggested that they head straight to Afters for a dance. She didn't want to get too drunk or stay up too late. She wanted to be feeling her best for Pete the next day, but Sam was insistent that they head into The Sun for a drink and then, after Zoe completely resisted a cocktail in The Feathers, led Zoe down the steps into The Cellar bar for a mojito. By the time they got to Afters it was already gone 11pm and Zoe was keen to be home before midnight to be fresh for her date the following lunch time.

'Just one drink then Zo' Sam smiled at her friend 'it's not like I will be getting you to myself for a while by the sounds of things' Sam laughed and Zoe joined in, excited at the prospect of nights and weekends with Pete.

As Zoe headed to the bar to buy their drinks, Sam headed towards Cal. She seemed to be laughing a lot as she chatted to him and there was something conspiratorial about the way she was leaning her head close to Cal to speak to him. Zoe frowned. It was odd. She was sure Sam wasn't likely to be unfaithful to Alex with Cal, but why would she have made a beeline for him and be so giggly. Zoe found it disconcerting and felt a little worried.

She grabbed their Prosecco from the bar man as quickly as possible and headed towards Sam, just as Sam left the DJ booth and Cal began playing Maniac, Sam was immediately by Zoe's side, extracting her drink from Zoe's hand as she began dancing. Zoe laughed and shook away her doubts. She had an hour to dance and enjoy herself with Sam before her first official date with Pete tomorrow, she didn't need to be inventing things to worry about!

The girls danced their hearts out to Maniac, Take on me and then I think we're alone now. Zoe had a tremendous sense of deja vu and frowned. Sam stopped dancing and took a sip of her drink. 'You ok Zo?' Zoe shook her head 'yeah fine, just felt a bit weird'. She felt someone's eyes on her back and turned to see Pete, standing exactly as he had back in August, less than a metre away, blue eyes gazing into hers and perfect white teeth smiling at her. He laughed as her eyes widened and winked at Sam in a conspiratorial way. He took a step closer to Zoe and leant to whisper into her ear. She smelled his familiar smell and couldn't help but reach up and touch his cheek with the palm of her hand. She couldn't believe this man had told her that he was hers. He was perfection.

Pete leaned in to speak to her over the noise of the Music, just like he had the first night they had met, but this time he kissed her ear before speaking. She shuddered at his kiss, it was electric. 'I love watching you dance and enjoying yourself Zoe. You look absolutely amazing.' Zoe smiled at him, disbelieving that she was here with him, just as she had been all those months ago. Sam tapped Zoe on the shoulder and indicated she was heading outside. Zoe nodded, her attention still firmly on Pete. He put his right hand firmly on her left hip and leant in to speak again, his breath warm against her cheek 'nothing to say?' He asked her, eyebrows raised.

Zoe laughed and put her left hand over his to make sure he didn't let go of her. she smiled as she spoke, the happiness inside almost overwhelming her, 'well, as it happens, you can watch me dance whenever you like!'

Pete grinned and led her to the side of the dance floor. He asked her about her week and told her that work had been busy for him, but that he hadn't stopped thinking of her. Just being with him made Zoe burst with excitement. As they chatted the sparks flew, just as they had that first night last August. She glanced around to see if Sam had returned and Pete frowned mockingly. 'Come on Zoe, you must remember how this goes.... she is outside with Alex'. Zoe laughed as she remembered him telling her that Sam was outside on the night that her friend had met her true love, Alex. 'Ready to go out to then?' Pete asked, continuing the pretence of their first night meeting perfectly. Zoe nodded and headed toward the door.

As they stepped out onto the terrace, Zoe looked to where Sam and Alex had been last August and there they were. Zoe grinned at Pete. 'Did you and Sam arrange all this together?' Pete smiled and tapped his nose, and pulled her into his embrace. He leant against the wall and held her tightly against his chest. She could feel his heartbeat and realised she had never experienced such intense feelings, neither with Ryan or Dan. Pete was something different. He was special and she would do everything she could to keep this feeling.

As he tilted her chin up, he looked into her eyes. He looked unsure and so Zoe reached up and kissed him. His mouth was warm and his kiss soft. Zoe reached her arms around his neck, standing on her tiptoes to get closer to the man she had longed for all these months. She kissed him like she should have on the first night they met. She paused as she thought back to that night, it seemed a lifetime ago and she seemed like a different person.

Pete put his hands on her cheeks and pulled away. 'Are you ok?' His question was quiet but his eyes showed concern. 'Tell me if you want to stop'. Zoe shook her head and kissed him on the lips again and then stood back, keeping her arms around his neck. 'No thanks' she smiled 'I've made that mistake once before and there is no way I'm running away tonight or ever again Pete Saunders'.

Pete grinned at her. 'Well that's a relief!' He was laughing as he said it but Zoe saw genuine relief in his eyes, and knew they had just passed their first milestone. Pete looked anxious as he spoke softly 'would you like to come back to mine Zoe?' Zoe smiled and kissed him again before nodding her consent. She stopped to tell Sam on their way past, and Zoe and Pete headed into the night, hand in hand.

\*\*\*\*\*

As they walked along the High Street, Zoe realised she had no idea where Pete lived. Sensing her hesitation, he stopped and faced her, bending down to kiss her softly on the mouth.

'You have no idea how much it means to be here with you Zoe' his expression was tender as he held both of her hands in his. 'There is nowhere I'd rather be' Zoe responded before Pete kissed her with more certainty and confidence than before 'well' he said, his eyes sparkling, 'I can think of one place I'd rather be'. Zoe blushed at his innuendo and he kissed her again before leading her further along the high street.

He stopped at the entrance to the towns most exclusive apartment block, and Zoe realised it was where he lived. He headed into the foyer of the building and straight to the lift, pulling her behind him. As they headed up to the top floor, Zoe tried to imagine what his apartment would be like and how many women he had taken up in this lift. For the first time, she felt embarrassed of her inexperience. She didn't want anything to come between her and Pete and she wasn't sure she would meet his standards in the bedroom. As though he sensed her sudden anxiety he squeezed her hand and smiled at her reassuringly. Zoe took a deep breath, she couldn't let anything ruin her chance of being with this man. The thought of going back to wanting but not having him was almost unbearable.

Pete opened the apartment door and they stepped into a large, spacious and minimalist open plan living area. On the wall opposite them were two sets of french doors with balconies directly overlooking the cathedral. 'Wow' Zoe exclaimed as she headed straight to admire the view. Pete opened the door and they stepped out onto the balcony. The cathedral was floodlit and festive white fairy lights hung in the trees around it. The view was stunning.

'Prosecco?' Pete asked her and she turned her attention away from the view to him. 'Yes, if you have some, then that would be perfect'. He gave Zoe a sheepish smile. 'Yeah I have some Zo. I've had a bottle chilling in the fridge since coming back from Italy. I bought it back for you.' Zoe looked up at him and frowned slightly recalling again what had happened on that Saturday afternoon in mid-December. Pete continued 'I came to your house that day to invite you over for dinner Zoe, I wanted to tell you how I felt, and ask you how you felt about me. You were all I had thought about in Italy'.

Zoe gulped as she felt a wave of emotion at what had played out that Saturday and all the weeks they could have been together since then. 'But why didn't you tell me? Pete, when Ryan turned up, I was completely staggered and then when you turned up too, I just didn't know what to do. I ended up sitting in shock all afternoon and Ryan took my silence to be acceptance of his return, but I promise we were never back together, not really. He knew that I had feelings for you, but kept telling me he could tell you didn't feel the same for me. His way of trying to keep us apart I guess'.

Pete slid his arms around her waist again, pulled her close and rested his head on hers. 'I'm sorry I didn't say anything Zoe. I should have, I just didn't want my heart getting broken. Like I said, I've been in self-preservation mode since I was fourteen. I thought I still had a chance of saving myself, but New Year's Eve I realised it was way too late anyway. Watching Ryan behaving like you were his property all night really hurt. That's why I had to leave'. He paused and sighed heavily before continuing 'I don't really know why I thought I could save myself, or why I thought I needed to…. The thing is Zoe, that first night I met you, I just knew that you were right for me. When we talked, I could feel how strong the connection was, and I kind of hoped then that you would be the one to save me from myself. Even when you ran away, I knew I had to keep trying….. but I'm not good at expressing myself, and all my attempts ended up with me saying things I didn't mean. I'm sorry.'

Zoe stepped back and looked up at him. 'You don't have to be sorry Pete. The way you spoke to me sometimes was really confusing, but no more confusing than me running away from you, or meeting Dan in Madrid, or Ryan being on my doorstep when you came back from Italy….. I wish some of those things hadn't happened, but I guess it happened that way for a reason and now here we are, together.'

Zoe looked into the face of the man she had wanted for so long. She couldn't believe he was being so open about his feelings, but his expression was serious, as though his confession was a weight, heavy on his mind. Zoe decided it was time to lighten the mood. She was determined to enjoy this time with Pete, she had waited so long to be with him and wanted him to feel the same elation she did. 'So anyway, Pete Saunders, yes, I'd love a glass of the Prosecco you brought from Italy for me!' Pete's face instantly relaxed as he smiled and stepped back into the apartment, leaving Zoe to admire the view and think about all he had said.

As Pete headed to the kitchen area, he picked up an iPad and moments later music began to play in the apartment. Zoe smiled as she realised the song playing was The long and winding road, the song that had played in Pete's car when he had driven her back from the airport. She felt a chill of cold through the thin fabric of her dress and stepped back into the apartment, heading towards the kitchen area where Pete was lifting two champagne flutes out of a cupboard.

She looked down at the iPad and saw the playlist titled 'Zoe's playlist', she picked up the tablet, curious at her discovery. The list included a whole range of music, Hey Jude and We can work it out, Take on me, Mr Brightside, I'm still Standing, Hungry Eyes. Zoe looked up at Pete questioningly as he re-entered the lounge area, Prosecco in hand. 'It's the songs of the time since we met' he said 'all the songs that remind me of you'. She smiled as she took her Prosecco from him, touched that he had remembered all of their moments together.

Pete headed to the sofa and sat down, patting the seat next to him. Zoe joined him, setting her Prosecco down on the side table. Pete turned and took her in his arms, 'this has been a long time coming' he muttered before kissing her passionately for the first time since August. She realised he had been taking things slowly tonight up until this point. Zoe kissed him back with the same intensity, as he pulled her to sit on top of him. Zoe was sure he could hear her heart pound as he kissed her harder, his hands moving up her thighs. He broke away from her momentarily, pausing with uncertainty before asking 'shall we take this to the bedroom?' Zoe nodded and stood up, collecting her Prosecco glass, as he held her hand and led her to the bedroom.

The bedroom was also minimalist with a large bed in the centre, bed side drawers and large fitted wardrobes. The playlist was already playing from a small WiFi speaker on the bedside drawers. Pete took Zoe's Prosecco from her hand and laid both their drinks on the drawers. He pulled the duvet back in a swift movement and then turned his attention back to her. They stood face to face and Zoe realised that she was already breathing heavily with both anticipation and nerves. Pete reached around behind her and slid the zip down the back of her dress, sliding it down her body and onto the floor.

He kicked his shoes off and pulled his T-shirt over his head before bending to kiss her again, his hands caressing her back and causing electric shocks to surge through her body. Zoe put her hands flat on his stomach and felt his toned torso. He was in amazing shape and she momentarily felt self conscious about her soft flesh. Pete was kissing her neck and breathed into her ear 'you're so sexy Zoe, I want you so much.' He turned her so that her back was to the bed and slowly lowered her down to lying, climbing on the bed beside her as he removed his trousers. He finished undressing Zoe as he kissed her. She was a total mix of emotions, full of desire and anticipation , but nervous and excited too.

Pete pulled the duvet part way over their naked bodies and lay kissing her until she thought she might explode. His hands were everywhere and Zoe was conscious of the uncontrollable gasps that kept escaping her lips. Finally he reached into his bedside drawer, looking at Zoe intensely and asking if she was sure, she nodded and kissed him hard to show him she couldn't wait any longer.

Pete was amazing in bed. He knew exactly how to touch her to turn her on, and took her to the edge over and over. She was ready to explode when he finally let her climax. Zoe realised she was trembling. She had never felt such intensity. She knew it was because of the way she felt about him as much as the way he was touching her. She pulled him close to her as he increased the intensity for himself. He looked into her eyes and she could see the desire in his face. He held her gaze and then kissed her again hard. Zoe sighed with contentment as Pete finally collapsed on her, breathless and sweating.

They lay side by side, faces almost touching. Pete smiled at her 'well, that was even more amazing than expected, and I already knew it would be amazing being with you Zoe', Zoe smiled back 'well, obviously I'm a bit lacking in experience, but I'd give it ten out of ten'. Pete laughed 'good to know, and just FYI, you are incredible. Experienced or not'. Zoe blushed and Pete kissed her as he reached past her to get their Prosecco. 'Here's to us, Zoe' he said, chinking her glass. 'To us, Pete' she smiled back, feeling truly content.

\*\*\*\*\*

When Zoe awoke the winter sun was shining through the apartment and she was alone in Pete's bed. She could hear the shower running and propped herself up on her pillow, pulling the duvet up under her chin and wondering what to do next. It was only moments before Pete emerged from the bathroom, damp skin glistening with a towel wrapped around his waist. He looked so relaxed and happy, she couldn't help but smile.

'Good morning!' He had an energy that Zoe was not accustomed to seeing or feeling in the morning. He moved around the bed put some music on and climbed on next to her. He kissed her face. Zoe felt self conscious. She had no idea how she looked but was very aware she was naked. 'Did you sleep well?' He was so chirpy Zoe mused, a real morning person, she had always wondered if there was any such thing. 'Tea'? He asked grinning again.

Zoe nodded and smiled 'Tea would be great. Do you mind if I grab a shower? And would you have a T-shirt I could borrow?'

Pete was immediately sliding off the bed and heading towards the wardrobe and as he found her a T-shirt continued talking, but this time with some uncertainty in his voice. 'So, Zoe, you know that Sam and I arranged last night together, and I didn't have any expectation that you would come back with me, but I really...... I mean really hoped you would. Anyway, Sam said you would definitely want some stuff here in the morning. I thought it was too presumptuous, but she insisted'.

He was rambling like Sam did. He wasn't looking at her but she could tell he was suddenly nervous. She cut in 'Pete, what is it you are trying to say'. He turned around and was holding a gift bag. 'Sam told me to get this, but now I have it here I feel panicked that you are gonna be offended' he passed the bag to her and she peered into the pink bag.

Inside were a collection of her favourite brand cleanser, toner and moisturiser, a pink toothbrush, shower gel and make up wipes. She looked up and smiled at him. 'I'm not offended Pete' he looked massively relieved 'besides, this is so Sam. In her head she would have been devising reasons for me not to leave straight away! She has a really romantic, and devious heart!'.

Pete sat back on the edge of the bed, 'I'm glad you didn't think it was because I assumed you would stay with me. But now, as I've already booked you for lunch, you have no reason to go anywhere!

Zoe laughed 'hmmm, just the small matter of my clothes Pete!' He looked at her and laughed back 'good point!'.

As they laughed, the playlist that Pete had made for their time together shuffled onto Golden Slumbers. Zoe rolled onto her side to face Pete as he lay down beside her. 'This song' she said, 'it's the song you were singing in my house that night'. Pete nodded, and explored her face with his eyes before speaking softly to her.

'This version is linked to another song called carry that weight. The way the songs are merged and the lyrics, they've always just resonated with me. The lyrics about carrying that weight for a long time.' He lifted his hand to smooth her hair from her face and left it touching her cheek.

'To be honest Zoe, I always thought that I would never meet

someone that I could let my guard down with. It felt like a weight put there by my parents break up.' Zoe could feel his hurt and wished she could take it all away. She put her hand over his and kissed his palm. He glanced down at their hands and smiled as he continued talking 'since last Tuesday, when I told you how I feel, and you said you had feelings for me too.... since then, it kind of feels like the weight has already been lifted'.

As he leaned into kiss her face, Zoe sighed with contentment and elation at his admission of his feelings. Pete threw his towel on the floor as he slid back under the covers with Zoe and made love to her again, golden slumbers playing softly in the background.

*****

Pete dropped Zoe at her front door on their way out to lunch and she dashed in to do her make up and get changed. She packed a small overnight bag in the hope that she could stay with Pete again.

Zoe didn't arrive home until Sunday evening. Pete had wanted her to stay over for another night, but she liked to have time to get things ready for the new term and was keen for some time to call Sam and Leyla. They had been texting since Friday night and Zoe was desperate to share her elation with her friends.

Pete had reluctantly parted on the agreement that he would come to hers the next night and stay over. Zoe missed him already, their first two days together had been intense and passionate and just amazing. Pete was relaxed, funny and really caring and showed no signs of the erratic man she had encountered over the past few months. She couldn't believe she had him in her life now, and was determined to keep it that way.

As she dialled Sam's number, she thought about the last five months since she had met Pete. She remembered all the snap shots of time they'd had together and smiled. All the heartache and joy, it had all been leading to this point and now here she was. At the beginning. The beginning of something that looked set to be amazing. She couldn't wait.

Epilogue: Hope for the heartbroken

Zoe looked at her reflection in the mirror. She loved the dress she had bought earlier that week. It was a deep burgundy red and wrapped around her, leaving just enough of her cleavage on show where it crossed at the top, and a little thigh where it crossed at the bottom. Her hair was back to chocolate brown and her eye make up in smokey greys complimented her dark hair and pale skin. She had her trusty black ankle strap sandals on and felt good. There was a definite glow about her these days, which she put down to the wonderful love affair she was experiencing with Pete. He was an attentive and loving partner who was amazing in the bedroom. He was everything that she had fantasied he would be for those long months and so much more.

As she smiled at her reflection, Pete open the bedroom door and entered. Music drifted in from the lounge and she could tell it was his Beatles number 1's album playing again. Zoe loved being at Pete's apartment. It felt like a fresh start away from the memories of Ryan that her own house held. They had been spending most of their time at Pete's apartment, mainly because of its amazing location for the town, but Zoe had been wondering about selling her house and buying somewhere new that didn't have all the memories of her past in it. Maybe she would mention the idea to Pete later.

Pete stood behind Zoe looking into the mirror with her and wrapped his arms around her from behind. He kissed her neck gently and smiled at her reflection. 'You look beautiful Zo', he spun her around to face him and kissed her intensely on the mouth. 'I'm gonna be the luckiest guy there, but it's a shame we're gonna be late'. He pulled her towards the bed as he whispered in her ear and tugged at the ties on the waist of her dress. Zoe giggled as she tumbled onto the bed, kissing him and pulling at his clothes as she sank into the mattress.

They were indeed late leaving the apartment, but Zoe had even more of a glow about her now! Pete held her hand as they stepped onto the pavement and began singing 'I wanna hold your hand' quietly. She had noticed how he would sing whenever he was happy. His voice was beautiful and Zoe found his way of expressing his happiness adorable. She squeezed his hand tightly.

They set off along the high street hand in hand, Pete serenading Zoe as they walked. It was Valentine's Day, almost six months to the day since Zoe had met Pete, and they were headed to a party. Pete's friend Matt had proposed to his girlfriend and tonight was their engagement party.

Going out with Pete and his friends was always something Zoe looked forward to. Alex always took Sam and Jake was always with Leyla. It meant that Zoe got to spend her nights out with Pete and her best friends, which was pretty much perfect in Zoe's eyes.

The party was in a function room above one of the towns newer pubs. There was a cheesy DJ that the girls were immediately up and dancing to, whilst the boys stood at the bar catching up. Zoe looked around her from her friends to Pete and felt as though she might explode with happiness.

As the DJ began playing Elton's 'don't go breaking my heart', the boys all crowded into the girls dancing circle. Pete snatched Zoe's hands up and pulled her to dance with him. She laughed as he sang to her whilst he danced and she sang back at him. As the song approached its end, Pete pulled Zoe off the dance floor and to a quiet corner of the bar area. Standing face to face he looked intently at her.

'You won't will you?' His eyes were scanning her face as though waiting for an expression to give her answer away. Zoe frowned 'won't what?' Pete still had some very cryptic and intense moments and Zoe realised that this was one of them. 'You won't go breaking my heart' his face was serious as he repeated the song lyrics to her. Zoe laughed trying to lighten the moment 'I couldn't if I tried' she repeated the next lyric of the song back to him, but his expression didn't lighten.

'I mean it Zoe' his expression was intense as he spoke and Zoe's playful laughter was replaced with confusion. Where was this coming from? She opened her mouth to speak but Pete continued 'its just that... well... Zoe, my self preservation mode, it seems to have evaporated since New year'. Zoe smiled and wrapped her arms around his waist. 'Well' she smiled up at him 'I see that as a very good thing'. She reached up to kiss him but he was still distracted and pulled away to carry on speaking.

'You know what that means though Zoe'. His intensity was starting to concern her. His face was serious and Zoe's heart started to race as she shook her head to indicate she didn't know what he was trying to say. 'Zoe', he looked so stressed as he spoke 'it means I'm basically defenceless. It means that I can't help myself when I am with you.' He paused and his face softened as he looked into her eyes. 'Zoe, I have fallen completely in love with you and if you did break my heart....' he stopped mid sentence and looked at her with his beautiful blue sparkling eyes, 'Zoe. I love you. That's what I wanted to say'.

Relief flooded Zoe's body. He was so intense, she wondered if he would ever completely relax into their relationship and move on from the hurt in his past. She took his hands in hers and gazed into his face. 'I love you too Pete Saunders. More than you could know'. His face was awash with relief as he reached down to kiss her. She had thought of telling him a million times in the last five weeks since their first night together. She had already known she loved him then. Zoe's heart swelled as she processed his declaration of love. They stood smiling at each other, both ecstatic at the others admission.

As the rest of their group suddenly joined them at the bar, their quiet reflection was interrupted and the moment was over.

Pete kissed Zoe softly on her lips, before turning to order the next round of drinks. As he ordered, Sam moved to stand next to Zoe, grinning in her friends direction 'Looks like all is going well' Sam nudged Zoe affectionately. Zoe beamed back at Sam as she responded 'definitely Sam. I'm so happy I could burst'.

Sam smiled a kindly smile at Zoe. 'Do you remember Zoe, last August when I said all would be ok and to give it six months?' Sam's eyes were sparkling and Zoe knew she was feeling smug. Zoe smiled at her friend. 'I remember. I remember clinging to the idea of six months.' Pete turned from the bar and winked at Zoe. Zoe grinned back before turning to Sam.

'I remember not believing you and thinking I would humour you and I remember thinking I would do anything to be back with Ryan'. Sam grimaced and Zoe laughed. 'But then Sam, you made me get myself together enough to go out and that night I met the man of my dreams.' Zoe squeezed Sam's hand to show her appreciation for all her friends love and support. 'Six months Sam, who would have thought that all it takes for true happiness is six months'.

As Pete returned from the bar with the girls drinks, he looked from one of them to the other 'what are you two talking about' he asked looking at them suspiciously. Sam and Zoe looked at each other and grinned before turning back to Pete and replying in unison

'Six months!'

Zoe's Playlist

Maniac, Michael Sembello, 1983

I think we're alone now, Tiffany, 1987

Take on me, A-ha, 1984

The long and winding road, The Beatles, 1970

Mr Brightside, The Killers, 2004

Wonderwall, Oasis, 1996

Hey Jude, The Beatles, 1968

We can work it out, The Beatles, 1965

I'm still standing, Elton John, 1983

All by myself, Eric Carmen, 1976

Be my baby, The Ronettes, 1963

Hungry eyes, Eric Carmen, 1987

Golden slumbers/Carry that weight, The Beatles, 1969

I wanna hold your hand, The Beatles, 1964

Don't go breaking my heart, Elton John & Kiki Dee, 1976

# ACKNOWLEDGEMENT

Thank you to my family and friends for supporting me in writing, and publsihing, my first novel.

# ABOUT THE AUTHOR

## Deborah Fullwood

Deborah Fullwood lives near Birmingham with her husband and young daughter. An Astrophysics graduate, she has been a Physics teacher for twenty years and a Headteacher for the last seven years. Despite a scientific background, writing has  become a passion of Deborah's and she spends her free time blogging or writing romantic fiction.